DONIPHAN'S TH(

Colonel Alexander Doniphan has endeavoured to create the finest fighting force he can from the wild, untrained, insubordinate, unorthodox bunch who comprise the 1st Missouri Mounted Volunteers. Nate Hatcher is a dedicated soldier, but is repeatedly dragged into trouble by Kirby: his comrade and uncle, and a gambler who dabbles in illicit trading of army goods. Stationed in Santa Fé, Nate encounters the beautiful young Spanish noblewoman Inez Torreón, though he is warned by her father not to approach her on pain of death. Despite this, Nate continues to attempt to devise ways of meeting her. Betrothed to an elderly man for an arranged marriage, Inez has been stirred by Nate's gentle advances. But Kirby also has his eyes on her, for different reasons — cultivating a relationship with her could be useful to his shady business machinations . . .

SPECIAL MESSAGE TO READERS

DONIPHAN'S THOUSAND

LES SAVAGE, JR.

SAGEBRUSH
Large Print Westerns

First published in the United States by Five Star

First Isis Edition
published 2017
by arrangement with
Golden West Literary Agency

The moral right of the author has been asserted

A catalogue record for this book is available
from the British Library.

ISBN 978–1–78541–390–2 (pb)

PUBLISHED BY
F. A. THORPE (PUBLISHING)
ANSTEY, LEICESTERSHIRE

SET BY WORDS & GRAPHICS LTD.
ANSTEY, LEICESTERSHIRE
PRINTED AND BOUND IN GREAT BRITAIN BY
T. J. INTERNATIONAL LTD., PADSTOW, CORNWALL

This book is printed on acid-free paper

Editor's Note

Doniphan's Thousand was the penultimate novel Les Savage, Jr., wrote before his untimely demise. The story, the way he wanted to tell it, did not meet with editorial approval at Doubleday, his principal book publisher. The biggest problem, according to Savage's editor, Barbara Ellis, was that he had, in her opinion, written an historical romance that did not end in a romance. The author was compelled to rewrite the book, especially the conclusion. In the interim, Savage had written what would be his final story, *Gunshy*. This would first appear posthumously in 1993 under the title *Table Rock*. What Savage had intended in *Doniphan's Thousand* was an historical novel that was honest and realistic, that sought to depict the Mexican War in the Southwest in terms of its military, social, cultural, and human aspects, a story that was true to its time, its characters, and the events it describes. For its appearance here, Savage's text for *Doniphan's Thousand* has been restored to what the author intended before the changes forced on him by editorial intervention. As such, it may well stand as the culmination and perpetuation of his extraordinary talent.

CHAPTER
ONE

"Reveille" woke Nate Hatcher before dawn. The tent was only a half shelter, and, although he had left his boots on, his feet were numb with cold. He doubled his legs up under the blanket in a futile attempt to get warm. There had been rumors of a battle today. Nate worried about how he would act in a battle. He guessed everybody worried about how he'd act in a battle. Everybody except Kirby.

"Reveille" never waked Kirby and Nate reached over to shake his uncle. Kirby wasn't there. Nate sat up, almost pulling the tent over. He saw that Kirby's rifle lay on his blanket, but the rest of Kirby's gear was gone. Nate crawled out of the half shelter and saw that the company street was in its usual morning chaos, the volunteers coming out of their little tents on all fours, cursing and grumbling. Most of them slept in their clothes and all Nate had to do to be fully dressed was to buckle his belt and button his cavalry coat. He couldn't see his uncle anywhere. Sergeant Hicklin came trotting down the line of tents, kicking at the feet of the laggards. He took his job seriously, and, if he wasn't carrying a manual in his hand, there was always one or two of them stuffed in his coat pockets to study whenever he got the chance. Nate grabbed him by the arm as he went by.

"Bill," Nate said, "you got to cover for me at roll. Kirby's got in one of those all-night card games again."

"I can't do it, Nate," Hicklin said. "We're in for a fight for certain. The Mexicans are holding a pass in them mountains ahead. Anybody who don't show up at roll will be posted as a deserter."

Nate said stubbornly: "Tell Hugh Long to answer for me and Kirby. Kirby's probably over in town with some of those traders."

"That's the worst place to go," Hicklin said. "The general's fed up with desertions. He's got Lieutenant Merritt and a detail scrounging around now for anybody that's strayed."

"You got to cover for me, Bill. You did it before."

"Nate, this is before a battle. They'll shoot you . . ."

Hicklin broke off as he saw Captain Reid appear at a distance and head toward them. Nate turned and plunged between a pair of tents, heading through the horse lines toward the cover of willows along the river. Behind him, spreading its tattered half shelters across the New Mexican plain, under a haze of dust that seemed to have followed it all the way from the Missouri River, stretched the Army of the West. Nate had joined it over two months before, not long after May 13, 1846, when President Polk had declared that a state of war existed between the United States and Mexico and had called for 50,000 volunteers. Missouri had formed her regiment by counties, and Nate had joined the Saline County Company at his home town of

Marshall. With 114 men enlisted, the company elected its officers and marched 100 miles to Fort Leavenworth, where General Stephen Kearny was organizing the Army of the West. The only regulars Kearny had were his 300 1st Dragoons. The rest of the force was made up of volunteers, green farm boys and illiterate tobacco rollers and ague-ridden bottom landers, raw recruits who didn't know an about-face from a column of fours. The whole army didn't amount to much over 1,600 troops. With such a force Kearny had been ordered to occupy the two northernmost departments of Mexico, while General Taylor's army drove into the mother country south of the Rio Grande. Nate thought they'd given Kearny a mighty little parcel of men to take on all of New Mexico and California.

As he slid down the crumbling bank of the Rio Gallinas, the brazen bleat of stable call came from camp behind him. The river was swollen from the rains and red with mud. It made Nate remember what Thomas Hart Benton had said about the Missouri — too thick to swim in but not quite thick enough to walk on. It had riled Nate because it was his river the senator was slandering. Nate had been born twenty years ago in the Missouri bottoms north of Marshall. His ma had said he would be a limestone man. He had lived up to the prophecy, tall, black-haired, his long face hollowed and ridged to a bony gauntness. When he was four, his first ague had taken him and ever after that his cheeks had the sallow color that marked the people who lived in the fever-ridden bottoms of the new country.

He had come a long way from that country — 740 miles from Fort Leavenworth, through the man-killing heat of the Kansas prairies, the waterless deserts south of the fur-trading post they called Bent's Fort, following the Santa Fé Trail, the same route the American traders had been taking to Santa Fé for the last twenty years. A lot of the traders had already started for Santa Fé when the war was declared. The Army of the West had caught up with their strings of white-topped wagons all along the trail, and Kearny had ordered them to stay under his protection until Santa Fé was taken.

The army had moved too slowly for most of the traders and they had spent their time cursing Kearny and champing at the bit and trying to sneak out ahead of him. Their wagons were corralled closer to town than the army camp. The teams were turned out to graze every night. Nate didn't think he'd ever seen such a big herd, hundreds of mules, maybe thousands, trampling through the bottom lands and deafening a body with their braying and *hee-hawing* as the wranglers rounded them up. Nate skirted the wagons, looking for some of the traders Kirby had played cards with during the trip. He saw Dr. Leitensdorfer. The doctor was a big name in the Santa Fé trade, owned a store on the plaza in Santa Fé, and had recently married Soledad Abreu, the daughter of a former governor of New Mexico. Leitensdorfer said that Kirby had come into camp that morning, wanting to sell him some cutlery. For some reason Kirby hadn't been willing to bring the cutlery to the traders' camp but had it stashed away somewhere

4

in town. Leitensdorfer wasn't in the market and turned Kirby over to a man named Jim Ganoe. Leitensdorfer thought they had gone into Las Vegas.

Between the camp and town was a hide-colored country, all browns and reds and yellow buckskin, patched with scrawny soapweed and burned creosote brush. Las Vegas stood half a mile or more from the river, a village of 300 people, the mud buildings scattered around the central plaza like a cluster of dingy brick kilns. Nate knew the New Mexicans called a tavern a *cantina*, and that would be the first place to look for Kirby. He followed the back streets, watching out for Lieutenant Merritt and the detail that was hunting deserters. He asked some children he met for directions to the *cantina*, and they pointed out a building on the square, looking more like a soddy than a tavern, its windows boarded up with puncheons, its mud walls crumbling and water-streaked. He was opening the door when he saw Merritt and four volunteers appear on one of the streets, coming toward the square.

Nate ducked inside. It was so dark they had to burn bay-berry candles. The barkeep didn't speak English, but there were a couple of traders having a drink. They said Kirby had been there and had gone out the back way with Jim Ganoe.

There was a muddy back yard backed by a long mud wall with a gate in it. Nate was almost to the gate when he heard his Uncle Kirby's drawling voice from the other side of the wall.

"Ganoe, you got to put the money on the line. You show me the cash and I can get you all the sabers you can tote. You ain't got a notion what a hate the volunteers got on these sabers. The most useless piece of equipment a man ever got harnessed with. Hanging down a body's back, beating his backbone to shreds, poking holes in his rump when he dismounts, not long enough to reach anybody when he's ahorse, too big to throw when he's afoot . . ."

Nate looked through the bars of the gate. He saw that the wall formed a big pen, filled with a dozen of the shaggy little Mexican burros. The two men were standing to one side of the gate. Kirby's back was to Nate. The other man was a big Missouri puke with bristly jowls and britches and a hickory shirt stained with the resin and tallow the teamsters used to grease their axles. He saw Nate and made a sharp sound.

Kirby wheeled around. When he recognized Nate, he relaxed, grinning. He had a sway-backed way of standing, with his boots planted widely and his head tilted off to one side. It was a shaggy head, the matted, curly, corn-colored hair streaked with white where the sun had burned it. There hadn't been enough uniforms for the volunteers and the only regulation thing Kirby wore was a blue jacket with yellow cavalry trim. Nate pulled the rope latch free and shoved open the gate.

"You got to git back," he told Kirby. "Lieutenant Merritt's over here with a detail looking for deserters."

"Nobody's deserting, Nate," Kirby said. "I just been over here drumming up a little business. Jim Ganoe has

6

offered me a dollar apiece for every saber I can get him. The Mexicans will give their soul for a good knife."

Nate moved inside the corral, looking at the heap of sabers in their scabbards, lying at Kirby's feet. He realized they were the same swords he had seen Kirby picking up along the trail, thrown away by the volunteers. Every night Kirby had kept them inside the tent and every day he had rolled them up in the tent and stowed them in the company wagon.

"You said you were a-going to turn them in," Nate said, "or give them back to the boys when they needed them."

"I tried that," Kirby said. "They just threw them away again."

"But Kirby . . . this here's government property."

"It ain't a-going to do the government any good, rusting away on the Kansas prairies," Kirby said. "I figured they might as well be put to some use."

Nate frowned at Kirby, trying to cipher it out. It all sounded logical, the way it always did with Kirby's deals. Sometimes Nate had the feeling that, if he talked the deals over with a parson, he'd come away convinced he was committing a mortal sin, but after Kirby explained them snow couldn't be whiter.

A sound across the yard made him wheel around. He saw the back door of the *cantina* opening, caught the flash of a blue uniform. He dodged back of the wall.

"It's the lieutenant," he said. "They probably told him we were out here."

7

Ganoe whirled and ran across the corral toward the opposite wall. Kirby stooped and started gathering up the sabers.

"Kirby," Nate said sharply, "we ain't got time for that."

"Sure we have," Kirby said.

He took one of the sabers and whacked a burro across the rump. The shaggy little beast reared up, letting out an ear-splitting bray, and headed at a run for the gate Nate had left open. Kirby ran on through the bunch, whacking others, till he had all of them in a stampede. They crowded through the gate, knocking mud loose from the walls, and Nate could hear somebody shouting from the yard beyond. With most of the sabers gathered up, Kirby ran for the back wall. Ganoe was already going over the top.

"You git up and I'll hand the swords to you," Kirby said.

The mud wall was head high and it took Nate two tries to gain the top. From its height Nate could see the back yard of the *cantina*, filled with the shaggy horde of milling burros. The volunteers must have run back into the alley to escape the stampede, but Merritt had returned now that the burros were in a mill. Nate could see the top of his blue cap beyond the wall, as he fought to get through the animals.

"He's almost at the gate," Nate said. "You'll have to leave the sabers."

"I ain't leaving them, Nate . . ."

"Halt!" Merritt called from beyond the other wall. "Who goes there? Stand and identify yourself!"

8

Kirby let out a curse, looking over his shoulder. He dropped the armful of swords and reached up to grab the wall. Nate caught his leg as it swung up and helped him over. They dropped off the other side. A shot made a sharp *crack*, and they heard the bullet thump into the adobe wall behind them. They ran through a maze of narrow alleys to the outskirts of town. They knew they would be too exposed crossing the open plain to the army camp. They went through the traders' camp to the river. They passed unnoticed in the bedlam of teams being harnessed and wagons getting under way. The willows in the river bottom covered them till they got to the edge of the army camp.

They found the same chaos there. Roll had already been taken, breakfast was over, and the men were striking their tents. Hugh Long had the tent next to the Hatchers. He was the schoolmaster from Marshall — a stooped, consumptive-looking man with sunken cheeks and weak, squinted eyes ruined with too much reading. The uniform that had been issued him was about four sizes too small; the frayed cuffs were pulled halfway to his elbows and his knees were poking out through holes in the ragged yellow-striped britches. He had covered for Nate and Kirby before, and said that, when he had answered for their names, the lieutenant attending roll call had been too sleepy to notice the difference. Nate hastily stowed the tent in the company wagon while Kirby gathered their gear and carried it to the horse lines.

Nate had a red roan named Strawberry. She was in better shape than most of the horses in Company D.

Nate figured that was due to the things Kirby had taught him. Kirby took better care of his horse than he did of himself. Usually it would take a cannon going off by his ear to wake him up in the morning, but, if his horse so much as whimpered in the night, he always seemed to hear it and broke his sleep to get up and find out what was the matter. One night in Raton Pass he had shot a wolf that was getting too close and had spent the rest of the time till "Reveille" wrapped in his blanket beside his horse. It was something the rest of the men didn't seem to understand. The volunteers took such miserable care of their horses that General Kearny had predicted he would have an army of infantry before he reached Santa Fé. Nate couldn't understand it. Most of the Missouri regiment were farm boys and should have known better. They let their animals drink too much at the river crossings and had to ride the bloated creatures the rest of the day; half the horses showed fresh gall sores at every evening camp; animals were going lame every hour of the day and forcing the men to lead them or ride double. So many horses had died or had gotten sick that it seemed half the regiment was dismounted by the time they reached Las Vegas.

Nate had his mare saddled when the call came to fall in. As D Company formed, Nate saw Colonel Alexander Doniphan mounting his chestnut mare at the edge of camp. The towering red-headed man was the commander of Nate's regiment, the 1st Missouri Mounted Volunteers. As Doniphan settled in the saddle, a rider came down the line of company wagons from the direction of Las Vegas. Nate saw that it was Lieutenant Merritt. His uniform was torn and caked with mud, and he kept wiping a bloody cut on his face with his yellow handkerchief.

Kirby smiled wickedly. "The lieutenant's a mite late. I'll wager he turned over every mud house in that town, looking for us."

Merritt checked his horse beside Doniphan with such a jerk on the reins that the animal reared and squealed. He bent toward Doniphan, talking fast, pointing toward Las Vegas and making savage motions with his hand. Doniphan grinned, sobered, and shook his head. He put a hand on Merritt's shoulder and said something. Merritt seemed to hesitate, then wheeled his horse and spurred it toward the regiment. He was a Saline County man and had enlisted in Marshall along with Nate and Kirby and the others. He had been a West Point graduate and had served a hitch in the 1st Dragoons before resigning his commission and going into Missouri politics. He took a position not twenty feet away, faced so that he was staring directly at Nate. His face, scabby and peeling and burned a brick color by the inferno of the Kansas prairie, was set in a rigid mold of barely controlled fury. Nate stirred uncomfortably.

"Kirby," Nate said, "you don't allow he got a look at us back there in town."

"Couldn't be," Kirby said. "We was behind that wall all the time."

Nate saw Lieutenant Colonel Ruff talking with Doniphan now. Like Merritt, Ruff had served five years

11

with the 1ˢᵗ Dragoons before retiring to civilian life. The regiment had elected him lieutenant colonel for the same reason that Company D had elected Merritt as their second lieutenant — they figured it would be good to have an officer who knew some soldiering. They were bitterly sorry for the decision. Ruff had proved a martinet, a more rigid disciplinarian than Kearny, a man who'd had somebody marching before the guard tent every hour since they left Fort Leavenworth. Ruff nodded at something Doniphan said, and turned to ride toward the ranks. Nate heard a soft groan go up from the men.

The lieutenant colonel halted before the regiment, straightened his long legs in the stirrups, and called to them in a parade-ground voice. "This morning before dawn, General Kearny was informed by our spies that the Mexican governor, Manuel Armijo, has command of the gap two miles to the west of us. His force is estimated at two thousand men."

"That's hogwash," Kelly Goff said. "He's jist telling us that so we won't turn tail. I heard in town it was twelve thousand men."

Nate tried not to pay any heed. Kelly Goff was always trying to make things sound worse. He was a big man with greasy black hair that got so tangled and matted with burrs it looked like an old buffalo coat. He had been a tobacco roller back in Marshall. Once Nate had seen him hoist a hogshead of tobacco, so big that nobody else had been able to lift it, and carry it a mile on his shoulders.

12

"You will be issued ten cartridges apiece," Lieutenant Colonel Ruff said. "I want you to make saber wristbands of your neckerchiefs. You will tie the neckerchief around your wrist and to the hilt of your saber. Before entering into action, and as soon as you are commanded to charge, discard your rifles and then use your sabers."

"Won't do no good against them spicks and their knives," Kelly Goff said. "Man don't stand a chance against them spicks and their knives."

"Don't they have no guns?" Nate asked.

"They wait till you shoot off your gun," Kelly Goff said. "Then they come in and rip your guts out. Nobody stands a chance against them spicks and their knives."

Nate began to sweat. He didn't put much faith in what Kelly said. Kelly always seemed to be one of the men with rumors. Kelly was the first to hatch a plot against the officers but he had never pulled anything off. Nate couldn't get the idea of the knives out of his head.

After a short wait they were marched into Las Vegas and halted in the street while Kearny mounted the flat roof of a house on the plaza and made a speech. Nate couldn't hear what he said but Captain Reid told them it was the first formal occupation of New Mexico. After Kearny finished, they marched out of town in a column of fours.

The volunteers had been issued a heterogeneous mass of arms. Ahead of him, Nate could see Hall breechloaders held across a dozen saddles, the more ancient flintlocks lashed under stirrup leathers, elbows crooked to hold Harpers Ferry rifles from the factory of Eli Whitney, Jr. Nate had been issued a Jenks breechloader without a scabbard, and, when he didn't keep it tied on the saddle under one leg, he had to carry it.

The Santa Fé Trail met the foothills south of Las Vegas. Nate had already seen the New Mexican mountains at Raton Pass. To a flatlander they were an everlasting marvel. The slopes were steep and broken and rust-colored, bearded with strange plants called by strange names. From the rocks and crannies sprouted a lonely sentinel that the Mexicans said was "The Candle of Our Lord". In the early morning when the sun was hot, the cluster of wax-colored flowers became a white flame burning above its circle of saber-like leaves. Higher up, twisted, gnome-like piñons, reminding Nate of ancient apple trees, clutched at the cliffs in patches of grama grass that glinted against the red earth like spilled hay. There was a smell to it all, the tickle of snuff, the syrupy sweetness of molasses, the sting of turpentine, filling Nate with a disturbing restlessness.

They came within sight of the gap, a red slash in the red mountains, and there was a lot of milling around while Kearny got them into battle formation. The 1st Dragoons, under the immediate command of Colonel Sumner, took the advance, along with the Laclede Rangers, a troop of volunteer cavalry from St. Louis. Major Clark and his two batteries occupied the center. Company B of the artillery battalion was under the command of Captain Woldemar Fischer, a native of

14

Prussia. The unit was made up of German immigrants from St. Louis who spoke very little English. They had been outfitted with gray coats of Kentucky jeans and gray britches with yellow stripes down the seams, but two months on the march had turned the fancy uniforms to rags. The artillery had trailed all the way from Fort Leavenworth, constantly bogging down at the river crossings, losing their horses, overturning their caissons, and causing general chaos. They had become a source of pain to General Kearny and a standing joke to the volunteers. Nate felt sorry for the sweating, pink-faced boys as they fought with their stubborn teams, struggling to wheel the long brass twelve-pound howitzers into line, suffering a barrage of catcalls and insults from the volunteers.

There was a bugle call from somewhere up front. Nate saw the infantry battalion move up the hill on the right flank, their bayonets fixed. There were two companies of them, from Cole and Platte Counties, marching on the holes in their boots and proud as hell that they had kept ahead of the cavalry for most of the way.

Sergeant Hicklin appeared on the flank of Company D, carrying one of his manuals in his hand. "We're going to move now," he said. "In four ranks, form company. By the left, double files . . . march!"

They'd had less than two weeks of training back at Fort Leavenworth and had mastered none of the drills. Half of them didn't pay much heed to the commands anyway, and those who did got all mixed up trying to execute them, and it always ended in a hopeless tangle.

Nate came out with most of his squad faced in the wrong direction, looking back down the slope toward the rear. He could see the long lines of white-topped wagons, belonging to the traders and the commissary, half hidden under their own haze of dust, with Captain Walton's Company B acting as rear guard.

"Hey, Bill," Kelly shouted at Hicklin, "you're using the wrong book! That's the infantry manual!"

Captain Reid joined Sergeant Hicklin. Reid had been a lawyer and a schoolteacher in Nate's home town, and had been elected captain by the Saline County men the day they formed their company at Marshall. He occupied a place in their affections second only to Doniphan, and by giving them a casual little talk he managed to get them into some semblance of a formation.

There was another bugle call from the front and Nate saw the dragoons break into a trot, up ahead of the Missouri regiment. The uniforms made a solid blue line across the road and the sabers flashed over their blue caps like the flicker of a sinuous silver snake.

Nate said: "I can't stop thinking about the Mexicans with their knives. Are they really such a terror with their knives?"

"Forget it," Kirby said. "Goff was just ragging you. A Missourian's worth ten greasers any day. Just remember that."

The order to load was passed back through the Missouri companies. Nate opened the breech on his Jenks. From his cartridge box he got a paper cartridge containing a ball and a measure of powder. He jammed it home in the breech. The saber tied to his wrist by his neckerchief clanged awkwardly against his rifle.

"Ain't you a-going to load your gun, Hugh?" Kirby asked.

"It's loaded," the schoolmaster said.

"It ain't loaded," Kirby said. "You gitting fritter-minded or something?"

"I thought it was loaded," Hugh said.

"Maybe he don't want to load it," Kelly said. "Maybe he has friends among these Mexicans."

"I don't know a one of them," Hugh said. "Didn't you ever think of that? We're going to kill a lot of men and we don't even know who they are."

The chief bugler blew the charge. It was repeated by the eight company buglers. Nate put the heels to his horse. They were galloping into the pass. The dust was so thick Nate could hardly see the company guidon. The men with flintlocks or muzzleloaders had to point their rifles skyward so the balls wouldn't roll out. Nate didn't have to worry about that with his Jenks. What he kept worrying about were the knives.

There was a lot of shouting and whinnying of horses and the dust boiling up to get in his eyes and he kept waiting for the sounds that would come when the dragoons met the enemy. Sergeant Hicklin's voice came out of the dust somewhere, repeating some order over and over again. Nate ran head-on into the man ahead of him and had to wheel aside to keep his horse from climbing the man's back. The men were stopping all about him and he realized that Hicklin was shouting at them to halt.

The whole regiment milled around for a while, and then Captain Reid came riding along the line. "It's all over, boys," he kept saying. "It looks as if there isn't going to be any fight, after all."

CHAPTER
TWO

The army marched sixteen miles that day, camping at a Mexican settlement near San Miguel Springs, where the officers were quartered for the night. Colonel Alexander Doniphan was among those who joined Kearny for dinner in one of the private homes. The main topic of discussion was the mystery of the empty gap that morning. There were all kinds of wild speculation among the volunteers as to why the Mexicans had not stayed to fight. Doniphan, as well as the other higher officers, was not so mystified, being privy to certain facts unknown to the rank and file.

It had happened at Bent's Fort, over 200 miles behind them. For almost twenty years the fur-trading post on the Arkansas, built by the four Bent brothers, had been the last American outpost on the frontier between the United States and Mexico. Early in August, Kearny had halted the Army of the West at the fort to reorganize for the last leg of his march. During the halt James Magoffin had arrived. He was a Santa Fé trader who had lived in New Mexico for the last twenty years. In Magoffin's opinion the Mexican governor, Manuel Armijo, could be subverted. Armijo had few regulars at his command, the bulk of his army being made up of untrained peasants, half of them armed only with swords or bows and arrows. Governor Armijo was a cynical opportunist, with no patriotism to sustain him, and Magoffin felt that he could convince Armijo of the foolishness of any opposition. Kearny had given Magoffin his chance, sending him ahead of the army with an escort of twelve dragoons.

By his preparations for battle at the gap Kearny had revealed what small faith his direct military mind put in Magoffin's devious methods. The failure of the Mexican army to appear had convinced Doniphan and some of the other officers that Magoffin had succeeded, and that Governor Armijo had abdicated. But Kearny was still not convinced. The villagers around the springs said that Governor Armijo had planned to meet Kearny at the gap but at the last minute had changed his mind and was now waiting with his army in Apache Cañon, fifty miles to the west.

Doniphan excused himself early from dinner and went to his quarters, a cramped room in one of the outbuildings of the settlement. He took off his coat and shirt and shoes and sat down with his sock feet propped on the desk, wearing nothing more than his walnut-dyed jeans that were held up by a single gallus made from a strip of bed ticking. He lit a bayberry candle in a tin sconce and got out a copy of *Tactics and Regulations for the Militia*. He doubted if he could apply much of it to the wild men under his command, but he had a tapeworm in his mind that needed constant feeding.

20

He had originally enlisted as a private in the Clay County Company. It had been mustered in at Liberty, where he had his law offices. When the regiment was collected at Leavenworth and the election of field officers held, Doniphan had been given command of the 1st Missouri Mounted Volunteers.

He wondered if any army had ever seen such a wild, untrained, insubordinate, unorthodox bunch as his boys. He doubted if any of them really knew why they were fighting the war. He was in doubt about some points himself. The threat had been hanging fire since Texas broke free of Mexico ten years ago. Mexico had never recognized Texan independence and had warned that any attempt of the United States to annex Texas would be considered a declaration of war. The United States had gone ahead with the annexation anyway and early in 1846 President Polk had ordered General Zachary Taylor into the newly acquired territory to protect American interests. There was still some doubt as to whether the Nueces River or the Río Grande was the southern boundary of Texas. When Taylor moved into the disputed strip, a Mexican force crossed the Río Grande and attacked him. Polk claimed that the Mexicans had come onto American soil and killed American soldiers and had left America no choice but to fight.

There were plenty of Whigs who thought that Polk was overstepping himself. Doniphan was one of them. He questioned whether the spot where the Americans had been killed was American soil. Mexico's claim to the strip south of the Nueces was based on some pretty sound arguments and Doniphan felt that Polk had deliberately provoked the attack by sending Taylor into the disputed section. But there was no stemming the war fever now and Doniphan wasn't the man to hang back over a technicality when the call came.

There was a knock at the door and Doniphan rose to open it. Lieutenant Taylor Merritt stepped in. He had washed and shaved and cleaned his uniform as well as he could, but he still bore some of the marks of his struggle with the burros that morning. There was a long scratch on his face, his blue coat was torn, and the plumes on his dress helmet looked as though the rats had been gnawing them.

"I wondered what you were going to do about those deserters?" Merritt asked.

Doniphan shook his head. "I had the adjutant check the roster books, Taylor. Everybody present and accounted for. It seems to me the only parties we could court-martial are those jackasses."

Doniphan didn't expect a laugh. He had learned long ago that Merritt had no sense of humor. He had always thought the man held himself in too tightly. A body could rarely tell what Merritt really felt. There was certainly no reading his face. It was as pale and expressionless as ever. The only sign of his fury was his restlessness. He started pacing the length of the cramped room, his narrow hands opening and closing.

"Ten sabers, ten new, perfectly good sabers. What were they doing there? You may be dealing with a conspiracy, Colonel, some kind of a Mexican plot. It's the type of thing this Hatcher would get involved in . . ."

"You said you didn't see him."

"Somebody called his name, just before I got to the gate."

"They called Nate Hatcher?"

"Nate, just Nate. Who else could it be?"

"There's a Nate in Company C, and a sergeant in Company F, as I recall."

"With his kind of record? How many times was Hatcher caught across the river after lights out? You remember how it was at Leavenworth. How many roll calls did he miss? Fighting in the barracks, insulting the officers, those card games in Weston. Every kind of hooraw known to man or beast. I don't know how he managed to skin out of it, but now we've got proof, something that perils the whole regiment. If you won't act on it, Colonel, I'll be forced to. I'll lay the whole matter before General Kearny."

Doniphan stuffed his hands in the pockets of his jeans and walked to the narrow window. He was six feet five and his tousled red hair almost touched the ceiling. Low rooms and short women always made him nervous. And men like Merritt. He wondered just how much of Merritt's fury came from suspicion of a conspiracy, and how much from hurt pride. He must have made an absurd picture, fleeing the stampede of the little burros. To have the fiasco witnessed by the volunteers he despised would be doubly humiliating. Doniphan had never known a man so proud. It was an obsession with Merritt. He made a fetish of his aristocracy. He was from a Tidewater family who traced an unbroken military service back to the Revolutionary War. Merritt could not forget such a background even though his experience in the regular service had been a disillusionment. It had been a time when promotion was so slow that a lieutenant had little hope of ever becoming a captain. There had been no vacancies for the sixty graduates of Merritt's West Point class and they had been attached to their companies as brevet second lieutenants. After holding the rank for five years Merritt resigned his commission and settled in Marshall and went into politics. Doniphan had first met him at a Whig convention in St. Louis. At first the man's dogmatism had irritated Doniphan. Later on he began feeling sorry for Merritt.

"Taylor," he said. "The kind of proof you have wouldn't stand up in a court-martial, and you know it. And what could you tell General Kearny? That you were ordered to round up deserters before a battle, and all you did was get attacked by a herd of jackasses. If I was the general, and one of my officers came running to me with his tail between his legs and told me that kind of story, I'd begin to wonder if he was really officer material." He saw Merritt frown, wavering. Doniphan went on, using the thing he knew would sway Merritt, hating himself for playing on the man's pride, yet knowing it was necessary. "If you keep this matter alive," he said, "the only thing you'll achieve is a standing joke for the whole army . . . named Lieutenant Taylor Merritt."

The Missouri volunteers were camped in the pass west of the springs. Kirby drew wood detail for their squad and Nate stayed in camp to pull their half shelter out of the company wagon and set it up. He learned at mess call that the supply wagons had not caught up with the army yet and they would have to go without dinner. It had been that way ever since Fort Leavenworth. Kearny hadn't been given adequate time to organize his commissary. There was so little food that most of the time the men had marched on half rations, and often the supply trains lagged so far behind that they had to spend two or three days at a stretch without enough food.

The squad huddled around the fire, hatching up ways to get even with their officers for starving them. It had become their favorite pastime. A man named Herkins wanted to put a burr under General Kearny's saddle so his horse would pitch him. A man named Hall had the measles and he offered to give them to Lieutenant Colonel Ruff.

"You're all making a lot of empty noise," Hugh Long said. "You've been hatching plots against the officers ever since the Missouri, and what've you done? If you had the courage to fix Kearny and his kind, you wouldn't have joined up in the first place."

"You shouldn't talk like that, Hugh," Sergeant Hicklin said. "We ain't out here to fight our officers. We're out here to kill the Mexicans."

Hicklin had his heap of manuals out. He had one called *Cavalry Tactics* and one called *Tactics and*

Regulations for the Militia and one by General Scott called *Instructions for Field Artillery, Horse and Foot,* although how he would apply that to the volunteer cavalry Nate couldn't guess.

"They who live by the sword shall die by the sword," Charlie Hayes said. "We aren't out here to kill anybody. We're out here to convert the Indian from his heathen sacrifices and the New Mexican from his Popish idolatry."

Charlie had been sitting in front of his half shelter reading his Bible. He was the son of a Baptist preacher and always spent an hour with the Bible after supper. He started reading them a verse from Exodus, but none of them was listening, and Kelly Goff broke in.

"The worst punishment I can think of for General Kearny," he said, "is to keep him from seeing La Tules."

Nate saw Kelly glance slyly at Bristol Graham as he said it. Bristol was only seventeen. He came from the back country near Marshall. When he was a child, a mule had kicked him in the face and left him in such shape that no girl could stomach the look of him.

"What's La Tules?" Bristol asked.

"It ain't a what, it's a who. This La Tules, she owns a tavern in Santa Fé. Men, they come a thousand miles jist to git a look at her. President Santa Anna come clear up from Mexico City to git her, and, when he couldn't do hisself any good, he went back and built a gold statue of her, thirty feet tall, smack in the middle of the square in Mexico City, naked."

Bristol cleared his throat. "Naked?"

"Plumb naked. Pilgrims come from all over the world jist to camp in the square and study that statue. The curious part is it ain't the handsome men this La Tules goes for. She hankers after the ugly ones."

"Kelly," Nate said, "this ain't a very funny hooraw."

"It ain't no hooraw," Kelly said. "I tell you, Bristol, if you promise not to go frothing at the mouth, or commit suicide because you can't touch the hem of her dress, I'll introduce you to La Tules."

"You would?" Bristol's mouth was hanging open.

"I can't do it for nothing. Let's say you rub my horse down every night between here and Santa Fé, and take my wood details and my guard duties . . ."

Bristol picked up a rock, throwing it savagely into the darkness. "I thought so, you're just hoorawing me, like Nate says."

G. M. Butler rode up and stopped his horse beside the fire. He was Doniphan's adjutant and he said that the colonel wanted to see Nate.

Kirby hadn't come back from wood detail by the time Nate got his horse saddled. Nate could guess what Doniphan wanted. He'd been worrying about the sabers all day, trying to cipher it out. It seemed different from Kirby's usual troubles, getting caught across the river after lights out, a fight over a game of cards. It bothered Nate. And he knew that he couldn't expect any special consideration because he had known Doniphan so well before the war. Nate's father, Asa Hatcher, had been friends with Doniphan. Asa had served with him in the Missouri Militia during 1838, when the strife between the Gentiles and the Mormons along the Missouri-Illinois border had reached the point of open warfare. That was the year Governor Boggs issued his Extermination Order. He decreed that General Lucas and the militia should either drive the Mormons from the state for good or exterminate them. Joseph Smith and other leaders of the Church of the Latter-Day Saints were captured and tried by court-martial. The verdict condemned them to be shot for treason in the public square of Far West.

Doniphan was then a brigadier commanding six regiments in the militia. When General Lucas ordered him to execute the condemned Mormons, Doniphan put his refusal in writing. **It is cold-blooded murder. I will not obey your order. My brigade shall march for Liberty tomorrow morning at eight o'clock, and, if you execute these men, I will hold you responsible before an earthly tribunal, so help me God.**

Joseph Smith was not shot, and Asa Hatcher marched back to Liberty with Doniphan, thinking that Doniphan was the greatest man since George Washington. Doniphan must have thought some of Asa, too, because he promised Asa that, when Nate was old enough, the boy could study law with Doniphan at Liberty. Two years later, on his deathbed, Asa made Nate promise that when he was eighteen he would take Doniphan's offer. Nate had lasted six months. By that time he'd gotten his craw full of office hours, he allowed that he'd kept his part of the deathbed bargain by giving Doniphan's offer a try, and he went back to tobacco farming with his Uncle Kirby.

On the road just outside the New Mexico village Nate was stopped at a sentry post. The officer of the day was there and he directed Nate to Doniphan's quarters. Nate found Doniphan shaving. There was no mirror in the primitive room and the colonel had drawn a line on the wall and was staring at it while he scraped at his red whiskers with a Bowie knife. After asking Nate to come in, he went on twisting his mouth around and making faces as he scraped at the bristles. Nate figured that he was working up to a speech. When Doniphan made his courtroom appearances, the whole county turned out just to hear him talk. Nate had never met anybody who knew such a power of things or who had so many crackling words to describe them.

Finally Doniphan said: "You're getting quite a woolly reputation, Nate. Back at Leavenworth it seemed I couldn't pass by the guardhouse without seeing your face at the window. I thought maybe you'd settle down on the trail."

"I guess I'm a little slow getting broke to the halter, Colonel."

"And now we've got some wild scheme about stolen sabers that Lieutenant Merritt found at Las Vegas. He thinks it's some sort of sinister, traitorous plot with the Mexicans or something. I see it as something simpler. A big part of the Santa Fé trade has always been cutlery. Suppose some trader figured he could get hold of a lot of new U.S. sabers at maybe one fifth of their value. Some enterprising volunteer could make himself some money."

"Well, Colonel, that does beat all."

"When you worked for me at Liberty, now, it seems Kirby always had some kind of deal going. That time he wanted you to trade your farm for a steamboat . . ."

"I guess I would have, if you hadn't argued me out of it."

"This business with the sabers . . . it's the kind of deal that would appeal to him."

"How could Kirby be in Las Vegas? He was in camp."

"I know. I checked Hicklin's roster book. Kirby was present and accounted for. So were you, Nate, at precisely the time Lieutenant Merritt swears you were in Las Vegas."

"He must've made a mistake, Colonel. I couldn't be in two places at once."

Doniphan went on scraping his face, and the sound set Nate's teeth on edge. "As I recollect," Doniphan said, "you were thirteen when your folks died. Your Uncle Kirby raised you ever since. You must feel a power of obligation."

"I owe Kirby a lot."

"And whenever you get in some devilment, Kirby seems to be lurking somewhere in the background. He's quite a gambling man, isn't he? Back at Fort Leavenworth . . . those card games in Weston . . . all the times you were picked up across the river without a pass . . . were you really over there in some hooraw of your own, or had you sort of tagged along with Kirby?"

"Colonel, when you were a young man, didn't you kick up your heels some?"

"This is different. Should he take a notion, Merritt could cause you real trouble, maybe even a court-martial. You don't owe Kirby that much, Nate."

For a moment Nate had the impulse to trust Doniphan, to tell him the truth. Then he was ashamed of his weakness. He couldn't betray Kirby. Doniphan glanced at him obliquely.

"Well, Nate, we know that somebody was in Las Vegas with those sabers. Maybe he didn't really steal the sabers. I know the volunteers have been throwing them away along the trail. Maybe this party just picked them up, and maybe, if a friend of his blundered in on the deal, it didn't seem so wrong to this friend, since the sabers would have been a loss anyway. But if there wasn't anything wrong, why did this party run off when Merritt showed up?"

"I hadn't thought of it that way."

Doniphan ran his thumb thoughtfully down the bright edge of the Bowie. He sighed thoughtfully. "Nate, I'll tell you how I feel about this war. I'm not fooling myself about the job I've got, making soldiers out of these boys. They aren't ever going to be the kind of soldiers Merritt wants, and he'll have to learn that sooner or later, and Kearny will have to learn it sooner or later. I'm willing to leave some slack in the rope. I guess I'll tolerate a little hoorawing now and then, just to let steam out of the boiler. But there are some things I won't tolerate. One of them is treason. And I look upon it as treason to sell government property. I think you have a little influence here and there among the boys. If there's something going on with these sabers, maybe you can stop it before there's any real trouble."

"I'll do what I can, sir."

"I own you will. I guess that's all. Case dismissed."

Nate saluted. "Thank you, sir."

"Don't salute so much, Nate. This isn't the regulars."

CHAPTER
THREE

Beyond the San Miguel Springs the mountains closed in on the Army of the West. They were towering mountains, bigger than Nate had ever seen, the piñon-matted shoulders gray with an undersea mist at dawn, the rock faces giving off a blinding glare at noon, the overwhelming cliffs dyed crimson by sunset. Nate learned that Captain Philip St. George Cooke had rejoined the army near Tecolote. Cooke was the officer commanding the escort of dragoons that Kearny had sent with James Magoffin under a flag of truce to Santa Fé. Cooke had seen the Mexican governor, Manuel Armijo. In Cooke's opinion, Magoffin's wiles had prevailed, and Armijo would probably abdicate. But as they passed through the mountain villages, the little brown people standing by the road said that Governor Armijo would take his stand at Apache Cañon and the number of his forces ran as high as 20,000 men.

Tuesday, August 18th, was dismal and raining. Nate crawled from his tent, soaking wet, and began the wearisome business of breaking camp. Kelly Goff idled around, lording it over Bristol Graham like an Oriental potentate, while Bristol struck Kelly's tent and loaded it in the wagon and saddled Kelly's horse and collected

Kelly's gear. Kelly had been talking so much about how beautiful La Tules was and how she hankered after ugly men and how he could fix it up for Bristol that he had finally convinced Bristol. He had arranged for Bristol to pay for the introduction by doing all of Kelly's work in camp. It made Nate mad because Bristol was the kind of jasper everybody was always hoorawing, and Nate tried to argue him out of it, but Bristol was too fired up to pay any heed.

Under a gray drizzle the army climbed into Apache Cañon. They tied their sabers to their wrists again and loaded their guns. But the cañon was empty. They passed redoubts and bastions made of felled timber, a whole series of fortifications without any defenders.

The scouts captured a frightened Mexican farmer watching them from the heights. He said that Armijo had been at the fortifications with several thousand men. But he thought it was just a show to save Armijo's face. There had been a quarrel among the officers and Armijo had fled south with his personal retinue of dragoons, leaving the demoralized peasants to return to an undefended Santa Fé.

The Army of the West moved out of the cañon into sloping sagebrush flats, a long line of emaciated men on emaciated horses, the sixteen brass cannon giving off a green shimmer in the overcast, the endless file of white-topped wagons fluttering like moths against the dark mountains.

Late in the afternoon Nate had his first sight of the town. He didn't know exactly what he had expected —

34

castles, towers glittering in the sunset, fancy battlements, or what — but, after all that talk, the end of the Santa Fé Trail, the capital city of all New Mexico, the sinful women, La Tules, money heaped on the tables, it kind of took the tucker out of a man to see it. Santa Fé was just another mud village.

They had come 821 miles according to the viameter on the wagon of the Topographical Corps. They had marched for almost two months just to see another brown mud town with brown mud houses that seemed to grow out of the ground. A creek meandered down out of the mountains and ran south of the main part of town. Nate couldn't see the water because it had cut a deep ditch and the ditch was choked with willow growth. South of the creek the houses were more scattered, separated by fields, patches of green against the brown earth. North of the creek the buildings clustered more closely, creating narrow streets that wandered crookedly between crumbling walls and spindle fences toward a central square. Just across the bridge an old woman stood on the trail that ran along the high north bank of the creek. She had a shawl over her head and was wailing.

"Captain Reid says they think we're a-going to rape all their women and brand U.S. on their cheeks," Kirby said.

"Which one is La Tules's house?" Bristol wanted to know.

"She lives on the other side of town," Kelly said. "She can't come out in the daytime. The governor don't have enough soldiers to protect her."

In order to get through the streets they had to break their fours and form in a column of twos. Ahead and behind of Nate the narrow passage seemed choked with men. They got jammed up near a corner and Herkins's horse slammed its rump against the mud wall of a house. The outer plaster crumbled away, revealing the long mud bricks underneath. Herkins slammed at the bricks with the butt of his rifle, knocking more chunks of the crumbling adobe away.

"Hey, Kirby!" he called. "Look at this. These houses ain't nothin' but mud." It seemed to fascinate him, and he kept slamming his rifle at the wall and gouging big holes in it. "It's nothin' but mud clear through, the whole thing's nothin' but mud top to bottom . . ."

"Herkins!" the sergeant called. "As you were!"

The plaza was a bare and sandy square, a sundial and a few scrawny trees in its center surrounded by a rutted road. It was jammed with troops. The infantry stood at parade rest. The six companies of the 1st Dragoons were drawn up in precise ranks before a long building that stood on the north side of the square. It had a low tower at each end and a gallery across the front with a roof supported by heavy posts planted every ten or twelve feet. Somebody told Nate that it was the Palace of the Governors. In the shadows of the gallery were the officials of the town, giving some kind of greetings to Kearny.

The sun was just setting. Its red afterglow creeping up the mountains behind Santa Fé made Nate think of blood. Major Clark had dragged his two batteries onto a low hill above town and they gave a thirteen-gun salute. The reverberations made a heavy sound against the mud walls of the town and Nate thought that he heard window glass shatter somewhere.

After the ceremony the troops marched out of town. Nate heard that they would make camp on the hill near the artillery. He was glad that it was over. They had marched thirty miles that day in the rain. He was wet and tired and ached all over. On their way out they passed a girl standing in the carriage entrance to a house. Kirby grinned at her, and she went back inside.

The gate in which Inez Torreón had stood was wide enough to permit the passage of a coach. When the yellow-headed *gringo* had smiled at her, she had backed into the patio. The house was built around the patio on all sides. It gave Inez the comforting feeling of standing in a square well, shadowed and safe from the outside world, looking up at the sky above. For over 200 years the Torreóns had lived in this house on the Río Santa Fé just south of the church. For the eighteen years of her life Inez had lived here.

The smell of honeysuckle was sweet and strong in the patio. A peppery sprinkling of red tamarisk seeds covered the parched ground beneath the trees. The finger-like pods of drying chile hung against the walls in red festoons. Above the flat roof of the house Inez could see the yellow aspens on the high red slopes of the Mountains of the Blood of Christ. But she could not forget the smiling soldier. He was so much taller than the men she knew. All the *gringos* were taller — and more violent. She had seen it in the face of the one with the yellow hair — something about his teeth when he smiled, something about the shape of his cheeks, the look in his blue eyes. The thought of his violence stirred her in a strange way. She touched her cheek. It would hurt when they branded her. She had seen the cattle squeal and lunge when they were branded. She had been nauseated by the smell of burning hair. Inez shivered and pulled her shawl around her shoulders.

She went inside. She had to pass through the parlor. The last of the red-tinged twilight coming through the narrow windows gave the whitewashed mud walls a luminous glow. In niches around the walls stood the family saints. In one corner stood the Man of Sorrows. Sometimes it frightened her to think of how long he had stood there with the thorny crown on his head and the agony in his eyes. Her father was a *penitente*. It gave a man great power in the community to belong to the *penitente* brotherhood. She had heard that in many matters her father was even more powerful than Governor Armijo.

To the brotherhood, Christ was not only the image on the cross but also the Man of Sorrows who had passed through the tortures of his passion and had come down from the cross to stand before mankind bearing the marks of his anguish. During Holy Week, deep in the mountains, the *penitentes* reënacted the Crucifixion. One of the brotherhood was chosen as Christ. On Good Friday the procession came from the mud-walled *morada* with the chosen one carrying his heavy cross. The *penitentes* marched behind the man with the cross. They whipped themselves with cactus scourges. They marched up the trail to the hill of Calvary. When she was fifteen, Inez had been chosen as one of the *verónicas* who walked beside the brothers and wiped their faces with cloths. Inez had seen her father whipping his bare back until it was covered with blood. She had seen him crying in pain that was atonement for his sins. She had seen Christ hanging from the cross at the top of the hill.

Inez was crossing the parlor when her father and *Don* Fecundo León entered from the other door. At first they did not see her in the dim room and she hesitated, filled with the impulse to turn back. But she knew that she would have to make an appearance before *Don* Fecundo. He was dressed in the old style, a ruffled Rouen shirt and a green corduroy jacket. His black kid shoes had a fringed leather piece at the heel to support spurs he had stopped wearing long ago.

When Inez's father saw her, he said: "You have dust on your feet. Was it kicked there by *gringo* horses?"

Guiltily she looked at her bare feet. Shoes were hard to come by in this barren land and even the daughters of the fine people went barefoot much of the time to save their slippers.

"You were forbidden," her father said. "Did I not forbid you to go into the street?"

She kept her eyes lowered. She knew that she could not explain her curiosity to him. She could not even explain it to herself. There had been so many strange stories about the *gringos* — all she had wanted was a peek. Her throat always seemed to go dry and close up before her father's anger.

Don Miguel Torreón's long face was rigid and pale and always reminded her of the wooden faces of the saints in their niches. He wore a dark velvet suit and queued his black hair. On one forefinger was a ring bearing the rubric of a Spanish house a thousand years old. In 300 years no Indian blood had tainted the Torreón family and *Don* Miguel had once killed a man for suggesting that it had.

Don Fecundo cleared his throat. *Don* Miguel looked at him. *Don* Miguel did not smile but his mouth relaxed a little. The two men had been *compadres* since childhood. The relationship of such fellow-godfathers was sacred.

"We will go into your disobedience later," *Don* Miguel told Inez. "At the moment we have something of great importance to announce. I have now formally acknowledged *Don* Fecundo's letter of proposal. I have given my consent. We have just set the wedding date. You will marry *Don* Fecundo on the Thirteenth of September."

Inez felt some need to react. The proper thing would be to smile, some sound of pleasure. But she could not smile. Her face felt numb. It did not matter. Neither of the men was looking at her. *Don* Fecundo smiled. His eyes were half closed and dreamy. It always gave him the look of smiling at some memory in the distant past. From his scarlet sash he took his packet of cornhusks and the little silver tube containing his tobacco. He looked at *Don* Miguel, clearing his throat.

"Of course," *Don* Miguel said. "Smoke."

40

Don Fecundo looked at Inez. Automatically she nodded in consent. She wondered if he would always be so gracious with her, seeking her permission for the slightest act in her presence. He had a reputation for great kindness but the fact that he gave it so indiscriminately did not do much to distinguish her from his favorite horse. She saw that he was making three *cigarrillos*. It was a celebration of the occasion.

Don Fecundo handed the first *cigarrillo* to her father, the second to Inez. Her mother often smoked with the men and even her aunts and elder sisters, but Inez had so far smoked only among the women. She crossed to the chest against the wall. From one of the drawers she got the little tongs of gold in which the women held their *cigarrillos* to keep from staining their fingers. She took one of the three burning tapers from the silver candleholder on top of the chest and carried it back to light the smokes for the men. Her hand was trembling and *Don* Fecundo steadied it with his.

There was no feeling of strength to his fingers. They had the soft smoothness of wax. She could not think of a lover touching her hand. She could think only of a father, or a priest. It did not make her heart jump as it had when Bernardo Gálvez touched her hand. Bernardo was only twenty and he had requested her as his bride in a letter to *Don* Miguel a year ago but *Don* Miguel had not answered the letter. The Gálvez family had been in Santa Fé for only 100 years and Bernardo's father was not a *penitente*.

She carried the candle back to the candleholder and placed her own *cigarrillo* in the golden tongs and held it to the candle flame. *Don* Fecundo would not smoke any of the imported tobacco. The native leaf had little bite. She would always associate its bland taste with *Don* Fecundo.

"We have been discussing the guest list," *Don* Miguel said. "We have decided to eliminate your uncle, James Magoffin. We all know he arrived in town with that Captain Cooke, ahead of the *gringo* army, and it is said that he was an emissary from the *gringo* general and was somehow instrumental in getting Governor Armijo to abdicate."

She was surprised that her father would take such a stand. James Magoffin had married her aunt, María Váldez, and had lived for many years at El Paso. He was loved and respected by the Mexicans, and, if he had really influenced Armijo's abdication, he had achieved one of her father's most cherished wishes. Governor Armijo was not one of the fine people and *Don* Miguel had hated having a peasant in the palace. Armijo's abdication had justified *Don* Miguel's contempt. The governor had marched to Apache Cañon with his whole army, and then had marched out again. He had fled south with all the loot he could carry and Santa Fé had been left undefended.

It put *Don* Miguel in a peculiar position. That morning at breakfast he had announced his intentions to the family. As a conservative he had never had any use for the *gringos*. But they were now the only ones strong enough to prevent the return of the Armijo regime. It was a matter of choosing the lesser of two evils. The Torreóns would bide their time. They would

42

wait to see if the *gringo* rule were an improvement over Armijo. They would keep a careful neutrality. They would not oppose the *gringos* but that did not mean that they would support them. They would certainly not invite the *gringos* into their homes. James Magoffin, in the last analysis, was a *gringo*. Even if he had helped overthrow Armijo, he had also opened the gates to a foreign conqueror. *Don* Miguel could never forgive him that.

"As you go to your room," *Don* Miguel told Inez, "stop and ask your mother to come here. We will require her help in completing the guest list."

Inez left the room with a bowed head. She was glad that the men took her acceptance of the betrothal for granted. If they had asked for some expression, she might have revealed her feelings. There was no reason why her father should consult her wishes. When he had married his wife, he had addressed the proposal in a letter to her father and her father had not consulted her wishes.

As Inez went through the door, she looked back at her bridegroom. The flesh of his hands had the color of the parchment they used for official documents. Then she was out of their sight and she turned to the wall and pressed her shawl against her mouth. She didn't know whether the sound it muffled was a laugh or a sob.

CHAPTER
FOUR

On the morning after the army reached Santa Fé, the volunteers who didn't draw duty had a look at the town. Only four men out of Nate's squad went. Sergeant Hicklin was too busy studying *Tactics and Regulations*, and Charlie Hayes said that he had seen enough poverty and dirt and Popish superstition to last him a lifetime. Besides he had to read his Bible.

The ragged soldiers were streaming down off the hill into the crooked streets, most of them ending up in the square. Indians stood in bright-colored blankets against the blank mud walls, watching the crowds impassively. In front of the long palace gallery, vendors sold pyramids of soap, goat's cheese, heaps of onions, freckled beans, firewood, buffalo hump, or anything else a body could imagine. It all smelled of the fresh-cut alfalfa that could be had for 25¢ a load and the rancid pork and the ague-colored chickens and bloody tripe that raised its stench from under protecting nettings of pink cotton. Nate thought that the noise was worse than a chicken coop, the shrill chants of vendors and the cursing of Missourians and the creak of the big two-wheeled outfits the Mexicans called *carretas* and the volunteers called bulger wagons.

Nate tried some of the chili and tamales a woman was cooking at a brazier, and thought he'd burned the lining out of his mouth.

Bristol was in a sweat to be introduced to La Tules and he badgered Kelly until Kelly led them all off the square onto San Francisco Street. Bristol's eyes were shining and he kept wiping the back of his hand across his moist lips.

"Kelly," Nate said, "this better not be a hooraw. You ain't got no right to make a hooraw out of Bristol this way."

"It ain't no hooraw," Kelly said. "It's the ugly ones La Tules goes for, I tell you. Last time I was here she had a hunchback Indian without no nose. Fair turn your stomach to look at him. Some women are that way, you know. An ugly man sends them crazy."

Nate couldn't argue with Kelly, because so much of it sounded like the things he'd heard about La Tules already. The Missouri settlements had been the eastern terminus of the Santa Fé Trail for over twenty years, and it seemed to Nate that for most of his life he'd been listening to the tales about La Tules brought back from Santa Fé by the traders. She was a New Mexican, born of the poor, and had gotten her start many years ago throwing monte. Her beauty, her skill at cards, and her talent for politics had lifted her to a dazzling pinnacle. The richest and most notorious woman on the Santa Fé Trail, confidante of rulers and rogues, mistress of Governor Armijo, she was believed to have been the real power behind the throne before the American occupation. The traders believed that it was her influence, even more than Magoffin's blarney, that caused Armijo to abdicate. Nate had been thinking about it till he wondered if he wasn't just about as excited as Bristol.

There were no sidewalks on San Francisco Street. It was hedged on either side by the blank and windowless walls of the houses, turning it to a crooked, dusty chasm. A few hundred feet west of the plaza the solid walls were broken by a passage called Burro Alley, where the woodcutters hitched their shaggy little animals. The door of the building beyond that was wide open. Nate could hear somebody playing a fiddle inside and there was a crowd in the street craning to get a look through the door. When Kirby tried to push through, a dragoon got in his way. It was a sergeant from another company who had been giving the volunteers trouble ever since leaving Leavenworth.

"How did you Missouri pukes get here?" the sergeant asked. "General Kearny told me he was going to keep you in a cage."

"He changed his mind," Kirby said. "He needed somebody dirty enough for latrine detail and he sent us down to fetch the regulars."

They exchanged some more insults and it was leading to a fight when a dragoon lieutenant named Noble appeared and broke it up. When Nate finally got inside, he saw a big room divided down the center by long beams and heavy supporting posts. An immense chandelier hung from the ceiling. Kelly told them that it had 100 candles. Against one wall stood long narrow mirrors that rose from white marble shelves, reflecting the red velvet hangings over the windows, the carved chairs, and the claw-footed green-topped monte tables. There was a shiny bar backed by another mirror and at its rear stood the high seat for the spotter who watched all the games. Beyond him was a platform where the squeaky orchestra played. A lot of traders and soldiers were dancing with the Mexican girls. The girls had dirty bare feet and ragged dresses. Their faces were pitted from smallpox and their teeth were stained yellow from the cornhusk cigarettes they all seemed to smoke.

"Where's La Tules?" Bristol asked Kelly. "You promised to show me La Tules."

Kelly found one of the bartenders who spoke a little English and the man said that La Tules would be out soon. None of the volunteers had any money but the man at the bar told them the brass buttons on their jackets were worth 25¢ apiece. They all tried something called Taos Lightning, and, by the time their buttons were all used up, Nate had a roaring in his head and Bristol was so drunk he had trouble standing up. He pounded on the bar.

"Where is she, Kelly? I took a dozen wood details for you. I been rubbing your horse down all the way from Las Vegas for this. I got my steam up now, I'm pounding harder'n a double-acting steam engine . . ."

The Mexican bartender touched Kelly's arm and pointed to the bandstand. A fat woman had climbed up on the platform beside the fiddler. She had on a red silk gown and over her shoulders was a purple-fringed shawl embroidered with pink roses. Her wig was about the same color as the roses. Her eyes were outlined with greasy black mascara and there was a chalky powder on her face that turned her bloated jowls lavender in the light from the overhead chandelier.

"Well, Bristol," Kelly said. "There's La Tules."

Bristol stared blankly at the woman. Nate knew how steamed up he had been, and he thought that, when Bristol finally understood the joke that had been played on him, he would really bust his boiler and clobber Kelly or something. But he didn't move. A strange, crumpled look came to his face, his throat started to twitch as if he had something he couldn't swallow, and he made a whimpering sound. Kelly was slapping his legs and whooping fit to bust, and all the other volunteers at the bar who had been in on the hooraw were laughing and pounding on each other. Nate thought about all the work Kelly had gotten out of Bristol, and how it must feel to be so ugly no woman would look at you, and it made him so mad that he turned around and hit Kelly.

It knocked Kelly back against the bar. He hung on with his elbows, blood coming from his mouth, and then he grabbed up the half-filled bottle of Taos Lightning and broke it against the bar. He lunged at Nate with the broken bottle held face high. Nate was trapped against the bar, and, when he tried to wheel away, a soldier got in his way. He tried to block Kelly's thrust, but Kelly knocked his hand away with his free fist. Nate had his back against the bar and he saw the jagged bottle coming at his face and knew he couldn't escape.

Then Kirby grabbed Kelly from behind. It stopped the bottle so close to Nate that a piece of it nicked his cheek. Kelly let out a bellow as Kirby twisted his arm up and back of his head. He arched Kelly so far backward Nate thought the man would break in two, and then Kirby kicked his feet out from under him and Kelly went down.

Lieutenant Noble came through the crowd, shouting at them, and some volunteer at a table picked up a chair and threw it at him. The chair hit Noble in the face and he went down.

Nate saw that fights had started between dragoons and volunteers all over the room. The sergeant tried to grapple Nate, but Kirby knocked him back into the crowd and grabbed Nate, dragging him toward the door.

"Time to light a shuck, Nate. Any volunteer caught in here after Noble got clobbered with that bottle is due for a court-martial, certain."

They got out on the street without being caught and headed for the plaza. Nate realized that he was trembling now. He'd never had a broken bottle so close to his face before. It made him think of how close he'd come to betraying Kirby when Doniphan had been questioning him about the sabers back at the San Miguel Springs. Maybe Doniphan was right; maybe half the trouble he'd gotten into back at Fort Leavenworth and along the trail had been because he was tagging along with Kirby. But it was Kirby who always got him out of the trouble, too, one way or another. Kirby had been getting him out of trouble ever since he was thirteen.

That had been the time Nate first met Kirby. Nate was abed with the ague. It was a common affliction and during the whole year hardly a month went by without somebody in the family being down with it. Nate's father, Asa Hatcher, thought that he had caught it plowing a virgin field. The rich soil emitted gases that poisoned his system, Asa said, and he had passed it on to Nate. There were the chills, the fevers, the headaches, the periods of delirium. It kept the whole family down till late in February. Nate's pa was so weak he couldn't crawl out of the house and he said if he didn't get the tobacco out they would have no crop that year. At last Asa wrote to Kirby in St. Louis, asking him to come and get the tobacco out. Nate had never seen Kirby and didn't know much about him except that he was Asa's younger brother, only twelve years older than Nate, and had traveled around a lot.

One night a long time after the letter had been written Nate came out of a delirium and saw a stranger lying on the floor near him. The man had long hair the color of fresh corn. The sun had burned white streaks through it and his heavy eyebrows were almost white. His pointed ears made Nate think of a wolf. He had his chin aimed at the ceiling and he was grinning and snoring louder than anybody Nate had ever heard. Nate went to sleep again, or passed out, and, when he came to another time, the stranger was at the wood stove cooking a big pot of soup. He saw Nate looking at him and grinned.

"Hello, button," he said. "I'm your Uncle Kirby. After you git this hot soup down your innards, I'll give you a big dose of Osgood's Cholagogue that I brought all the way from Saint Looey. It'll send your ague shouting home to glory."

It seemed that Kirby had his hands so full nursing them that he never did get the tobacco out. Kirby finally caught the ague himself and Nate could remember waking up many a night and seeing Kirby shaking with chills, the sweat pouring off him, grinning and trying to make jokes, as he piled blankets on Asa or tried to get some medicine down Nate's mother. Nate's baby sister died, and then his mother, and finally his father. Afterward the neighbors told Nate that he would have died, too, if it hadn't been for Kirby.

Nate and Kirby were halted by a crowd where San Francisco Street entered the plaza. The swarm of barefoot brown people and the smells of the town and the strange talk was so all-fired different from anything Nate had ever encountered that he forgot Kelly and Bristol and the fight, just wanting to stand and gape. But Kirby seemed to be looking for somebody now.

Nate followed him through the mob, past a crumbling mud building on the south side of the square that some volunteer told them was the military chapel, to an inn on the southwest corner named La Fonda. It was one story high, built of the inevitable buckskin-colored, water-streaked adobe. There was an enormous main barroom with smaller rooms opening off of it for private games. The larger room was blue with smoke and jammed with dragoons and volunteers and

51

barefooted Mexicans. Nate was used to the splintery deal tables and penny-ante card games of the two taverns at Marshall. He'd never dreamed of such fancy layouts as he saw now. The faro dealers had ivory card boxes inlaid with silver, the chuck-a-luck cages looked as though they were pure gold, the monte games were painted in gaudy colors on the bright green covering of handsome walnut tables with clawed legs and silver inlay and intricately carved edges.

"Alza," somebody kept shouting, "the blond queen rides toward me!"

Kirby saw how Nate was gaping and chuckled softly. "What'd I tell you, Nate . . . the doings they have here and the women they have here and the deals a man can make . . ."

It was the way Kirby had talked all the way from Missouri. Nate guessed that was mostly why he had joined, because of Kirby's talk, and because Kirby had joined. He wanted to stop the Mexicans from killing Taylor's boys, and wanted to win the war, but he hadn't thought about that so much as he had about Kirby's talk.

"You sure weren't hoorawing me, Kirby," he said. "I guess I've never seen such fixings."

Kirby saw somebody at the bar and started toward him. Nate recognized Jim Ganoe, the Missouri trader Kirby had tried selling the sabers to back at Las Vegas. He had shaved clean and changed his stained hickory jacket for a blue fustian, but he still smelled of wheel dope and mules. Kirby took out his plug of tobacco, offering it around. It was cased with licorice and molasses, and, when Ganoe took a chaw, it made Nate's mouth water. Nate took the last chaw and handed it back to Kirby. Ganoe was in a sour mood.

"I'll tell you boys," he said, "I could've made a killing. About ten years ago the Mexican government put an embargo on a list of goods as long as your arm. Candlewick, cotton drillings, shoes, cutlery . . . we couldn't bring none of it in. The demand built up something sergiverous. These people went without some things so long they'll pay almost any price. You seen how many of 'em are still barefoot. Soon's the war was declared I knew the U.S. would take off the embargo. Shoes is what I stocked up on, ten wagonloads of shoes. If a man takes wool for the shoes, and trades for it at five cents a pound here, and sells it for fifteen cents a pound back in Missouri, it adds up nigh onto a thousand per cent on the original investment. And who kept me from it? The U.S. Army."

Nate knew the trouble the traders had been having with the army. Ever since the Missouri River they had complained that Kearny moved too slowly for them. He had a constant battle to keep them from rushing ahead of his protection and taking their chances with the Mexicans in order to sell their goods at the best possible prices.

"I had my deal all set up here," Ganoe grumbled. "A buyer for the shoes and enough wool to fill my wagons. If I'd started three days earlier, the army wouldn't have been able to catch me. I lost the whole deal to Speyer and some of them other smart jackasses that got onto the trail before Kearny put the brakes on. Time we pulled in here all the decent wool had been traded, and not even enough hides left to make a dollar on."

"There must be some wool around," Kirby said. "What about those big flocks of sheep we saw on the way through Apache Cañon?"

"If it's still on the sheep, you can bet we'll never get it," Ganoe said. "There's a bunch of ranchers and big mucky-mucks here that you might call the conservative element. They hate Americans, they've never accepted us, and they'd kill their sheep before they'd do any business with us."

"What would it be worth to you if one of them would make a deal?" Kirby said. "Ten per cent of your Missouri profit?"

"I'd give that and more," Ganoe said. Then he made a sputtering sound and glared at Kirby. "Now you're talking hogwash."

"I've got some connections," Kirby said mysteriously.

"Not in this country, you ain't," Ganoe said. "I can't afford to get involved in one of your tricky deals, Kirby. The only thing for me is to go on south to Chihuahua City. The big market is there anyway, and under ordinary circumstances I wouldn't mind it, but with this war on a man's taking his life in his hands."

"If you're going down there, you'll be able to sell the five hundred sabers," Kirby said.

"You ain't got no five hundred sabers."

"Now you're backing out," Kirby said. "You told me a Mexican would sell his soul for a good knife. You offered me a dollar apiece for every saber I kin git."

54

"I didn't figure you was going to sell the whole army out."

"Nobody's selling the army out. The army will lose every one of those swords anyway, the way the boys have been throwing them away. I guess I talked to every man in the volunteers. Ain't a one of 'em wouldn't sell his saber for fifty cents."

"Kirby," Nate said, "I thought you learned your lesson. Colonel Doniphan says it's treason. It ain't just the fact that it's government property . . . it's the Mexicans . . . you're putting knives in their hands to stick our boys with."

Ganoe chuckled. "Not these knives. You boys will never see them Mexicans down in Chihuahua City, Nate."

Kirby led Nate away from the bar and said: "You circulate out on the square. Tell all the boys you kin see that I can git them fifty cents apiece for their swords."

"Ganoe offered a dollar."

"Nate, Nate, you and me got to make our profit, too. They wouldn't even have this deal if I hadn't drummed it up. Five hundred sabers at fifty cents apiece . . . that's nigh onto two hundred and fifty dollars. There was some years we didn't make that much on our whole crop. Ganoe will have his wagons parked on the flats south of the river, and you tell the boys if they bring their swords to me down there . . ."

"Kirby, when you get to talking so fast, it's like my eyes git full of smoke or something, and I can't cipher anything out clear. There's something wrong with this. I ain't a-going to do it. Can't you see there's something wrong with this?"

Kirby kept on talking and came up with a dozen reasons why there was nothing wrong with the deal. He came so near convincing Nate that Nate finally had to leave for fear he'd weaken and agree to help Kirby. He went out into the square alone, wondering what there was about this particular deal that plagued him so much. Kirby had always been making sharp trades.

There had been the time he sold the team of mules with the Monday-morning disease to the deacon. It had seemed all right because the deacon was one of the shrewdest horse traders in the country, had done the same kind of thing to other men a dozen times, and anybody who could put one over on him was sort of a local hero. There was another time when a flood had ruined the Hatcher crop and Nate thought that he was going to lose the farm. A St. Louis manufacturer named Fenton stopped off at Marshall on an upriver trip and somehow started the rumor that he meant to build a cigar factory in town. By selling direct and saving their shipping costs to St. Louis, the local farmers could double their former profits. It started a lot of speculation in good tobacco land and Nate was able to sell a piece of his flooded farm for enough to save the rest of it. Fenton never came back, the factory was never built, and a couple of years later Nate found out that Kirby had worked for Fenton in St. Louis as an auctioneer.

Nate wondered why he hadn't added it up then. Maybe he had been too young. Or maybe he hadn't wanted to see it. When a man saved your life and raised you like he was your own pa or your big brother, it was hard to believe that he could do anything wrong. Even when one of Kirby's schemes seemed too ornery and Nate tried to argue him out of it, Kirby had ended up convincing Nate that it was the most innocent business deal in the world. Next to Doniphan, Kirby was probably the most powerful talker in the county. He would have made a booming lawyer had he put his mind to it. He always said that it was a land of sharp dealers, and, if a man didn't stay on his toes, he'd be plowed under. It always seemed to work out that way. If it hadn't been for Kirby, they would have lost the farm more than once. Nate would have lost his life.

The clanging of the church bell drove the thoughts from Nate's mind. The brazen sound came from the massive church of St. Francis at the east end of the square, its twin towers rising taller than any other building in the town. A company of dragoons was riding through the crowd and drawing up in ranks before the Palace of the Governors. The officers were all decked out in yellow silk sashes and white-plumed dress helmets. Nate knew that General Kearny had asked the people of Santa Fé to assemble in the square for some more ceremonies, and figured it was about to begin.

General Kearny and some of his staff were gathering on the roof of the palace. There were some Mexicans with them in black suits covered with fancy gold braid. Kearny had been suffering with a fever since Las Vegas and his face looked yellow in the bright August sun.

One of the Mexicans talked to the crowd till they quieted down. After that Kearny began his speech.

"New Mexicans. We have come among you to take possession of New Mexico, which we do in the name of the government of the United States. We have come with peaceable intentions and kind feelings toward you all . . ."

Nate soon lost interest. He had heard too many of Doniphan's rampages in court. Beside them anybody else's speechifying wasn't much more than a squeak. Nate pushed on through the mob.

On the south side of the plaza was a long line of mud store buildings. On one of them Nate saw the sign for **E. Leitensdorfer & Company.** Leitensdorfer had been one of the traders who brought his wagons in with the army. There was a commotion going on in front of the building. Nate saw that it was Herkins. He had a girl pushed against the wall and was struggling with her. He kept offering her two pesos to take him home with her. The Mexicans in the crowd hadn't noticed yet because they were still listening to Kearny's speech.

"We come as friends, to better your conditions and make you a part of the Republic of the United States. We mean not to murder you or rob you of your property. Your families shall be free from molestation, your women secure from violence . . ."

The girl tried to get away and Herkins pushed her back, tearing her shawl away from her face. Nate could see that she looked different from the girls he had seen at La Tules's. No pox marked her face. It was fragile and very pale. Her eyes were black. He didn't think that he'd ever seen such big eyes. Her hair was black, too, so glossy in the sun that it looked wet, all pulled up into a mother-of-pearl comb. Herkins tried to kiss her. She turned her face away, trying to twist free.

"Herkins!" Nate called. "Let her go!"

Nate didn't know what made him call out. Herkins was a big broiling jasper and Nate had seen him break up more than one man in a fight. Herkins didn't seem to hear. He was drunk and pawing at the girl. A couple of Mexicans had seen him and they tried to pull him off, but he pushed them back into the crowd. The girl tried to get away, and he stopped her again.

Nate elbowed through the Mexicans and grabbed Herkins. He was stronger than the Mexicans and he managed to pull Herkins away. Herkins got out his saber. Nate grappled him to keep from getting stabbed. They struggled around a while, with Herkins trying to pull free and get his sword into play, and finally Nate got him off balance and tripped him.

Herkins went down hard but he hung onto his sword and jumped up again. Nate thought that he was going to get stabbed for sure, but some soldiers had seen the trouble and Major Swords came up from behind Herkins and tried to stop him. Herkins swore at the quartermaster and cut at him with the saber. It missed and Captain Turner came in from the flank with his saber out. He dueled Herkins and disarmed him and held him against the wall by the point of his saber.

While the fight was going on, the girl got away and ran around the corner. Nate followed her. She was going down the narrow street toward the river. Her red satin slippers were not meant for running. One came off, and she tripped and fell to her knees.

Nate went after her. He picked up the shoe and reached her just as she was trying to rise. He took her arm. She was on one knee and tried to pull away.

"Look, ma'am . . . no hurt . . . understand? No hurt you."

He felt foolish trying to work the broken English. She was breathing heavily. Her eyes had looked black from a distance, but he could see that they were really dark brown, filled with little golden flecks. They revealed none of the panic he had expected. The dilated pupils made him think of a mad cat. She looked at his belt.

"You forgot your buckle," she said. "You will not be able to brand me."

He gaped at her, surprised by her English. He felt even more foolish. "I don't have no U.S. buckle," he said. "Some of the volunteers got a belt with a U.S. buckle, but I didn't. You didn't really swallow that yarn about us branding you on the cheek, did you?"

She didn't answer. He went to one knee and she had to steady herself on him while he slipped her shoe on. Her hand made a soft pressure on his shoulder. It made him realize how long it had been since a woman had touched him.

"You got a mighty little foot," he said.

She pulled away, looking over her shoulder. He saw that some Mexicans had left the crowd and were coming down the street toward them. The girl moved off. He had to hurry to catch up.

60

"Let me walk you home."

"Please go away. I can get home by myself."

"I want to apologize. What I mean is . . . all us volunteers ain't as ornery as Herkins. He'll get hell . . . I mean he'll get punished for what he did. General Kearny really meant it when he said we wouldn't harm your women."

She glanced at him quickly, then looked down. She pulled her shawl over her head, hiding the glossy hair. Her head was bowed, her face turned away, hidden by the shawl. It made her look frightened for the first time. The anger in her eyes had hidden it, but now he saw how small she was and how young and how frightened. He tried to make his voice soft. He tried to make it sound the way Kirby's voice sounded when he was gentling a spooked colt. There wasn't a man in the world could take the fright out of a colt the way Kirby could.

"Your English . . . where'd you learn to speak it that good?"

She did not look at him. For a while he thought that she did not mean to answer. They walked along. There was a hot dusty smell to the street. A climbing rose ran along a wall but its leaves had yellowed and fallen in parched little heaps on the ground. Nate looked over his shoulder and saw the Mexicans still trailing after them.

"James Magoffin taught me to speak English," she said.

Nate looked at her in surprise. "Jim Magoffin? The trader? I know him."

"You do?" she asked. She was looking up at him. Her mouth was open a little and her eyes were big. Curiosity seemed to have made her forget her fear.

"Jim Magoffin used to come into the offices sometimes when I was studying law with Colonel Doniphan back at Liberty. How come Magoffin taught you? English, I mean."

"He is my uncle." She sounded out of breath and got to talking faster and faster. "Not really my uncle. The woman he married is only my aunt by marriage. It has much complication. But he is also my godfather. I think . . ."

She stopped. She was looking at him and her mouth was still open. She blushed and looked at the ground.

He couldn't quite understand it. "Well . . . uh . . . how come you were outside? Today, I mean. If you thought we'd brand you."

She waited so long that he thought she wasn't going to answer again. When she finally spoke, she did not look up at him. She kept looking at the ground and she spoke lower. She seemed to choose her words carefully.

"General Kearny asked that the people assemble in the square. At first my father said he would refuse, but then he said he could not allow the *gringos* to think they were making us hide in our house and he took us onto the plaza. I got separated from my duenna . . ."

"Your what?"

"My duenna. A woman who always goes with me."

"Always? How do you git any sparking done?"

"Sparking?"

"Making love. A girl and a boy, fixing to make love, they go for a walk along the river, they don't want a third party tagging along. We sure don't put up with no duennas in Missouri."

"This is a fact very interesting," she said. She let her shawl slip away from her face. He could see that she was frowning, her lower lip held in a pout. It made him think of a little child concentrating.

"You wear shoes and have a fine horse and money to buy things," she said. "You are a man of the law so you must read and write."

"I guess I do. Tolerable good, anyway."

"You cannot be poor, or a slave."

"No, I guess I ain't what you'd call poor."

"Then you must be one of the fine people."

He gave it some thought. He chuckled. "Well, if you say so, I won't give you an argument."

There was some commotion behind them. Nate turned to see that the Mexicans were still following him, but a new man was coming from the plaza and hurrying to catch up. He wore a black coat and knee britches and the look on his face made Nate think of the schoolmaster that had preceded Hugh Long. He had caught some of the boys playing hooky down at the river. When Nate came home with his back all bloody from the whipping, Kirby went after the schoolmaster and gave him such a beating that he was in bed for two weeks. After that Nate could play hooky about any time he wanted and nobody did anything about it.

Inez looked over her shoulder and saw the man in the knee britches. She made a little sighing sound. Nate had seen plenty of irate fathers before. He knew he didn't have much time left.

"What's your name?" he asked.

"You must go now," she said. She seemed out of breath. "That is my father . . . *Don* Miguel Torreón."

They had been walking along a wall that ran for half a block down the street and had reached a big carriage entrance. The gates were closed. She knocked on one.

"I've got to know your name," Nate said.

"Inez Torreón."

"Mine's Nate Hatcher. When kin I see you again?"

The gate was swung open from inside. Inez stepped through and disappeared. He would have followed but *Don* Miguel was only two feet away. The man stopped in front of Nate. He spoke in English.

"You will not approach my daughter again," *Don* Miguel said. "If you see her on the plaza, you will not go near her or speak to her. If I hear of any of these things happening, I will seek you out and I will kill you. Is that clear, *señor?*"

When he got into a spot, Nate always tried to think of what Kirby would do. He knew Kirby would pull some kind of hooraw. He couldn't decide exactly what it would be, but just thinking about it made him start to grin. He could almost see the smoke come out of *Don* Miguel.

"You must be a Whig," Nate said.

Don Miguel looked surprised. "A Whig?"

"No Democrat would talk to a Missouri volunteer thataway," Nate said.

CHAPTER
FIVE

Camp was in an uproar when Nate returned. Herkins had been brought from town under arrest, was tied to a wagon wheel, and had been swearing at the officers so much that they had ordered him gagged. Sergeant Hicklin said that he was going to face a court-martial. There was also going to be an inquiry about what had happened at La Tules's. Lieutenant Noble's face was all cut up. He couldn't pin it on any one man because he hadn't seen who threw the chair, and after the fight the only volunteers remaining in the saloon were a couple of men from Company A who had been left unconscious on the floor when everybody else ran out.

The trouble brought a tightening of discipline on the whole regiment. They were moved off the hill to a camp on the flats south of the river. Doniphan ordered three roll calls, one at daybreak, another at sundown, and a third at tattoo. Drill was called twice a day on foot. Everyone had to have a pass to get into Santa Fé. A strict guard was set up around camp and a patrol kept in town.

Kirby's deal about the sabers still plagued Nate. He knew that it was wrong, but he couldn't bring himself to betray Kirby by reporting him. He tried to argue

Kirby out of it that night after dinner, but Kirby said the deal was set, tomorrow the volunteers would start taking their sabers to Ganoe, and there was nothing more to say. The next morning the thing was taken out of Nate's hands. So many of the volunteers had already thrown away their sabers that the officers took all the names of those who couldn't produce them at morning drill. Doniphan held one of his first general courts-martial and the men on the list were sentenced to march in front of the guard tent, two hours on and two hours off, carrying their saddlebags on their backs loaded with forty pounds of sand. The regiment was warned that inspection would be held daily and any other men found without their sabers would receive the same punishment. Nate figured that it would discourage anybody from taking Kirby's offer.

Something else was plaguing Nate, maybe even more than the deal with the sabers, and that was the thought of Inez Torreón. It only made it worse when he couldn't get a pass into town.

Word had gotten around that Kearny was going to build a fort and name it after the Secretary of War, and that Saturday at roll call Captain Reid announced that the men working more than ten days in a row on Fort Marcy would get 18¢ a day over their regular pay. It only drew jeers from the men. It was just another empty promise to troops who hadn't received a cent of their pay yet. None of them would volunteer and Captain Reid had to order his first shift out. Kirby had just finished his penance in front of the guard tent, and he and Nate both drew duty at the fort. The details

66

from the eight companies marched across the river and up the hill overlooking town. At the site they found Corporal McClean with Lieutenant Emory and Lieutenant Gilmer of the Topographical Corps. McClean told them that Emory had been assistant engineer in building Fort Schuyler at New York Harbor. The volunteers were not impressed.

Fort Marcy was going to be built of adobe blocks and the engineers had gotten some Mexicans to show the volunteers how the bricks were made. They mixed the mud and straw in a hole and poured it into wooden forms. After the mud was dry, the forms were lifted off and they had a brick sixteen inches long that weighed forty pounds. It was hard work handling the heavy bricks in the sun and after lunch most of the Mexicans took a nap. They said that it was their custom and the officers couldn't get them back to work with threats or bribes.

Finally Kelly Goff figured out a way to wake them up. He tied a rope to one of the Mexican burros and made a slip noose at the other end. Kelly dropped the noose over the foot of an old Mexican sleeping under one of the company wagons. Nate looked at the rocky ground the old man would be dragged over and got to feeling bad about it. He went to wake the old man, but, before he reached him, Kelly jabbed the burro with his knife. The burro squealed and took off. Nate pulled his Bowie and slashed the rope just as it snapped tight and jerked the old man from under the wagon. The Mexican blinked and sat up. He looked blankly at the cut rope noosed to his foot.

Kelly came toward Nate. His jowls were bristly with whiskers and sweat gave them a greasy, gun-barrel shine. He had torn all the buttons off his blue jacket to buy drinks in town and it was stained with tobacco and food and the brown mud they had been working in all morning.

"What did you go and do that for?" Kelly asked.

"I don't think it would have been a very good hooraw," Nate said.

"I think it would have been a prime hooraw," Kelly said. "It seems to me you're a-bustin' in on too many of my hooraws lately. I guess you figured I'd forgot how you hit me on the jaw that night at La Tules's. Well, I ain't forgot."

"I allow you deserved it. Life already stuck the knife deep enough in Bristol, without you a-giving a twist to it."

"I don't like the way your nose is put on," Kelly said. "I think it would look better bent over to one side of your face."

He spat on his hands and started coming for Nate. From somewhere behind, Kirby said: "Kelly, you lay a hand on my nephew and I'll bust you open like a sack of meal."

Kelly stopped and Nate turned to see his uncle standing a few feet behind him. Kelly stirred around uncertainly, looking from Kirby to Nate. Before he could make any decision, Lieutenant Merritt came riding up from camp on inspection.

"Are you three men on this detail?" he asked.

"Yes, sir," Nate said.

"Then either get back to work or go on report."

Kelly hesitated, finally spat at Nate's feet, and turned to go back to the mud pits. Nate and Kirby followed more slowly.

"You don't have to take up my fights," Nate said.

"Nate, maybe you forget, I been taking up your fights since you was thirteen."

"Kirby, I don't aim to sound ungrateful . . . but I ain't thirteen any more."

Kirby laughed and clapped him on the back. "That you ain't, Nate, that you ain't. All right. Next time I'll let you turn your own wolf loose. Kelly Goff'll think he stepped in a bear trap."

Nate tried to grin. "I thought maybe you were mad about those sabers."

"No, Nate, not really mad. Appears I couldn't have pulled it off anyhow, the way things turned out. I got another deal a-going, a hundred times as big. You heard Jim Ganoe say he'd give ten percent of his Missouri profits to anybody that'd hook him up with one of these big sheep ranchers that won't sell their wool to the Americans. Well, I been trying to cipher out a way to swing it."

As they started back to work, Kirby went on talking about how there were some Mexicans in town who would do business with the Americans, and how he planned to use one of them as a middleman, so the big rancher would never know he was selling his wool to an American. Nate didn't pay much heed to the details; it seemed that he had heard so many of Kirby's deals.

While Kirby was still talking, the old Mexican that Kelly had tried to hooraw came over to thank Nate.

"I am named Jayán," he said, "and I have sixty years. I think the joke of them would have made me many broken bones. You have much youth to be so kind."

"It ain't that exactly," Nate said. "I guess you reminded me of my pa. He was taller then you, but just as skinny, and he had that little stoop to his shoulders. Too much plowing, maybe. Uncommon big hands, too, with knobby knuckles same as yours."

It was curious. Nate hadn't thought of his father in a long time. But he realized that it was probably the reason he had moved so quickly to help the old man. Jayán even had the same thick white hair Nate could remember on his father, although Jayán's skin was darker. Nate pulled out his plug and offered Jayán a bite. Jayán said he did not chew, but he would be pleased to smoke. He had not made enough money in a year to buy tobacco. Nate took out his Bowie and shredded some of the plug. Jayán borrowed a corn shuck from one of the other Mexicans and rolled himself a cigarette. He then announced that he and Nate were *compadres*. Nate asked what that was. Jayán said it meant they were co-godfathers, which was even better than being blood brothers.

"Will your folks like that?" Nate said. "Being *compadres* with an American."

"There are good *gringos* and there are bad *gringos*. You are one of the good *gringos*."

"I sort of expected you'd hate us all."

"There are some Mexicans who for you will have the hate," Jayán said. "Such as Governor Armijo or Colonel Archuleta or the Torreóns. The *ricos* who lose their fortune or the *gente de fina* who lose their power. But what have the poor to lose? Armijo was *un tirano* who from the poor had already take all. *Ciertamente*, the rule of the *gringo*, it could be no worse. Maybe better. *¿Quién sabe?* Already it seem that way. Do I not have tobacco, after the lack of a year? Has not General Kearny already do away with so many of the taxes and *derechos* that were giving us the ruin? It may have the strangeness, *compadre*, but there are some among us who welcome the conqueror . . . and most of these are the poor."

Nate hadn't thought about it that way. He had thought it would all be cut and dried. How could you fight a war if you didn't hate each other? It was all too complicated to cipher out, but a name that Jayán had mentioned stuck in his mind. The Torreóns. He asked Jayán about Inez Torreón. The old man said that she came from one of the finest families in Santa Fé and there was no possible way of Nate's seeing her. Jayán said that he had learned to speak English as a mule driver on the Santa Fé Trail, but he didn't do too well and he threw in so many Spanish words that Nate had to keep stopping him and asking him about them. After a while Nate figured that, if the army were going to be here long, he ought to learn to talk the language and he made a deal to keep Jayán in tobacco if he would teach him Spanish. Kirby told Nate that it was a waste of time. Kirby didn't like a man who talked a foreign language.

On Monday morning Kirby and Nate had to report to work again but they got off early to be paraded with the regiment while Herkins was drummed out of the service. Herkins was brought from the guard tent by six volunteers with bayoneted rifles. The adjutant read the sentence of the court-martial condemning Herkins to be dishonorably discharged from the service for molesting a woman in the square and attacking two officers with his saber.

When it was over, Nate and Kirby went back to work on the fort. Nate heard that General Kearny had made an announcement in town about throwing a grand ball next Thursday at the palace. All the finest families had been invited. That meant the Torreóns were sure to be there. It gave Nate an idea how he could see Inez. He tried to get Kirby to go along, but Kirby balked.

"How can you make it?" Kirby asked. "This ball is just for the officers and high mucky-mucks in the government. They won't let a volunteer near the place."

"We won't be volunteers," Nate said. "You know how close the dragoon camp is to where we've been working. You've seen those company wagons parked about fifty feet from Fort Marcy. That's where the dragoons keep their extra gear. There's a lieutenant in Company G sick with scurvy and a couple other dragoon officers down with typhoid. They ain't a-going to be using their uniforms for that fancy ball, certain for sure. I'll bet I could outfit us proper."

72

"Nate, don't be crazy. Impersonating an officer. You want to git drummed out like Herkins? They might even shoot us."

"I got to git to her somehow, Kirby. I tell you, once you clap your eyes on her, you'll understand why I'm in such a sweat."

Kirby shook his head. He couldn't see risking their necks just to meet a girl. He was involved in something far more important. If he could hook Ganoe up with a load of Mexican wool, they'd all go back to Missouri rich men. Nate could see that it wasn't any use arguing. When Kirby was working out a deal, he got single-minded as a mule.

On Wednesday morning after "Reveille" Nate managed to borrow a handful of buttons from among the men who still had a few left on their coats. He gave them to Hugh Long, who had a pass into town. Hugh bought some Taos Lightning with the buttons and brought it back to Nate. On Thursday Nate took the bottle to work with him on the hill. Jayán didn't understand all of what Nate tried to explain to him, but the old man considered Nate his *compadre* now and would do anything for him. Lieutenant Emory had gotten the detail excused from evening parade so they could work until nightfall, and, when it got dark, Jayán talked the dragoon sentry into moving away from the wagons for a drink. While they were busy, Nate rummaged hurriedly through the gear till he found the dress uniforms he wanted. In hope that Kirby would still join him, he took an extra helmet, boots, saber slings, and coat and trousers.

He hid them behind a pile of bricks till Jayán came back, and told the old man to take the uniforms to the bridge just outside the volunteer camp. When he told Kirby about it, Kirby still scoffed.

"Nate, I got a deal in town. I can't waste time on such hijinks as this. You ain't crazy enough to go through with it anyway. You'll get in a hundred feet of that palace and see all those officers in their gold braid and all those Mexicans in their fancy cutaways, your knees will turn to water, and you'll turn tail and run."

It made Nate mad. He remembered what Doniphan had said, about his getting into most of his trouble because he was just tagging along with Kirby. It seemed that he had been tagging along with Kirby most of his life, doing things because Kirby did them, and, now that he was trying to do something on his own, Kirby was laughing at him. He was glad that Kirby wasn't going along. It would give him the chance to show Kirby. He didn't need Kirby's help. He had to admit that Kirby was right, it did seem crazy, but something had gotten into him. Maybe it had started with just wanting to see the girl, but now it was all mixed up, like he had to prove something to himself, or Kirby; he didn't know which.

The volunteer sentries didn't keep much of a watch and it was easy for Nate to slip by them after dinner. Tattoo was at ten and Nate figured that he could see the girl and get back to camp in time for the last roll call. He found Jayán huddled under the bridge. The uniform didn't fit too well. When Nate got all rigged out in the plumed dress helmet, saber harness, jack

74

boots, orange silk sash, and yellow-striped britches, he felt so self-conscious and awkward that even Jayán had to grin.

A Mexican was firing the torches set on poles in front of the palace and their smoky yellow light played eerily over the crowded plaza. Red-skirted women were still selling cheese and soap and tamales in the market underneath the western tower of the palace and the usual loud mob of trappers and soldiers were gathered around the stalls, poking at the fresh cuts of buffalo and pork or buying bundles of hay for their horses. A string of dust-grayed army freight wagons stood in a long double-ranked line before Leitensdorfer's store. The hickory-shirted drivers were gathered in a boisterous bunch around the bonfire near the sundial in the center of the square. The somber, twin-spired shadow of the church towered above it all, a woman drifting now and then from its half open door to disappear into the crowd. Nate wondered why it always seemed to be women who came from the church; no matter what time of day or night, they were always there, with their faces hidden behind their shawls.

Nate kept to the shadows under the church as he crossed the square. As he neared the palace, he began to get skittish. His mouth got dry and his hands were clammy. He stopped against a wall, wondering what had made him so foolish. If they caught him . . . Just a girl, just a girl like any other girl, there were hundreds of them in town, why should he act like a mule with the blind staggers over this one? He could still go back. He would take the uniform back to work with him tomorrow and get Jayán to replace it in the wagon.

He remembered how small her foot had been. He remembered how black her hair had been, so glossy it had looked wet in the sun. He remembered how Kirby had laughed at him.

"You better stay here," he told Jayán. "From here on I'm a real dragoon."

He pushed through the last thin edge of the crowd. The palace building actually formed the front wall of a big quadrangle — the other walls running back from the palace for several hundred feet to enclose the rear patios. There was a dragoon sentry at the open wagon gate. Near him stood half a dozen dusty coaches and Dearborns and some horses stamping at a rope line. A party of Mexicans was getting out of one of the coaches and some Missouri traders in beaver hats and fancy fustians were heading for the gate. Nate moistened his lips, swallowed, wiped his hands on his trousers, and moved into the group of people. It was so dark he could barely see the sentry's face. The soldier glanced indifferently at Nate as he passed through into a courtyard that looked about as big as the parade ground back at Fort Leavenworth.

There was an army of Mexicans in black velvet coats all hung with enough gold braid to sink a flatboat. There was a line of Mexican women sitting on the benches against a far wall. The way they dressed was a caution. Nate hadn't ever seen so much bosom displayed. Half of them were smoking, holding their cigarettes and cigars in little golden tongs. One fat hag

76

was using an Indian slave for a footstool. Nate saw General Kearny in his double-breasted dress coat with rows of gold buttons and bullion epaulettes. His dress hat had a white horsehair plume that kept waving around in front and tickling the ladies when he bowed over their hands.

Nate was surprised at the number of Mexican officers. Technically, he supposed, they were prisoners of war. They had surrendered and had been demobilized and had given up their arms. But they still had their uniforms, and they put the dragoons to shame. Patent-leather shakos with red pompons, black horsehair plumes, brass buckles, gold aiguillettes, scarlet saber sashes — it made Nate squirm to see the way they posed and swaggered in front of the ladies.

There were a lot of candles on the tables and hung in tin sconces from ropes stretched across the courtyard, but they still didn't give much light. The crowd was in shadow most of the time and several dragoon officers passed near Nate without recognizing him. He thought that maybe Inez would be in the main ballroom, and worked his way around the edge of the patio to the rear of the palace. He glanced in through one of the narrow windows and saw a long room jammed with people. A Mexican moved through the crowd, tapping various ones with a cane. The people he touched were forming lines in the center of the room, the men in one line facing the women in the other. When the orchestra on the platform started a squeaky waltz, the women advanced toward the men and bowed.

Nate saw a squatty Mexican woman dancing with Colonel Doniphan. The colonel was about twice as tall and every time the woman said something he had to jackknife to hear it. Nate saw La Tules in her red wig and purple taffeta dress. She had just gotten choked up on the champagne and had dropped her uppers in her wineglass. Nate saw Lieutenant Merritt heading his way.

He whirled and crossed quickly to a long table loaded with silver punch bowls and clay platters heaped with food. His back was turned when Merritt passed. There was a crawly feeling between his shoulders and a lump in his throat fit to choke him. He knew he had to quit now. He knew he had to get out. As he turned from the table, he saw Inez.

She was near the end of a long line of women who sat on the benches against a far wall. In all the bold display of powdered flesh and billowing curves she looked no more than a child. Her black hair was drawn glossy-tight against her small head and in it she wore a tall tortoise-shell comb with a mantilla thrown over it to fall in a white froth of lace across her gleaming shoulders. For a moment he got a feeling — he didn't know whether he was sick, or dizzy, with his mouth going dry and a strange ache in his throat.

He moved through the deceptive patches of light and darkness, keeping to the edge of the crowd, avoiding the officers, trying to get closer to Inez. Across from the benches, in a shadowed corner of the courtyard that was avoided by the other guests, he saw a little tile-roofed well. He had just reached its protection when he saw a dragoon officer following him. He ducked behind the well. The officer continued coming directly toward Nate, and Nate thought that he was finished. Then the man passed through a patch of candlelight, and Nate saw that he was Kirby.

Nate couldn't believe it. Kirby looked more at home in the uniform than General Kearny. The cavalier ease with which he moved through the crowd obscured the fact that his blue cuffs stopped two inches above his wrist and his pants bagged in the seat. If Nate hadn't known him, he would have sworn that Kirby had just stepped out of West Point.

Kirby stopped by the wall, grinning sheepishly. "Well, I got to thinking it over, and I figured I'd better follow along and see if you'd really do it. I couldn't let you get into any real trouble, Nate. When I saw you come in here, I allowed you might need some help getting out again. I figured you'd left this other uniform under the bridge. If you've had your fill now, we can just start strolling back toward the gate, and maybe get out without a court-martial."

"I can't go yet," Nate said.

He turned to look at Inez again. Kirby made a soft sound. "Is that her?"

"Inez Torreón," Nate said.

"Torreón," Kirby said. "You just called her Inez. You didn't tell me her name was Torreón." A shrewd expression had come to his face. Nate had seen the same look when he was trying to swing a deal, the way he moistened his lips and squinted. "Look at her eyes shine," Kirby said. "I ain't seen a woman's eyes shine that way since the octoroon in Natchezunder. She used belladonna."

The man with the cane had come from the palace and was touching people, meaning to start another dance in the courtyard. He walked down the line of benches, touching various women with his cane, and finally reached Inez. She didn't giggle or make a fuss like the other women who had been touched. She was sober and very grave as she rose and went to join the line of dancers. The mantilla hanging to her waist and the spreading skirts of looped velvet could not hide the slender lines of her body. Yet there was something about the way she moved that was not childish. It was grace, or pride, the way she held her head, or the curve of her white neck; it made Nate think of a very fine, proud horse.

The squeaky fiddles had begun a new dance in the palace and the dancers in the courtyard began going through some motions, advancing, retreating, pairing off. Nate allowed it wasn't like any hoe-down he'd ever seen. After a few whirls the couples re-formed into lines and the women began making a circuit of the whole set. One man after another spun Inez around. As she pirouetted through the flickering patches of light, Nate saw how breathlessly she kept her mouth open, and how shimmering and red her lips looked. The dance was carrying her toward the well.

"I guess you ain't so crazy, after all, Nate," Kirby said. "There's something about her."

"I got to talk to her," Nate said.

"It can be done," Kirby said.

80

Inez whirled into the arms of a young Mexican artillery officer in a red coat with green turnbacks. They took a spin that carried them within five feet of the well. Kirby stepped from behind the well and the next spin whirled Inez directly into his arms. The officer gave her up, obviously assuming that Kirby was the next man in line. As Kirby danced the girl away, the officer turned in the other direction, his arms held out to receive the next woman. When none appeared, he wheeled back, glaring after Kirby, his empty arms held out foolishly.

As Kirby spun Inez past the well, Nate saw her struggling to pull free. "No, no, you must let me go. My father warned me against dancing with American officers. I only danced because there were no American officers in the line. Please . . ." She broke off, looking up at Kirby with a strange expression. "I . . . you are the one with the yellow hair."

"I could get another color, if you don't like it."

"No . . . that is, on the first day, when you came . . . the army, I mean . . . I think I saw you."

They were out of Nate's earshot by then. The Mexican artillery officer had started following them, pushing through the other dancers. Kirby was dancing Inez out of the circle and into the shadows. She had quit trying to get free and was staring up at Kirby with her lips parted and an odd, blank look to her eyes that was neither fear nor anger, yet held a little of both. It made Nate understand something he had been too surprised to realize before — Kirby had taken her right out of his hands. He started after them, forgetting any caution. The music quit. Kirby and Inez stopped dancing, and Nate got close enough to hear them talking again.

"Honey, can't we go somewhere else?" Kirby asked.

"I cannot. You do not understand. My father . . . if he sees me with you . . . at first he did not even want to come to come tonight, he was not going to allow the family to come until he heard that all the old friends of Governor Armijo had refused invitations. He could not stand to be classed with them. He said anything was better than that, even being with the *gringos* . . ."

She broke off as the music started again. Before Kirby could whirl her away, Nate reached them, pulling his uncle's hands off the girl.

"You showed me how it's done," he said. "Now go find your own girl."

Inez stared at Nate, her eyes wide and startled. Before he could say anything more, the Mexican officer appeared, pushing through the crowd. He faced Kirby and rattled off something in Spanish.

"What'd he say?" Kirby asked the girl.

Inez touched her fingers to her mouth. "He . . . he offers you his sword."

"Tell him thanks, I got my own."

"You do not understand. He is asking you for the duel."

"How can he duel?" Nate said. "I thought all the Mexican officers gave up their weapons."

The Mexican started talking Spanish again, his face flushed a turkey-wattle color. Nate saw Colonel

Doniphan and Lieutenant Colonel Ruff come out of the palace.

"Time to skin out, Nate," Kirby said.

Nate turned to Inez. "Ma'am, where can I meet you again? Please tell me where I can meet you."

Kirby took Nate by the arm, pulling him away. The Mexican officer grabbed Kirby, trying to hold him there and jabbering more Spanish in his face. Kirby hit him. The man staggered backward and fell.

Another Mexican grabbed Nate from behind. As Nate struggled to get free, half a dozen more closed around, trying to get a punch at Kirby or Nate, and some American officers Nate didn't recognize got mixed in with the Mexicans, trying to pull them off.

The battle carried Nate against one of the long tables. The surge of struggling men upset the table and it crashed over into the crowd, spilling food and candles in every direction. The candles were snuffed out beneath a dozen trampling feet. In the darkness and added confusion Nate felt somebody grab him by the elbow and pull him violently free of the clawing, kicking, punching knot of men.

"You're pointed at the gate, Nate." It was Kirby's voice. "Let's light a shuck."

Together they stumbled through the press of panicked women and confused men on the fringes of the fight. Everybody was moving in different directions and officers were running back and forth, shouting orders, with nobody obeying them. A couple of sentries had come inside from the gate but one had remained behind.

"Halt!" he shouted. "Who goes there?"

"Lieutenant Emory!" Kirby shouted. "Git in there, soldier. Them spicks are trying to kill General Kearny."

Nate heard the sentry curse, running past them in the darkness. They got outside, dodging among the coaches and into the narrow street. Behind them they could hear some officer calling the patrol. The palace sounded like an hysterical hen house. Running ahead of Nate, Kirby pulled off his coat and dropped it, tearing at the patent-leather sword belt and the orange silk sash that was wound twice around his waist under the belt.

"They better not find us in these fixings," he said.

They were in the back streets of the town, circling behind the church. By the time they reached the river, all they had on was their dragoon boots. They kicked them off and ran for the volunteer camp in their bare feet and underdrawers.

CHAPTER
SIX

The ringing of the Angelus bells woke Colonel
Doniphan on the morning of August 30th. He was
quartered in one of the bedrooms at the west end of the
Palace of the Governors. The old building had aroused
his insatiable curiosity. He had spent hours poking
through the series of dank chambers that extended for
350 feet between the two towers. The Mexicans said
the palace had been built almost 250 years before,
when the Spaniards had first come up from Mexico. It
fascinated Doniphan to think of the pageant of history
the ancient fortress had seen, the plots, the intrigue, the
governors betrayed, imprisoned, the Indians hanged.
The volunteers had found a dozen Indian ears hanging
on a string in Governor Armijo's office, and some
Spanish names scratched on the walls of the dungeon
in the west tower, and a date: 1621.

Doniphan rose from the narrow tester bed, and
stretched hugely. He pulled on his trousers, slipping his
gallus over his shoulder to hold them up. He knew that
he could call his striker to fetch him some hot water,
but he always hated to be ordering the boys around. He
went to the kitchen himself, still wearing nothing but
his long underwear for a shirt, and got a basin of hot

water from the cook, along with some of the amole root the Mexicans used for soap. He carried it back to his quarters and started shaving with his Bowie knife. He was about finished when one of Kearny's adjutants knocked and extended Kearny's invitation to join him at breakfast.

Doniphan was reluctant to go, because it meant dressing up, and Kearny would want to talk about the mess at the ball the other night. Doniphan found the general dining alone in the anteroom adjoining what had once been Governor Armijo's bedroom. Kearny was seated at a small table, all decked out in his long blue coat piped in gold, with bullion epaulettes on the shoulders and twelve gold buttons down the front. The wings of a narrow white collar were folded across the black stock under a set of jaws that looked hard enough to grind rocks. He was fifty-two years old and his gray hair was brushed forward on his brow and temples in a style that had been fashionable during the War of 1812. It always made Doniphan think of Andrew Jackson.

"Sit down, Colonel," Kearny said. "None of those tamales to make a holocaust of your insides this morning. Eggs and coffee and a rasher of bacon, all Missouri style."

Doniphan sat down, and after some carefully chosen small talk Kearny said: "I would like to know your decision about that atrocity at the ball the other night."

"I've had my adjutants investigating, sir. They've been unable to turn up anything. It seems nobody recognized the men who started the brawl. How about your dragoons?"

86

Kearny looked up sharply. He had to look up, to meet Doniphan's eyes. Doniphan wondered if that was part of Kearny's attitude. Doniphan had always thought that a small man resented a big man.

"It is not necessary to investigate my dragoons," Kearny said stiffly. "They would not descend to such horseplay. It's the kind of an outrage your volunteers have been perpetrating all the way from the Missouri River. If you are incapable of a solution, I will have to take action. I want you to issue an order. The men responsible for causing all that trouble at the ball are to confess their guilt, or the whole regiment will be punished, every man jack of them to spend twenty hours marching in front of the guard tent with a forty-pound pack on his back."

Doniphan cleared his throat. He knew what he was risking, opposing the general, but he had to speak his mind. "In the first place, we have no proof that my boys are responsible. And in the second place, I never did believe in punishing a whole regiment for what one man might have done. You've got to understand these boys, General. They're not regular troops. You don't realize what such a thing would do to their morale."

Kearny shoved his chair back sharply. His lips were pinched, gray. "Colonel, I have listened to your dissertations on the nature of these tavern bullies long enough. You have shielded them and protected them and defended them and apologized for them all the way from the Missouri River, and I can support it no longer. If it wasn't for your misconceived notions of humanity, these men would be a body of disciplined soldiers instead of a mob of disorderly, insubordinate, riotous pranksters. It is time that we put a stop to all this nonsense."

Doniphan felt the heat in his face. He understood what he was up against. Kearny had been a soldier for thirty-four years. He had obtained a commission in the War of 1812; he had become a captain when he was only nineteen, and his assault on Queenstown Heights was a military classic. He had been with the 1ˢᵗ Dragoons since it was established in 1833. Doniphan had found him surprisingly flexible and lenient for a regular, but there were limits beyond which the orthodox mind could not be pushed.

And Doniphan had his own limits. "General, I would rather resign my commission than do this to my boys."

Kearny stood up. He stared at Doniphan blankly, unbelievingly. "Colonel Doniphan, it will not end with your resignation. We are at war. We are dealing with a matter of discipline that affects the whole force. A court-martial under these conditions would wreck your career, not only in the service but in civilian life as well. I cannot believe that you will refuse my order."

Doniphan stood up. "You already have my refusal, General."

The two men stared at each other. Kearny's hands were locked behind his back. Strain made twin grooves around his mouth. The silence was broken by a discreet knock. Kearny hesitated, a little muscle knotting in his jaw. Then he crossed and opened the door. An aide told the general that James Magoffin wished an audience. Again Kearny hesitated, scowling, but Doniphan knew that he could not afford to turn Magoffin down. The man was one of the most influential traders on the trail. As early as 1825 Magoffin had taken his wagons to Chihuahua, had become American consul there, and in 1830 had married into one of the most important families in New Mexico. When war was declared, Magoffin had been called to Washington for some mysterious meetings with President Polk and Senator Thomas Hart Benton. He had returned from Washington in time to catch up with Kearny and the Army of the West at Bent's Fort, still 250 miles from Santa Fé. Doniphan had been in on the meeting there when Magoffin had revealed his mission to subvert Governor Armijo and his officers. Kearny had given him an escort of twelve dragoons, led by Captain Philip St. George Cooke, and Magoffin had gone to Santa Fé ahead of the army, paving the way for the bloodless conquest.

After the army's arrival in Santa Fé, Doniphan had heard rumors that the main reason the Mexican governor abdicated was a $50,000 bribe received from Magoffin. Magoffin had not mentioned any money at Bent's Fort and would not be pinned down about it now. The implication was that the War Department had supplied the bribe. Doniphan's private opinion was that the American traders had put it up. It would be worth $50,000 to ensure an American victory and get Armijo's staggering import taxes off their backs.

Kearny told the aide to admit Magoffin. The trader entered after a moment, smiling genially. He was an Irishman from the boots up, big-boned Ulster stock, a florid-faced man in a sky-blue fustian and a handsome beaver hat, an epicure, a wit, lionized by the Mexicans, known to them as *Don* Santiago. He greeted the two officers effusively.

"It's good to have this town in such competent hands, after the news from the south," he said.

"What news?" Kearny asked.

"You haven't read your dispatches?" Magoffin asked. "A regiment of Maryland volunteers has mutinied on the Río Grande. These atrocities in Mexico . . . General Taylor seems absolutely incapable of controlling his volunteers. Plunder, murder, rape . . . they're laying waste to the whole country. The officers are apparently helpless to stop it. The whole campaign has become one big drunken orgy. It makes our town sound like a country church. I tell you, General, you're lucky to have Colonel Doniphan. I wager Taylor would give his pantaloons for the kind of magic the colonel has with these volunteers."

Kearny glanced sharply at Doniphan, his eyes narrowed, a mixture of suspicion and wonder in his scowl. "Is that what you came to discuss?" he asked Magoffin.

"Not quite," the trader said. He crossed to a chair, carefully spreading his coattails before he sat down. "I wondered if you had done anything about Colonel Diego Archuleta?"

Kearny stirred irritably. "I haven't been able to contact him yet."

"As you know," Magoffin said, "I'm about to leave for Chihuahua. The War Department hopes I can pave the way there for General Wool in the same way I did for you here. Before I go, I'd like to be sure you take care of Diego Archuleta. As the ex-governor's second-in-command he still carries a lot of weight among the New Mexicans. He's a different breed from Governor Armijo. While from the very beginning Armijo didn't want to fight you, Archuleta did. I couldn't appeal to him with the same things I used on Armijo. I told you money wouldn't buy him off. But the promises I made must have had some value. He certainly didn't fight us at Apache Cañon. But now you've already broken one of the pledges to him. I had assurances that the United States wouldn't claim any land west of the Río Grande. I told Archuleta he could be governor of a Mexican department there. Your proclamation last Saturday, claiming both sides of the river, just about took the underpinnings out of everything I did."

"Mister Magoffin, no pledge of mine was broken. What possible authority did you have to guarantee that the United States would make no claim on land west of the Río Grande?"

"The river has been the historic boundary line in all the disputes. Even Texas didn't claim any land beyond it. Senator Benton assured me . . ."

"Then Senator Benton and the War Department ought to get together. My confidential orders of June Third from the Secretary of War are for the occupation of the whole Department of New Mexico. What general in his right mind would march to California and leave a strip of enemy territory at his rear from which he might be attacked at any time?"

Kearny had to stop and clear his throat. Magoffin merely smiled and tucked his thumbs under his lapels.

"I can't argue with you on military tactics, General, but the political damage has already been done, and we've got to patch it up somehow. I think you could save the situation if you offer Archuleta some high post in the new government you're setting up here. I know you plan on putting other New Mexicans in positions of responsibility. Face is enormously important to the Mexican. In that way they are very Oriental. It's why these fine people can put on royal airs while they're standing barefoot on a mud floor. As long as a man has a fancy cloak, he can hide a starving belly. But you never want to pull aside that cloak. It is a mistake that can get you killed. That is the kind of a pride they have. Everything must be done in style. That is their word for it. Style. It might seem strange to you at first, a pretense. But it isn't. To understand them you must realize they are living in the past. When you enter this country, you step through a door into the Middle Ages. Their customs, their traditions, their laws, their food, their clothes ... none of it has changed in four hundred years."

"Mister Magoffin, I think it's pretty obvious how backward these people are."

Magoffin seemed to look beyond Kearny for a moment. Then he smiled, almost to himself, and said: "What I'm getting at is that Diego Archuleta has lost face. He is humiliated, defeated, hiding as a thief would hide. He will not take that for long. Unless you give him a chance to regain face, to get back some of the power that means so much to him . . . he'll cause you trouble."

"I can't conceive of returning Archuleta to a position of power," Kearny said. "Would General Taylor conquer Mexico and then make Santa Anna president again?"

"The situation here is a little different," Magoffin answered. "You are planning to go on to the conquest of California with your dragoons in a few days. That will leave only the volunteers in Santa Fé. Archuleta could easily gather enough forces for a revolt. As much as I admire Colonel Doniphan, his volunteers might well be overwhelmed without your dragoons to back them up."

Kearny locked his hands behind his back, frowning intensely. Finally he crossed to the table and shuffled through some papers by his plate. "In a way, Mister Magoffin, I have already done something about Archuleta. You might as well hear this order I dictated earlier." He picked up a sheet of paper and read in a crisp voice. "'The general will leave Santa Fé, for the Río Abajo, on the second proximo. He will take with him five hundred of Colonel Doniphan's regiment of Mounted Volunteers, one hundred of Major Clark's Battalion of Horse Artillery, and one hundred of Major Sumner's Dragoons. Colonel Doniphan, being now engaged on highly important business in this city, will remain in command of all the troops left in this city.'"

"Do you think Archuleta is downriver?" Doniphan asked.

"He may be," Kearny said. "I have heard rumors that Governor Armijo is gathering another Mexican army in the downriver district. If what Mister Magoffin feels about Archuleta is true, Archuleta may be involved. The purpose of this march is to settle the whole matter before I go on to California. If the rumors turn out to be facts, and we have a battle, an American victory would certainly finish whatever chances Archuleta had of mounting a revolt."

"I hope you are right, General," Magoffin said. "Unfortunately, if you are wrong, it will be Colonel Doniphan who pays for your mistake, and the price will be dear."

Magoffin's genial smile had disappeared as he shook hands with both of them and excused himself.

After he had gone, Kearny stood by the table, frowning to himself and shuffling through his papers. "I'll have to speak to my adjutant," he said absently. "Those dispatches from Mexico . . . they should have been brought to my attention." He looked at Doniphan. "Colonel, I may disagree with Magoffin about Archuleta, but one thing he said made some sense." He smiled tightly. "After thirty-four years on a parade ground, a man's mind can get pretty petrified, can't it? Will you kindly forget that order I gave you earlier?"

Doniphan saluted gravely. "Thank you, sir."

A frosty glint came into Kearny's eyes. "But if you should happen to discover the clowns who caused that

94

mess at the palace, give them an extra slice of hell for me, will you?"

CHAPTER
SEVEN

The next morning at roll call Kirby heard about the order to march south. They weren't supposed to start till Wednesday and that gave him two days to figure out a way to be left behind. He had done the groundwork in town for his deal to get Ganoe some wool, and he knew that he would lose out completely if he had to march off and leave everything hanging fire.

What had happened at the palace the other night only added to the possibilities — learning for the first time that the girl Nate had wanted to see was a Torreón. *Don* Miguel Torreón was one of the big sheep ranchers who wouldn't sell their wool to the Americans. If his daughter took a shine to Nate, chances were that she could convince the old man what a good thing it would be to make a deal. Kirby tried to show Nate how it might work out, but Nate wouldn't listen. He thought it would be cheap to use the girl in such a deal. Kirby couldn't understand that. He guessed it was because he had never really cared that much about any woman. In fact, when he got right down to it, the only person he'd ever felt very close to was Nate. Kirby's brother Asa had been twelve years older than he was, and had left before Kirby was old enough to know him well. His father had been away most of the time, and his mother had left Kirby to tutors and servants while she occupied herself with the Mozart Society, the Louisville Conversation Club, the Benevolent Association, and just about every other organization in the city a woman could join.

Kirby had been born thirty-two years ago in Louisville. He couldn't actually say that he was quality, because his father had started as a deck hand on one of the river boats. He couldn't say that he was trash, either, since, by the time he was born, his father had worked his way up to captain. The steamboat captains lived well along the Ohio. The Hatchers owned a big brick house on Green Street and had a fistful of servants and went to church in a twelve-quarter coach with red leather seats. Captain Hatcher was on the river most of the time but he tried to provide an education for his two boys. Asa had taken to it dutifully if unimaginatively, and just as dutifully Kirby had avoided it. He supposed that was why he was such a strange mixture of the things he had learned from his tutors before he was old enough to escape the boredom of lessons, and the things he had learned when he could begin frequenting the deadfalls and taverns along the waterfront. Some of the early book learning must have rubbed off. When he got all fired up and talking thirteen to the dozen, some of the most astonishing things came out. He had a way of using and embellishing what knowledge he possessed that deceived Nate and a lot of others into believing that he could sit in the same pew with men like Alexander

Doniphan or maybe Senator Thomas Hart Benton. Sometimes he even thought so himself. It seemed that he could move just as slickly with quality as he could with trash. Then again, the way he heard himself using language sometimes, a body might think he'd been born in some shack in the Gut, or Natchez-under, never heard a gentleman talk, never opened a book. A woman had told him once that he was like a patchwork quilt, all spots and pieces, with nothing to hold them together.

When Kirby was only ten, Asa had left home to seek his fortune in the Missouri settlements. When Kirby was eighteen, his father had been killed in a boiler explosion, and the fever took his mother a year later. A will divided the estate equally between the two boys. By the time Kirby had squandered his share away in the deadfalls, he had picked up enough knowledge of cards to make a passable living as a faro dealer. Through all those years his only contact with Asa had been a hastily scrawled letter now and then. The last one had come when Kirby was in St. Louis, saying that Asa and the whole family were down with the ague and they needed Kirby's help the worst way.

Kirby had never dreamed that it would saddle him with a boy to raise. Looking back, he wondered why he stuck with it, after Asa and the rest of the family died. There had been times when the responsibility got to be too much, or the itch in his feet got unbearable, and he thought that he had to leave. But he never left. Maybe what had developed between him and Nate was what he might have had if his father had been home more, or if his brother had been younger. Or maybe it was the way Nate worshiped him. It did something to a man to have somebody believe in him so blindly. Maybe it got him to believing a little more in himself. Kirby and Nate had been able to hire their labor most of the time, but there was still a lot of work to do, getting a tobacco crop in. Planting, billing, weeding, suckering, cutting, hanging — things he never would have dreamed of doing before.

Sometimes, when he got to thinking about it, he allowed that he must be fooling himself. He couldn't have done all that just because of his feeling for Nate. He couldn't believe that he had that much good in him. And maybe he was exaggerating Nate's feeling, too. He had noticed a change in Nate lately. The way he'd acted up over the deal with the sabers. A year ago he might have argued against it — but in the end Kirby could have talked him into it.

Well, that was all behind him now. He had a bigger deal on the fire than a few rusty sabers. That first night in town, after learning how much Ganoe would give to make a deal for wool, Kirby had gone to La Tules. During the Mexican regime, if a man wanted to slip a wagonload of goods past customs without paying the duty, or wanted to meet a certain woman, or ruin somebody politically, or have somebody put out of the way — he went to La Tules. She had interviewed Kirby in one of her back rooms, and his proposition had interested her. She had asked a couple of days to make her contacts. The time had passed now and Kirby meant to see her.

He made out that he had hurt his back lifting the adobe blocks at the fort and gave such a good show that the surgeon put him on sick call. When Nate and the others had marched off to the fort, Kirby went to one of the abandoned buildings at the edge of camp that Company D was using as an orderly room. Sergeant Hicklin spent most of his spare time there studying his manuals. Kirby badgered him till he issued a pass just to get rid of him. Kirby snitched some buttons off a coat in the storehouse and went into town, heading for the place on Burro Alley.

There were only a few people in the gambling hall at this time of the morning. A faro dealer sat at his empty table, fiddling with his dealing box and staring emptily out the window. There was a distinctive smell to the room — stale tobacco smoke, stale whiskey, stale perfume — the residue of a thousand nights' debauch. The bartender told Kirby that La Tules didn't usually wake up till the afternoon. Kirby's buttons were worth 25¢ or one drink apiece. He made the drinks last till La Tules came walking out of the back room about two o'clock. It was hard to believe that she had ever been beautiful. She hadn't applied the mascara and ghastly lavender powder she wore at night, and in the dim afternoon light her face looked pasty and bloated. She looked badly in the need of a drink and Kirby offered to buy her one.

"You have the advantage, señor," she said. "You know that a woman of Mexico such beautiful yellow hair can never resist."

100

"Well, you got the advantage on me," he said. "I bet I got a bigger weakness for red-haired women than you got a weakness for blond-haired men."

She giggled. "*Por favor*, do not pinch me there, *señor*. A man I have who would kill you."

"It'd be worth dying for," he said.

She giggled again. He knew that she was too wise not to realize he was honey-fuggling her, but she loved it anyway. He had a way with women gamblers, madams, and girls who got afflicted with the holy laughs at revival meetings. He wondered how long it had been since this fat old woman with her false teeth and her red wig had been romanced by a man.

"Well," he said, "I got Jim Ganoe all talked into it. He's willing to give you half a wagonload of shoes for your part in the deal. How are you coming with the ranchers?"

She took her whiskey neat and left her mouth open while it went down. Then she let out a sound of escaping steam. "It does not seem to have the possibility. I have approach all of them, Chavez, Otero, Torreón, Archuleta . . . wool they will not sell to me. I have certainty they suspect I mean to turn it over to some *gringo*."

It was a big disappointment, and it turned him ornery. "I got a bad feeling. You sold Governor Armijo out. Maybe you're selling me out."

"What I do with Armijo has nothing to do with this," she said. "The star of Armijo, it was descending. It was obvious that nothing could stop the *gringos* from coming. Those who fight them lose. Those who do

101

business with them win. There are many who think James Magoffin gave Armijo a bribe of fifty thousand dollars to leave. *Pues*, that has a possibility. All I know is that Armijo came to me and ask . . . 'Tules, what you do?' . . . and I say . . . 'Manuelito, you no can win, the time of the *gringo*, it is here, and the time of Armijo, it is gone. If you fight, they beat you and put you in prison. If you run, you can take with you enough to live in richness the rest of your fat, greedy, selfish life.' He always listen to me, Manuelito. Did he not run?" She hiccupped, and her stays creaked softly. "If I profit by the coming of the *gringo*, who can blame me? A lover I have been, a gambler, a politician, but above all a businesswoman. Many changes have I survive. When I first come to Santa Fé, almost thirty year ago, it belong to Spain, *sabe*? Then the revolution, and it become a part of Mexico. Many Mexican governor, the good, the bad, and finally Armijo. And always me. This, it is just another change of government to me. I am not sell you out, *chico*. If I could do business with you, I would."

Kirby wasn't paying much heed. His mind was already working at something else. He remembered the thought that had come to him when he found out that the girl Nate was interested in was a Torreón. Maybe something could be worked out through her. If Nate wouldn't do it, Kirby was willing to take a whack.

"You said Torreón was one of them ranchers you talked with," he said. "It seems he has a daughter. Inez, or something."

La Tules smiled wistfully. "A rose of Castile. Betrothed to that old man."

"Old man. What makes her want to git hitched with him?"

"It is our way. The will of her father. Ashes where there should be a fire. The pity of God on her."

It had started out as a germ, a vague thought, the way most of his schemes began, but now it began to gain focus. "What do you call it?" he asked. "A dowry?"

"There will be a big dowry. *Don* Miguel is rich."

"Some sheep, maybe."

"If they were a part of the arrangement."

"How many sheep?"

She must have understood what was on his mind. She threw her head back and let out a cawing laugh. "Enough sheep to fill Jim Ganoe's wagons three or four times, if the groom wishes. But you it will do no good, my friend . . ."

"Why not? You said Inez couldn't love this old man. Suppose she falls in love with somebody else before the wedding. There'd still be a dowry, wouldn't there?"

"No, no, no, my friend. Our ways you do not understand."

"Maybe we can change your ways. How well do you know Inez?"

"We are better friends than we should be," La Tules said. "There was Indian trouble here about ten years ago when the Pueblos, they revolt. Many of us flee south for safety. It was in the house of James Magoffin at El Paso that I met Inez. Magoffin married one of her aunts, you know. It was against the wishes of *Don* Miguel, but there was little he could do about it. When

Don Miguel heard that I had met Inez at the house of Magoffin, and had befriended her . . .”

La Tules broke off, a glittering look coming to her eyes. Kirby asked her what had happened, but she couldn't go on. He had to give her another drink before she would talk again. He said that, if she knew Inez that well, she should be able to rig a meeting between him and the girl. La Tules said that it was impossible. She gave him an illustration. She told Kirby about a boy named Bernardo Gálvez, who gambled at her place. Bernardo was in love with Inez, but *Don* Miguel had ordered him away from the girl. Bernardo had devised a way of seeing her secretly. The Torreón family always observed Vespers in their chapel, which was at the south end of the patio and shielded from the rest of the house by willow trees. It was known that Inez had the habit of remaining alone in the chapel for a short time after the others left. There were some trees outside the wall, and, if a man climbed one, he could get onto the wall and drop off inside. If he timed it right, just at dusk, he would be unseen, and might find Inez in the chapel. But Bernardo knew that *Don* Miguel might shoot anyone he found there, and had never found the courage to carry out his plan.

Inez was in her bedroom when she heard Vespers ringing in the church. She joined her family in the parlor and her father led them across the patio to the chapel. The Spanish crown was carved on one of the chapel doors and the keys of St. Peter on the other. On pedestals and in niches around the wall stood the wooden statues of the family saints. Every statue carried its burden of little silver *milagros* offered by the family in their appeals for intercession. When Inez had burned her hand in the kitchen the week before she had hung a silver hand on *Santa* Rita. It had taken a long time for the pain to leave but it would have taken much longer if her namesake had not interceded.

The family knelt before the altar with its silver candlesticks and the image of Christ on the cross. *Don* Miguel led the prayers. Inez saw that her Aunt Maximiliana had brought some cactus candy and was nibbling on it secretly between prayers. During the Lord's Prayer, Inez kept seeing the face, the yellow-bearded face, and the look of violence in the blue eyes. When the Acts were finished, they all crossed themselves and rose from their prayer cushions. They were used to Inez's remaining after the others left. The only one who glanced at her was her brother Agustín. He was only twenty-one years old but he had been a lieutenant in the presidial company for two years. He still wore his dragoon uniform as a gesture of defiance against the *gringos*. He was much like her father. He had run more than one horse to death, and, when he grew angry with the servants, he whipped them personally.

"You will be here long?" he asked.

"I have many prayers to say," she said.

He frowned, pulling at his lower lip. He went out, closing the door softly behind him. There was something on his mind, she knew, but she could not keep thinking of it. She had something on her mind, too. It had been on her mind ever since the ball at the palace. She was still not clear about what had happened. There had been so much confusion and General Kearny trying to smooth it over, and out of all his explanations she got the impression that the soldier she had danced with did not belong at the party. She did not know his name. All she could tell them was that he had yellow hair. There were many *gringos* with yellow hair. She kept remembering what he had said about how badly he had wanted to meet her. Did it mean that he had broken into the party just for that? They were talking about court-martialing him if they found him. No man had ever taken so much risk just to see her. He seemed to have some connection with the boy, Nate Hatcher. At least he and Nate had apparently known each other. What Nate had been doing there she could only guess. Such escapades seemed typical of young men. Kearny's talk of court-martial had kept her from mentioning Nate's name. She knew that he was a volunteer and had no business in a dragoon uniform, and did not want to cause him trouble.

"Dear *Santa* Rita," Inez said, "most beloved namesake, why can I not put this out of my mind? Is this what *Padre* Antonio meant when he spoke of the evil power of the flesh entering my life . . . ?"

She heard a sound behind her. She turned. A man stood in the doorway. The candlelight glinted in his yellow beard. She stood and backed against the frontal of Dutch brocade that covered the altar.

"*Señor*," she whispered, "I did not want . . . I did not mean for you to come. I was not asking *Santa* Rita for that . . ."

Kirby laughed softly. He crossed and stopped before her. The masculine smell of leather and the flavored tobacco he used made her think that she could not breathe.

"I learned about the trees at the back wall, and the time you'd be alone in the chapel," he said.

Her throat closed up. She could hardly speak. "You must go."

"You don't want me to. I guess it's a crazy way of sparking but I couldn't figure out any other manner of seeing you."

She wondered why she did not run. Sparking. The boy named Nate had used that word.

"You must not say it," she said. "I mean . . . you cannot mean it. When a man . . . he does not court in this way."

"Well, it's time they started."

He put his hands on her arms. She twisted free, pulling the frontal off the altar. He blocked her route to the door. Her hands were against her cheeks.

"*Señor* . . . all I have to do is make a sound, one small sound. There are a dozen servants."

"Honey, if you was really afraid of me, you would have let out a howl long ago."

She knew that he was right. It wasn't fear she felt. It had all the symptoms of fear but it wasn't fear. Moving very slowly, he reached out a hand and touched her cheek.

"There . . . soft as a feather. Now that don't hurt, does it? That's the way it's a-going to be all the way through. Soft as a feather."

"It is no good. I am flattered that you should take such great risk to see me but . . . but I am already betrothed."

"La Tules told me about him. She said he was about ninety years old."

"Fifty-six."

"You ain't telling me you love him," he said. She did not answer. He said: "I'll bet he never even kissed you."

"That . . . that is not done till after the marriage."

"You ain't never been kissed?"

She did not answer. She could not make her eyes meet his. He cupped her chin with his hand and lifted her face till she had to look at him.

"Now," he said, "soft as a feather."

He leaned forward and put his lips to hers. It created a feeling in her stomach. It made her legs tremble. Then she realized what they had done and she groaned and put her hands to her face.

"Honey . . . what in the nation . . . ?" he said. "That didn't hurt. You can't tell me it hurt and you can't tell me it didn't pleasure you."

"But now we will have . . . there will be . . . I mean, the yellow hair . . . *Don* Fecundo . . . how can I make the explanation . . . ?"

He threw back his head and laughed so loudly it startled her. "You don't really believe that," he said. "You don't really think kissing makes a baby."

"It is what my aunt told me, and my mother. It is wrong to kiss young men. Young men will only hurt you and give you babies the way the serving girls who are not married have babies and you will be a disgrace to your family and never have a husband."

"Honey, I don't know whether you got it all mixed up, what they told you, or whether they mixed it up on purpose, but I never heard tell such a clabber. Hark from the tomb. Let me tell you, kissing won't make babies, nor smoking a cigar, nor looking over your left shoulder at a quarter moon on Friday the Thirteenth. Now own up . . . ain't nobody ever kissed you?"

"My father never kisses me."

"Your brother, then. You got a brother, ain't you? Ain't you ever seen him kissing somebody?"

"My aunt . . . she kisses him sometimes."

"And did they have a baby?"

She frowned and pouted her lower lip out, considering it. "No."

"Well, then . . . ?"

She saw that he meant to kiss her again. She put her hands against his chest.

"I must think," she said. "I must ask somebody."

There was a sound from out in the patio. Inez felt his hands tighten on her arms.

"Stay here," she said. "It is perhaps my mother. If I go to her, she will not come inside here."

He refused to let her go. "I got to see you again."

She knew that she could not see him again. She knew that it would be a sin and impossible. "Sunday," she said, "early Mass . . . the family and most of the servants will be at the church. I will pretend the sickness. Here . . . I will be here."

She touched her mouth, surprised at what had come out. It seemed almost as though someone else had spoken the words. He kissed her again. She could feel his teeth and the kiss hurt and his grip on her arms hurt. When he released her, she whirled and hurried to the door, closing it after she was outside.

She stood against it, trembling. There was a sick feeling at the pit of her stomach. She didn't think it was fear any more. She thought it was just excitement. The patio was empty. The shape of the willow trees and the little tile-roofed well and the colonnade around the edge of the patio were all half lost in the silver haze of dusk. She moved toward the carriage entrance, hearing voices beyond the gate. She had almost reached it when the gate was swung open. She had a glimpse of Agustín talking with a taller man. Under his velvet jacket the man wore a Rouen shirt with drawn-work inserts. Over a shoulder was flung a serape with the old Saltillo stair-step design. It was a handsome serape that she had seen at many public functions before the *gringos* came. It belonged to Colonel Diego Archuleta.

Agustín saw her. He stepped through the gate quickly, swinging it shut behind him and bolting it. He crossed to Inez and grasped her arm so hard that she made a small sound of pain.

"You did not see anything," he said.

"Agustín," she said. "You are not mixed up in this thing."

"What thing?" her brother asked.

110

"There has been talk . . . the servants . . . that was Colonel Archuleta . . ."

"You did not see him. You did not see anything."

He squeezed her arm till she said: "Very well, I did not see anything."

"Swear it . . . the Virgin . . ."

"I swear by the most holy Virgin, I did not see anything."

CHAPTER
EIGHT

That evening Nate got back from Fort Marcy with the work details in time for a late mess call. Kirby told Nate that he had gotten a pass into town but had been unable to figure out a way to see Inez. At the Wednesday morning roll call Hicklin told them that a portion of each company was to go with Kearny on his march downriver. The men counted off. Kirby was a one, Nate was a two. Hicklin said that all the even numbers were to report for duty in fifteen minutes, ready to march.

Nate didn't want to go. He had his craw full of the boredom of camp life and the hard work on the fort but he hated to think of marching off without seeing Inez again. He knew what little chance he had of seeing her even if he stayed in Santa Fé, and that only made it worse.

Nobody had much idea where they were going or why. Somebody said that they were marching to California. That first day they marched twenty miles and camped on the Galisteo, red sand country, scant grass, poor water. The August heat came early the next morning and many of the volunteers piled their coats in the company wagons while breaking camp. As the wagons moved off, Kearny arrived for inspection. He found half his troops in shirt sleeves and immediately issued an order that all men were to appear in proper uniform. Sergeant Hicklin ordered those in Company D who still had their coats to put them on and told Corporal McLean to take a detail after the wagons and bring them back. The corporal named Nate as one of his detail.

"Dammit, Corporal," Nate said, "I ain't wearing no coat in this weather. The general ain't a-going to have no war in California if half his army dies of heat stroke."

The rest of the detail stood with Nate, and the corporal went back to Sergeant Hicklin. Hicklin bullied and bawled and threatened. Even the ones who had their coats would not put them on. They sat in their saddles, wiping their wet faces with soggy neckerchiefs. The sweat made stains in the armpits of their shirts. Many of them had their sleeves rolled up or their shirts unbuttoned to the waist. Finally Hicklin went to Captain Reid. While the sergeant and the captain were talking, General Kearny approached in his inspection.

"Captain, have your men no jackets?" Kearny asked.

"Some have," Reid said, "some have not."

"Captain Reid," Kearny said, "make your men put on their jackets, or I will dismiss them from the service. The government has paid them commutation for clothing, and expects every man to dress in a manner wholesome to military discipline."

Nate saw Captain Reid turn red. "My men, sir, came here not to dress but to fight the enemies of the U.S.A., and they are ever ready to be of service to you and the country in that way. As to the commutation, which you say the government has paid my men for clothing, I must inform you that you misapprehend the truth. My men have never received one dime since they entered the service, and what money they brought from their homes with them they have already expended for bread while on half rations, owing to the neglect of your chief commissary."

Captain Reid had been a lawyer in Missouri, and, when he got excited, he reverted to his courtroom style. His voice got louder and his neck swelled up and he made wild gestures with both hands. It reminded Nate of the oration he had made at the Marshall courthouse when he was elected captain and had taken on a little too much corn whiskey.

"As to being dismissed from the service, sir, we do not fight for wages. If there is no place for us in the army, then by Almighty God, President Polk, Thomas Hart Benton, the Whig party, and every red-blooded patriot in this land, we shall furnish ourselves and fight the enemy wherever we may find him!"

When he was finished, Company D began to cheer and Nate was so excited that he rode up with Bristol and Squire Dille to gather around Captain Reid, clapping him on the back and shouting congratulations.

Kearny had not said a word. Nate saw his hands twitch a little on his reins. There was no color in his face. It bore a pinched, gray look. He waited till the uproar died down. He looked shrewdly at Captain Reid, sent a glance toward Nate, and turned to ride

114

away, followed by his guard and retinue of officers. Lieutenant Colonel Ruff rode over to Reid.

"My God, Captain," Ruff said, "are you crazy?"

"Better than that," Reid said. "I'm a First Missouri Mounted Volunteer."

On the Sunday after Kearny marched south, Kirby saw Inez again. Kelly Goff had a sentry post from midnight to "Reveille" and he could be counted on to sleep on duty. Kirby sneaked past him just before dawn and followed the miniature cañon of the Santa Fé River to a spot 100 yards behind the Torreón house. He waited there till the family left for Mass.

He couldn't stop shivering. He cursed these freezing mountain mornings. It seemed ten times colder than a Missouri morning this time of year. He hated the altitude. They said it was 7,000 feet. He hated the little brown people who were always saying things about him that he couldn't understand. He hated the dry, burned smell of the land and the food that scalded the lining out of a man's mouth and the bells ringing all day long. He'd give a month's pay for some mucky Missouri river bottom where a man didn't start shivering unless he had an honest-to-God attack of the ague.

Kirby thought that it was an everlasting marvel what a man would do for a woman. There had been a whole parcel of schemes in his mind when he first had come to see Inez at the Torreón house. The one thing he'd known for certain was that a man getting close to her would be one step closer to the wool. A man had to grope his way along in a situation like this, following whatever strings he came on. No telling what they would tie into. Maybe he could get her to talk her father into dealing with the Americans. He had gotten a girl in St. Louis to talk her sister into paying off one of his gambling debts once. Or it could work the other way. He remembered another girl in Natchez. She came from quality, up on the bluffs, and, when her father had found out about the girl and Kirby, he had paid Kirby to leave town and avoid a scandal. This time Kirby's price would be wool. There were lots of possibilities. And there was the girl. Maybe, after that moment in the chapel, he'd be doing this if there wasn't any wool involved. He reckoned he'd never seen anything quite like her. Something so virginal, so untouched, so fresh and new that it almost frightened him. And yet, underneath, something else, something else . . .

Pretty soon after sunup the bells began ringing for early Mass in the church on the square and San Miguel's south of the river. Kirby saw the Torreóns leave the house in their coach with the barefoot servants following afoot. He didn't have to climb the wall. Inez came out the little back gate and met him in the willows. Three feet from him she stopped. It was a strange game, approach and retreat, the same maneuvering a man went through trapping a wild thing.

"I told Father I was sick," she said. "I prayed in the chapel last night that you would come. I asked *Santa* Rita to make you come and then I asked the Virgin of Guadalupe to keep you away. Why is that? What is the matter with me?"

"It's just new to you," he said. "We're all afeared of something new. You just got to git used to me."

He could feel no breeze on his cheek, yet there must have been one for the yellow aspen leaves were whispering on the bank above. They made him think of her — painfully shy, set aflutter by the slightest stir, right on the brink of something. He took another step toward her. She faced him wide-eyed. There was none of the coy sparring he had met among the girls back home. There was something frighteningly honest about her complete lack of pretense.

He took her hand. He expected her to start, to pull back. She didn't. Gently he kissed her.

Her eyes were closed. "Kirby," she whispered. "Kirby . . ."

Her accent made his name sound as it never had before. He kissed her again and was surprised at the passion she showed. He held her tightly against him.

"Honey, when you shake thataway, I'm scared you're a-going to fall apart."

"I tried to confess," she said. "I tried to tell the priest, but I could not. I wanted forgiveness . . ."

"What for? I thought we decided kissing wouldn't give you no baby . . . and, if it was a crime, everybody in Missouri would be in jail by now."

"You make a joke. It is not funny. It is evil to lust."

"You talking about how you feel for me?"

"I do not know. I am frightened by the way I feel about you. I know you think I am a child, but there are things . . . I know what this is. I cannot help what I feel

117

. . . I try to fight, I pray, I do not want to be like these girls of La Tules's . . ."

"You've got to get something straight. I don't come to you the way those boys are going to the girls at La Tules's."

"You have not said you love me."

"I love you, Inez. I love you."

He kissed her again. He let his weight pull her down and she sank onto the sloping bank with him. His hands moved down her body and for a moment she permitted it. Then she grew rigid and pushed him away.

"No. It is not different. No matter what words you use, it is not different."

"How can I prove it?" he asked. "What can I do? You know I'll do anything."

"It is no use. It would be no good. You are not of the faith."

He saw how her mind was working. "Who says I ain't?" he asked. She looked in surprise at him. He said: "Well, my ma, good as she was in her way, didn't give me much chance to go on with the beliefs Pa meant me to have."

"Your father was a Catholic?"

"He was a steamboat captain. He was away most of the time, and didn't get to see to my religion the way he wanted to, and what with Ma gallivanting all around, I didn't get raised in the faith the way Pa wanted, and after he died it was too late."

His father had been a Methodist and his mother had been a hard-shell Baptist who spent most of her time at camp meetings and revivals, and about all Kirby could remember of the Bible was that, whenever his father had been home from one of his downriver trips, he had given both the boys a quarter for memorizing from the books of the New Testament. Inez was looking at him so intently that it disturbed him.

"Well, if you're born one," he said, "you're always one, ain't you? I can't help it if Pa died before he could fix it in my mind. Losing out so young, I don't remember none of the prayers or anything, but you can teach me again. Pa would like that."

"And a priest will marry us?"

"A priest, candles, a party, the whole fixings," he said. Well, he had made the same promise to plenty of other girls without ever marrying them and it had gotten him what he wanted. "And when the war's over, we'll go back to Missouri. I'll set you up better'n a princess. Talk about fine people, you'll see how they should really live. A place called the Pillars. Fifty pillars across the front, pure white marble, brought from Madagascar." He had been inside such houses, up on the bluffs above Natchez-under. "Thirty bedrooms . . . can you imagine it . . . solid gold beds, one of 'em shipped clear from France, Napoléon Bonaparte's own bedstead. It was kept special for Andy Jackson when he visited. That's when he was President."

"I saw a bedstead once," Inez said. "General Armijo had a bedstead at the palace. Only it was brass . . ."

"You'll see things you never dreamed about. You'll have a carriage for every day in the week."

"Every day. But I could not go out every day. I mean, my father says . . ."

119

"Honey, you got to git over the idea of being locked up behind walls. In Missouri a woman is as free as a man. You can come and go whenever you please."

She seemed to be looking at something beyond him. "It is hard to believe. The way we live . . . I thought it was so with all the women of the world. You cannot imagine how it is . . . a prisoner . . . sometimes I think it affects the mind."

"Well, it won't be that way. No father to keep you at heel the way he would a dog. No duenna, nobody to watch every move you make, no spy dogging your footsteps. When you go visiting, you can do it alone. When you go shopping, you do it alone. And you'll go shopping. I'll buy you things you can't imagine. They got dresses made all of diamonds. Or pearls. I'll show the whole world how much I love you."

He began kissing her as he talked and moving his hands over her body. He thought that the words would have their familiar effect. She responded to his kisses. Her fingers dug into his back.

She pushed away. He tried to pull her back.

"Honey, I'm not lying. I love you, honey. I'll show you how much, let's get married right now, run off and git married."

She stared at him blankly. He was holding her by one arm. With her free hand she touched her mouth. She began to shake her head from side to side.

"Ever since you danced with me at the palace I have been thinking things I would never have dared think before," she said. "I have been dreaming things while I was asleep and dreaming things while I was awake, I have been defying my father and lying to my mother and doing things that would have made me run to the priest and confess before, and I haven't been able to confess. This must be a part of those dreams, Kirby. I will wake up and find that it does not have the realness . . . we are talking about something that simply cannot be."

"Why?" he demanded. "Why can't it be?"

"Because I have fear," she said. "Can you not understand that? I have more fear than ever before in my life."

She pulled free, with her hand still at her mouth, and turned and ran down the river. He followed her, but she reached the gate, not even looking back, and disappeared inside. He stopped in the damp sand, looking at the gate. He began to curse softly.

As soon as she entered the patio, Inez saw the family coach standing in the stable yard. She stopped for a moment. She was still shaken and her mind would not work. Why should she have so much fear? Was it that she had fallen in love with an enemy? Love — enemy — she recoiled from both words. How could she call it love? How did she know? It was a thing of the flesh, not the spirit. If she had the courage to confess, that's what the priest would tell her. She could not think of Kirby as an enemy, simply because he was a *gringo*. The *gringos* had been a part of her town all her life, had lived as friends among her people for a generation. There had been no fighting, no war. The *gringos* had done nothing an enemy was supposed to do. And Kirby was of her faith. She could not think of a Catholic as an

121

enemy. It had surprised her to learn the truth about him, but now it filled her with a wonder, a sort of guilty excitement. It seemed to melt away so many barriers. It seemed to bring him, frighteningly, so much closer.

Finally she crossed to a servant who was unhitching the team. She asked if any of the family had gone to look for her in the chapel. He told her no. It had been a short Mass and the family had gone into breakfast upon returning. Sighing with relief, she went into the dining room.

At the head of the table sat *Don* Miguel. At his left sat his younger son, Agustín. At his right sat his eldest son, Ybarre. Six months ago Ybarre had married Leonor Espejo, bringing her to live in his father's house. Another room had been built for the new family. Leonor was big with child. There were two other daughters besides Inez but they were married and had gone to live in the houses of their husbands' families.

"Where have you been, Inez?" her father asked.

"In the chapel, Father."

"If your health has improved enough to go to chapel, then you may join us at breakfast."

"I . . . I do not feel that well."

"It is my wish that you join us."

"Perhaps she really does not feel well enough," Inez's mother said.

Don Miguel looked at his wife. *Doña* Prudencia was a slender woman and of such a close size to Inez that they sometimes exchanged dresses. She had thick black hair that was turning gray at the temples. People commented very often on what a fine carriage Inez had

122

and told her that she must have inherited it from her mother. If her mother had ever walked proudly, Inez could not remember it. *Doña* Prudencia had a stoop to her shoulders now that gave her the look of someone troubled with consumption or the cough, although she never coughed. It was rare that she looked directly at her husband. As soon as he turned to her, she looked down at her plate. It was where she usually looked during the meal.

Don Miguel did not raise his voice. He never raised his voice. "Sit down, Inez."

Inez sat beside her Aunt Maximiliana, picking absently at the blue tortillas and the mutton and eggs. Aunt Maximiliana didn't talk much at the table. She was usually too busy eating. None of them ever talked much at the table. Everything seemed unreal to Inez. She could think of nothing but Kirby. She was oppressed by her fears and her sense of sin.

After the meal the men retired to the patio for cigars while the women went into the parlor for their morning hours of gossip and knitting. Aunt Maximiliana was crocheting a frontal for the altar at San Miguel. With a variety of breathless little sounds, creaking stays, and comments to various saints she got herself seated. She made sure there was a plate of prickly-pear candy at hand before she started.

"This will be my seven hundred and ninth Lady of Guadalupe," she said. "I hope to make a thousand before I pass on to my reward. My mother only made nine hundred and ten Sacred Hearts, but I always take into account that she was not allowed her full span, being taken early by the pox." She looked at Inez. "You must have made a dozen coverlets by now. You should begin to keep count. When you are as old as I am, it is a comfort to have an exact record of your achievements."

"I do not care how many coverlets I have made," Inez said.

Leonor was outlining roses of Castile with a chain stitch of cochineal red. "You should have come to Mass with us this morning, Inez. We were trying to decide whether the trees on the plaza had really grown any bigger since Governor Armijo put them in."

"Did we not discuss that yesterday?" Inez said. "Did we not spend almost an hour deciding that the trees had grown bigger?"

Her mother glanced sharply at her. Inez stood up. The coverlet fell off her knees and gathered around her feet. She looked at the ceiling.

"Why can they not give us higher ceilings . . . as in a church?" she asked. "Why must they build these rooms so small?"

Her mother frowned at her. "These rooms have been big enough for two hundred years."

Inez kicked her coverlet aside and started across the room.

"Where are you going?" *Doña* Prudencia asked.

"I am going for a walk."

"The men are in the patio."

"Outside . . . I want to go outside . . . where there are no walls."

Aunt Maximiliana wheezed and started to rise. "I will go with her."

"No," *Doña* Prudencia said sharply. "It is forbidden." Inez had reached the door, but the tone of her mother's voice stopped her. *Doña* Prudencia leaned forward in her chair, staring intensely at Inez. "You know your father has forbidden us to appear on the streets, even with a duenna. These *gringos* have made it impossible."

Inez closed her eyes. She pressed her hand against her chest. She returned to her seat, picking up the coverlet.

Leonor smiled sympathetically at her. "I know what it is. During the time of my betrothal I was the same way. I had swoons and flutters of the heart that not even *dedalera* would cure. But it will be all right when you get married. Let me assure you."

"You should consider yourself lucky to get such a husband," Aunt Maximiliana said. "*Don* Fecundo is a kind man. We will all come to visit you often. We will knit in the parlor while the men smoke in the patio. Nothing will be changed."

Inez did not answer. A kind old man and sympathetic duennas and little white-walled rooms, two centuries, a thousand Ladies of Guadalupe. Nothing would be changed.

CHAPTER
NINE

On September 13th, Kirby had sentry duty from noon till stable call. He knew that it was Inez's wedding day and half the time he was at the point of deserting his post and going down to the Torreón house. But it wouldn't do any good. He couldn't just walk in and carry her off. There would be a big parcel of Mexicans around the place. He wouldn't get past the gates.

He had seen her several times since last Sunday. He had gone down the river almost every evening and waited behind the house. More than once she hadn't come out to meet him. She had said that there were too many people watching. She told him one night nobody was watching but she hadn't come out anyway. She had stayed in the chapel and prayed, knowing that he was waiting just beyond the wall. He had the feeling of a struggle going on in her all the time. There were moments when he seemed to be getting through, when she seemed to believe whatever he told her and her own desires were becoming too much for her. But she always stopped short of the breaking point. She wasn't a tease. He knew that. She was fighting herself more than she was him. He got the feeling that if he had been given just a little more time, one or two more meetings — but now it was over. Time had run out.

About an hour before stable call an Indian appeared at Kirby's post. He said that La Tules wanted to see him right away. The Indian wouldn't say why, but it got Kirby in a sweat. It had to be something about Inez. He wondered if the wedding had been postponed for some reason. He left his post and went with the Indian to the place on Burro Alley. Inside, he was met by the red-wigged woman.

"Well, señor, you must be the great lover."

"Certain for sure," he said. "What's this about?"

"I want you to have the understanding," La Tules said. She put her hand on his shoulder. A dozen glittering rings dug into the puffy flesh of her fingers. "I have much power in this town. If you do not observe the correct thing with this girl now . . . I have a man who would kill you."

"Girl? You mean Inez? You know I wouldn't do her no harm."

"Ai, what is the use? Why is it always men such as you who hurt us?"

She took him down the hall to a room. The floor was black and white tile and there was opaque glass in the windows and against the wall hung red damask drapes. At a marble-topped table with clawed legs sat Inez. Before her was a half-filled cup of chocolate and some untouched pastry.

Inez remained in the chair for a moment, staring at Kirby. Then she rose and came blindly into his arms. "I thought . . . I did not know . . . Kirby, when I first knew it, I was very calm. I mean when I knew what I was going to do . . . I did not understand why, but I was very calm. I took some jewels . . . I knew we would need money . . . and my little silver knife . . . and I told them I wanted to pray alone in the chapel. *Don Fecundo*, I thought they would see me, but those little trees by the chapel hiding the gate . . . everything so strange and far away, I don't know . . . I could not understand it . . . how I could be so calm until I got outside, and then I got afraid . . . if I did not run then, I would not have the courage to do it. I ran, all the way . . . Kirby, make me not afraid."

"Certain, honey, certain. Now just try to calm down. Nothing kin happen to you now. I'm here and I won't leave you again, never again."

He held her and talked to her and stroked her. Gradually her trembling subsided and she stood, heavy and spent, against him. La Tules wheezed and lowered herself into the chair by the table. From a gold box she thumbed snuff and jammed it up her nostrils, sniffing loudly.

"Inez," she said, "you must have the understanding of one thing. Marry this one, marry *Don* Fecundo, it does not matter, in either case you will get hurt, you will get hurt in many more ways than I can tell you. Mother of God. But this way . . . at least you will know love."

At seven o'clock that evening Colonel Doniphan was in his quarters at the Palace of the Governors. Because of his legal background he had been chosen to put together the collection of statutes that were to govern the new territory. He had gathered a staff to help him, but tonight he was alone.

It had been a peck of work added to his regular duties — up into the small hours every night arguing with Kearny and other officials, getting what grudging help he could from the Mexican lawyers in town. He was beginning to feel the effects. There was an ache in him that went clear down to his bones. His eyes burned as he tried to read the first page of the statutes they had roughed out.

ADMINISTRATION

Section 1: The laws heretofore in force concerning descents, distributions, wills and testaments, as contained in the treatise on these subjects written by Pedro Murillo de Lorde, shall remain in force so far as they are in conformity with the Constitution of the United States.

He grew so dizzy that the words blurred and he had to lean back. He was afraid that he was going to be sick. He wished that Beth were there to rub the back of his neck and put a hot towel on his eyes. Just about this time she would be putting John and Aleck, Jr., to bed. Maybe there would be a pillow fight before she could get them settled down. John was only eight and still rambunctious. But there was no reason to worry. It was just natural animal spirits. It was Aleck, Jr., he worried about. He wondered if Aleck had gotten the fever again this fall. The doctor had insisted that it was just the ague, but Doniphan was beginning to suspect that the boy had inherited his own weakness. He wished that he could look in on them for just one evening and make sure everything was all right. After the boys were in bed, he and Beth would spend an hour by the fire reading aloud to each other out of Byron or Shelley. Beth liked Shelley.

The sergeant major came in with some reports. He said that one of the sentries had been missing from his post since stable call. A search was being made but he hadn't been found. It was a man from Company D, Kirby Hatcher.

Doniphan wondered if Kirby had deserted. He wouldn't be surprised. He had expected it before this. In a way he wouldn't mind if it were true. He thought that Nate would be better off without his uncle.

Later the palace grapevine brought Doniphan other news. It seemed that Inez Torreón had run out on her wedding party. They hadn't found her yet, either. After that Doniphan couldn't work. He paced his room, trying to piece together a dozen vague suspicions. The one fact that had come out of the mess at Kearny's ball was that the soldier who had danced with Inez had yellow hair. At the time it hadn't helped much. But Doniphan knew Kirby's reputation with women. Breaking into the general's ball to see a girl was just about the kind of a hooraw Kirby would pull, and now Kirby and Inez, missing on the same day.

Doniphan wanted to talk with Nate. He knew that Nate was back in camp. Kearny had returned from his downriver march about two that afternoon. The rumor of Armijo's collecting another army had proved false. Kearny had quieted the downriver people by his show of force and by promises that he would give them protection against marauding Apaches and Navajos.

Doniphan sent for Nate. He was putting his papers away when the young man arrived. Nate was obviously uncomfortable. He performed a sloppy salute.

"Uh . . . looks as though you been working pretty hard . . . those new statutes, I mean."

"We're calling it the Kearny Code," Doniphan said. "We're using some of the Missouri statutes, what we can from the laws of Texas and Coahuila, the Livingston Code . . . oh, it's quite a clabber."

Nate tugged self-consciously at his clothes. He tilted his head to look at the colonel. "Are those fever spots in your cheeks? You shouldn't let them drive you so hard, Colonel. You'll come down with fever the way you did after the Turnham case."

Doniphan shuffled the papers and put them in a drawer. It bothered him to have Nate know his secret. Not many men knew. It made him ashamed. It was something he couldn't explain to his men. They would have accepted ague or scurvy. But it bore no relation to the ordinary fevers. It might even have made more sense to them if he were average size. But he was taller than any man in the 1st Missouri, stronger than most. He knew that they looked upon him as a giant. They thought of him as invincible and indefatigable, in a dozen places at once, always on the spot for whatever was needed, able to outmarch or outfight any man in the regiment. He realized what it would do to morale if they knew his weakness. They wouldn't be able to understand a man his size and strength being in such precarious balance, fighting such a thing off all the time, never knowing when it would strike him down. It was his private fear that they would find out someday and his grip on the regiment would go to hell.

"Just overwork, Nate," he said. "Not enough help, maybe. Why don't you sit in? We could use somebody who knows his Missouri organic. I told the boys you were up to the hub on that when you were at my offices in Liberty."

Nate grinned. "Well, I guess I forgot most of it by now."

Doniphan frowned at the floor. He wondered where he had failed Nate. He felt that he hadn't kept his obligation to Nate's father. Asa Hatcher had been one of his most valuable militia officers during the Mormon war. They had been close during those troubled years. But it was more than his debt to Asa. He had become fond of Nate during the six months the boy had spent in his law offices. Nate had a good mind. Doniphan hated to see it wasted on hooraws.

"I guess you know about Kirby," Doniphan said.

"Kirby just went into town," Nate said. "Lots of volunteers go into town. Git drunk or something."

"It's curious. It always seems to be you that covers for Kirby. It never seems to be the other way around. You've got so much loyalty it sticks out your ears. Trouble is, a virtue headed in the wrong direction can become a vice. It can become almost a disease, Nate."

132

"Colonel, you know what Kirby has done for me."

"He stuck with you through thick and thin, didn't he? He showed you how many tobacco crops you could lose if you spent your time hunting and fishing and loafing around in the taverns."

"Those weren't good tobacco years. Everybody was going broke."

"They were good years for selling off all your stock, though, and your best parcels of land. Was that your idea or his, Nate?"

Nate flushed. "Colonel . . . it was this kind of lecture you'd started giving me when I left your law offices at Liberty."

"It isn't as easy as running out on my lectures. I think you're at a fork in the road, Nate. Did it ever strike you how much you're getting like Kirby? We're fighting a war. We didn't come out here just for a big hooraw. There comes a time when a man's got to decide on his set of values."

Nate did not answer. He looked beyond Doniphan. The colonel closed his eyes and pressed his fingers against them. He felt too sick to struggle any longer. He knew Nate's stubbornness.

"I really asked you down here for your help and not to give you a lecture," Doniphan said. "We've got a problem. The feeling of these Mexicans is changing toward us. Kearny quieted them down some in the south, but now it's cropping up here. There's talk that this Colonel Diego Archuleta is stirring up some sort of a plot. If he gets *Don* Miguel Torreón in with him, we've got real trouble."

"Torreón?"

Nate spoke so sharply that Doniphan looked at him. But the young man's face had gone blank. "The Torreóns are one of the most powerful families in the country," Doniphan said. "Don Miguel is the most conservative type of New Mexican. Naturally he has no use for us. But he hated the government that was here before we came. Governor Armijo was corrupt, tyrannical, he bled the rich families as dry as the poor. Chances are the same thing would happen again if Colonel Archuleta got back in power, since he was Armijo's second-in-command. That's what has kept Torreón neutral. You can see what a position that puts us in. As long as Torreón is on the fence, we're safe. But it would be real bad if something turned him actively against us. The only way he could go is with Archuleta. And if the Torreóns went to Archuleta, half the people in Santa Fé would follow. It might mean the start of a rebellion."

"What would turn Torreón against us?" Nate said.

"Maybe his daughter running off with your Uncle Kirby."

Doniphan had hoped for some reaction. He hadn't expected such a violent one. He had seen the same expression on a man kicked by a mule.

"Then it's true," Doniphan said.

"No! I mean I don't know. How would I know? Kirby was already gone when I got back today. I ain't seen him since I left."

Doniphan studied him narrowly. "Well, the fact remains that Inez Torreón ran out on her wedding

134

today just about the same time your uncle deserted his post. It isn't as simple as finding your uncle and shooting him for desertion. If this girl's with him, he's put himself in a position to thumb his nose at the whole damned army. We can't take a chance on humiliating *Don* Miguel. We've got to pussyfoot, Nate, and it fair makes my skin crawl." Doniphan took a turn around the room. "And there's something else that doesn't jibe. A peasant, one of those barefoot half-breeds from La Tules place . . . we've got plenty of them running off to sleep with a soldier, even marrying some of the boys. But a girl of this kind, one of the fine people . . ."

Nate didn't answer immediately. He was staring beyond Doniphan. It seemed to be taking him some time to digest the whole thing. When he finally spoke, his voice had a faraway sound. "They all hanker after Kirby."

"In the States, maybe. But here . . . you've got to understand, Nate . . . these women are different. It's hard to explain. They're living in the past. They don't think the way our women think. This girl, Inez. I met her at the general's ball. Virginal, innocent . . . innocent in a way our women could never be. She wouldn't dream of doing something like this. If the thought so much as occurred to her, she'd have to spend an hour with her priest asking forgiveness."

"Maybe she's got something we ain't seen."

"No, it's inconceivable," Doniphan said. "You've got to put yourself in their minds to realize how inconceivable it is."

"Are you saying Kirby took her off by force?"

The colonel shook his head. "I don't know. There's something here I just don't understand." He closed his eyes. His headache was getting worse. Finally he said: "I doubt if anybody besides us has connected Kirby and Inez yet. Only a few men in the regiment know that Kirby's gone. The Mexicans in town probably think the girl simply got cold feet and ran out on her wedding. If we could keep it that way, if we could get the girl back to her father before the whole story becomes known, we might save the situation. Now you're the one best suited to deal with Kirby. If you could find him, make him see the light . . . I'm making him an offer. If he gives that girl up and comes back, he won't be posted as a deserter and shot. He will return to his company as though nothing has happened and the whole incident will be forgotten. My word on it."

"What about General Kearny?"

"I haven't spoken to him yet. I couldn't be sure I was right about Kirby till I talked with you. The general understands how ticklish the situation is. This is the only way out. He'll realize that. He'll back me up."

Nate looked at the floor, massaging the end of his nose between a thumb and forefinger. Doniphan remembered the habit well. He remembered Nate's rubbing his nose in the offices at Liberty every time he read from Byron. Doniphan believed that reading aloud from the classic poets developed a man's power of oratory in the courtroom. Nate had hated Byron.

"If I go, I'll need some help," Nate said. "There's an old Mexican named Jayán . . . he's been teaching me Spanish and such."

136

"A good idea. Somebody who really knows the country. You can offer him a *peso* a day and rations. I'll give you a requisition if he needs a horse."

Nate pulled on his nose again. "Well," he said, "I'll see if I can find Kirby."

Nate still had a numb feeling about Inez when he left Doniphan. He didn't want to believe it. He didn't think he could believe it till he saw it. He didn't want to see it.

Nate found Jayán in his mud house near the chapel of San Miguel, south of the river. Jayán agreed to help. He took Nate to the square and went around the *cantinas*, talking to his friends, and finally found out that La Tules's coach had been seen going north earlier that evening but that La Tules was known to be at her saloon. Jayán said that it might mean something. La Tules had befriended Inez many years ago in El Paso. She was about the only one in town who would dare *Don* Miguel's wrath by helping Inez. She was notorious for being the go-between in escapades of the heart.

Jayán went to one of his nephews who was a monte dealer at La Tules's. After a lot of arguing and pleading, he got the nephew to take them to her sitting room.

From behind the closed door, studded with brass and carved cherubs and sacred hearts, they could hear a singsong murmur, a wheezing, and the creaking stays of a corseted woman. The nephew knocked discreetly. There was a long pause, then an answer from the inside. The nephew opened the door.

La Tules lay on the haircloth settee, half buried in a heap of red velvet pillows. Her wig had fallen onto the black and white tiles of the floor. She had cut her own hair short and she was losing so much of it anyway that her naked skull showed through everywhere. It made Nate think of a yellow eggshell. Something red had been smeared on her jowls, reminding Nate of the pokeberry juice the girls back home had painted their cheeks with. The rest of her face was pasted up with a concoction of egg white and chalk the New Mexican women used as a cosmetic. It had a lavender color and was streaked where tears had run through it and where liquor had dribbled from the corners of her mouth. The garters on her white crocheted stockings had come loose and the stockings hung in soiled loops around her swollen ankles. Beside her on the floor stood a half empty bottle of Pass brandy. She held a cut glass goblet in one hand, waving it back and forth in time to the singsong chant. Nate had picked up enough Spanish from Jayán to understand her when she spoke.

"You from *Don* Miguel?" she asked. "Tell him I cannot help. Go back and tell him I cannot help. La Tules cannot help."

Nate tried to tell her who he was. She raised up, squinting at him. Her eyes were bloodshot and filmed and she had trouble keeping them open. Nate was still talking when she cut him off with a raucous laugh. She lay back in the pillows, laughing uncontrollably. She choked and had to stop laughing. She fought for breath, wheezing and spewing.

"Go back and tell *Don* Miguel," she said. "I have given him wounds that will not heal. My whip wounds, they have healed, the scars are still there, but the wounds are healed, there is no more pain . . ." She paused, gasping for breath. She pawed for the bottle on the floor and knocked it over. "He will have them all his life, not scars, such as my scars, he will have wounds, *Don* Miguel, wounds that you cannot hide from the town, whenever you appear you cannot hide them, we will see, the whole town will know."

"You're talking about his daughter," Nate said. "Inez. Inez and Kirby."

She threw the glass from her and it shattered against the wall. She began laughing again. "That flower, that little flower, she will not be imprisoned behind the walls, she will not fade and die in the old man's house as her mother has faded and died. *Don* Fecundo has been cheated and *Don* Miguel has been cheated and all those stupid old men whose hands shake when they see a young girl."

"Where'd she go?" Nate grabbed her shoulders. "You let 'em use your coach. Where'd they go?"

Her eyes were closed and tears were running through the white paste on her face. Nate couldn't tell if she was laughing or crying now.

"Tell *Don* Miguel," she said, "this is my message to him. He has been whipped in the plaza. After all these years somebody has finally whipped him in the plaza."

Nate began to shake her and shout at her, but Jayán pulled on his arm. "Please, *señor*, the coach, she is well known throughout the department. She will not be hard to follow."

Nate released the drunken old woman. She was still laughing. It sounded hysterical and he was afraid she would choke to death if she didn't stop. Jayán pulled Nate out of the room.

"What was all that about?" Nate asked.

Jayán said: "Many years ago *Don* Miguel sent his family to El Paso to visit James Magoffin. When *Don* Miguel heard that La Tules was there, also, and had befriended Inez, *Don* Miguel went down and whipped La Tules in the plaza."

Nate looked back at the room. La Tules had subsided. All he could hear was a wheezing and something every now and then that could have been a sob.

"Well," he said, "I guess she's got her revenge. *Don* Miguel sure won't ever git over this."

Jayán sighed. "It is hard to believe that once she was very beautiful. She was the mistress of Governor Armijo and entertained him often in this room. Before that she entertained many other great men in this room."

"Did she ever entertain *Don* Miguel?"

"Once, a long time ago, I think she entertained *Don* Miguel."

CHAPTER
TEN

Nate and Jayán started north that night. Doniphan had given Nate a requisition for an extra horse. It was an old zebra dun from Company C. It was a windsucker, a kicker, had galls and bog spavins and splints, but, the way Jayán carried on, a body would think it was the greatest horse in the world. Jayán said that he had not ridden a horse since he was twelve. Only the fine people and their retainers rode horses.

He told Nate that the valley north of Santa Fé was the Upriver. Most of the villages in the Upriver belonged to the Pueblo Indians. At Tesuque, about ten miles out of Santa Fé, an Indian told them that he had seen La Tules's blue coach pass by a few hours before. About dawn they reached the turn-off to Chimayo, one of the few Spanish settlements along the Upriver.

They lost a few hours trying to find someone who could tell them which fork to take. Near noon they met a farmer who had seen the coach going on toward Taos. At San Juan they lost more time on a false lead so that they didn't reach Taos till the second morning. At sunup they met the coach just south of the Mexican village. La Tules's coachman was alone. Jayán knew him and got him to talk. He had raised a particular hate on

Kirby. He said that Kirby and Inez had been married by Father Martínez yesterday afternoon. The priest knew the Torreóns and had first refused to perform the ceremony, but Inez had threatened to live with Kirby anyway. The priest had finally thought it better to marry them than to let Inez live in sin. The coachman had refused to take them any farther and didn't know where they had gone.

Again Jayán began questioning people in the town. At Estes's tavern they talked with a boy who had seen smoke coming from a house that had been abandoned for a long time. The house was on the road between Taos and Pecuris. It was still early morning when Nate and Jayán got there.

It was a small house. It looked old. Some of the wall had crumbled and lay in heaps at the corners. The outer plaster had washed away in big patches to expose the adobe bricks beneath. Smoke was rising from somewhere in the building. Its smell was a perfume Nate would always associate with this country. The smell of piñon smoke and the sound of bells. He wondered why he was thinking about these things. Maybe because he didn't want to think about other things.

"Well," Jayán said. "Shall we go in?"

Nate realized how long he had been sitting his horse before the house, staring at the building. He dismounted. "Kirby!" he called. "It's Nate! Can I come in?"

Inez appeared in the opening that had once been a doorway. She was barefoot. She had on nothing but a

142

wool skirt and a short-sleeved blouse pleated around its low neck. Her bare feet looked pale and fragile against the dark earth. Her black hair was let down. It had always been carefully groomed before, hidden beneath a mantilla or swept up into a tortoise-shell comb. Now it hung almost to her waist. It made Nate think of the bed. It changed her from a child to a woman.

"God give you good morning, Nate," she said.

She showed no surprise. Her smile was dreamy and far away. Her eyes were dark and so shining they looked wet. He had the feeling she was looking at him from another world. He had seen the same look in other women after that first night with Kirby. He remembered how he had felt when Doniphan first told him about Inez and Kirby. He hadn't thought that it could be any worse.

"Our house is yours," she said.

He couldn't answer. There was a crushed feeling in his chest. She looked at him curiously, then took a step backward into the room. He looked at Jayán. The old man swung down and took the reins of his horse. Nate followed Inez inside.

A fire was burning in the remains of the cone-shaped fireplace at one corner of the room, the smoke rising through a hole in the roof. Kirby lay on a serape. His shirt and shoes were off. His hands were back of his head and he grinned up at Nate without offering to rise.

"Don't this beat the volunteers?" he said. "No 'Reveille' breaking your ears, no sergeant kicking you out of the hay. You oughta get hitched yourself, Nate."

143

Nate didn't answer.

"Light and set a spell," Kirby said. "We ain't got fancy vittles, but I guess there's enough to go around. The parson at Taos, he give us some corn and beans and such. Even fixed me up with tobacco. Honey, roll us some."

Inez got a little silver tube and some corn shuck. From the tube she poured tobacco in the corn shuck, then rolled cigarettes. She got a burning stick from the fire and lit the cigarettes for the men. Kirby lay back with his eyes closed and let smoke stream from his nostrils.

"A chawing man has got to be pretty far gone to smoke his tobacco in a corn shuck, I'll admit. He's got to be even further gone to use this Mexican tobacco. But I been so long without a decent plug I'd've smoked old rags."

Inez was smiling at Nate. It was a strange smile and it disturbed him. He remembered a girl who had looked at the ground when she talked to you and who sounded breathless and who broke off in the middle of sentences and flushed if you stared at her too long. A body didn't change so much overnight. He remembered how Doniphan couldn't understand her running off, and what he had told Doniphan: "Maybe she's got something we ain't seen." He had a strong feeling of it now, something deep down, beyond the little girl, something that belonged with this country and that none of them would ever really understand.

"Take the hobble off your jaw, Nate," Kirby said. "I admit it's some of a shock, your Uncle Kirby gitting

144

hitched, but it had to happen sometime." Kirby stretched and grinned, waiting for some comment. When Nate didn't speak, Kirby quit grinning. He frowned at Nate. Without looking at Inez he said: "How about them corn cakes, woman?"

Inez looked down quickly, turning away from them. Nate thought that he saw a hint of color come to her cheek. She knelt with her back to them before the oven. There was a rock heating in the fire. From a broken bowl she poured a paste of water and corn onto the rock, and then patted it into shape with her fingers. The thin cake cooked fast and within a few seconds she was peeling it off and putting it on a slab of wood they were using as a platter.

"Kirby," Nate said, "I've got to talk with you alone."

"I've got no secrets from my wife."

"No, I mean it. I want to see you alone."

Inez looked over her shoulder at them. Kirby got up, yawning. The hair on his chest was curly and yellow in the shafts of sunlight slanting through holes in the roof. He and Nate went outside. Kirby put a hand on Nate's shoulder.

"Nate, I know how you feel . . ."

Nate pulled away from the hand. "Then let's not talk about it. Doniphan sent me up here. He said, if you'd come back now, you won't be posted as a deserter."

Nate told him about the rumors of conspiracy, Doniphan's fear that Torreón would go over to Diego Archuleta. Kirby looked beyond Nate, his eyes squinted. He scratched the curly mat of hair on his belly and shook his head.

"Might have been different if you'd caught us before we were married. Torreón might have taken her back then."

"He'll still take her back. They don't recognize this marriage. Doniphan tried to explain it . . . you didn't get any dispensation, did you?"

"I didn't need any. This priest, he somehow got the idea him 'n' me was of the same faith."

"How'd he get that idea?" Nate asked. There was a strange glint in Kirby's eyes, filling Nate with a quick suspicion. "Kirby, you didn't tell him . . . ?"

"Tell him what? I don't speak their language. Inez had to do all the talking."

"Then she must have told him. What gave her the idea? She wouldn't lie about something like that to a priest. Did you tell her you were Catholic?"

"Not exactly. We talked about religion, she must have got it all clabbered up somehow. Nate, I don't know how it all happened, I couldn't tell what she was a-jabbering to that priest and she didn't tell me what she told him till after the marriage."

"That doesn't sound right. It sounds like another one of your deals. I still don't think you're married. The ceremony doesn't mean anything to them if you ain't a Catholic, and it sure don't mean anything if you lied about it."

Kirby looked at the ground and shook his head. "Nate, I'm all mixed up. It all happened so fast . . ."

"It didn't jist happen," Nate said bitterly. "You must have been seeing her. All that time I was trying to cipher out ways of seeing her . . . you were seeing her."

146

"When it first started, Nate, I was doing it for you. You got to believe that. I was trying to rig up a way you could meet her. Then it sort of got twisted around. What I mean . . . the way she acted, the way she talked, well, I realized . . . I mean . . . well, a girl can't love two men, Nate."

"No, jist the one that lies to her and honey-fuggles her and spreads the molasses on up to the hub . . . he's done the same thing about a hundred times before with a hundred other women, he knows jist how to do it. This girl . . . I've seen the way they live, Kirby, locked up behind those walls, never seeing what the world's all about. She never had a chance."

"That's what I'm trying to say, Nate. Maybe neither of us had a chance. It all happened so fast . . . I mean, if she'd come to you, just run out on her wedding, you couldn't send her back to that, could you? What would you have done?"

"That's different."

"How is it different? When she says she loves you. When she's done something like that for you. I couldn't run out on her then, and I can't run out on her now."

"So you'll keep her a while, and then git tired of her when it's too late for her to go back. I won't let you do it, Kirby."

The skin looked shiny and stretched across Kirby's cheek bones. His eyes were almost closed. "There must be some other way, Nate. I won't give her up."

Nate felt himself tremble. His rage and bitterness and sense of betrayal had been building up ever since

Santa Fé, and he didn't think that he could hold it back much longer. He stepped past Kirby to the door.

"Git your shoes on," he told Inez. "You're going back." She rose to face him. Her hands were still covered with cornmeal paste.

"I don't want to go," she said.

"You're going," he said, "if I have to take you barefoot."

He crossed to her and grabbed her by the arm. She did not struggle as he pulled her across the room. Kirby stood in the door. Nate had his craw full. Without stopping, he lowered one shoulder and let the point ram into Kirby as he lunged through the door. It only knocked Kirby part way aside. Kirby caught himself and with one hand tore Inez free from Nate. With the other he hit Nate.

It knocked Nate back into the room. Before he could recover, Kirby followed and hit him again. Nate fell into the fire.

He let out a howl and rolled away, beating at the burning embers on his shirt. He rolled into the bowl of moist cornmeal and got mush all over his face. He heard Kirby start to laugh. He scrambled up, pawing at his face, and rushed at the sound of Kirby's laughing.

The mush was still blinding him when he went into Kirby and struck for the body without seeing where he hit. He heard Kirby grunt and felt him stagger backward. He followed, hitting him and hitting him. Kirby finally wheeled free. He was just out of reach and Nate could see his face smeared with blood and how glassy his eyes looked.

148

"Well," Kirby gasped, "cub's growed up all on a sudden."

Nate went after him again, but Kirby wheeled aside and caught him with a blow that doubled Nate up. He lunged at Kirby while he was still jackknifed, butting Kirby and knocking him backward. Nate plunged helplessly after him and they both crashed into the crumbling wall so hard that it gave way and they fell out with it.

The bricks seemed to come from everywhere, showering down on Nate, half burying him. Stunned, sickened, Nate dragged himself out from under the débris. He saw Kirby trying to get up, swaying and bloody. Nate got to his hands and knees.

"That's enough, Nate," Kirby gasped. "I don't want to fight you no more. I don't want to hurt you."

Nate made a dive for him and went into him while he was still off balance. He drove Kirby back across the room and Kirby never recovered enough to block any of Nate's blows or to hurt Nate with his own. Nate got him against the wall and kept hitting him. He didn't know when Kirby quit fighting. He kept hitting him till he couldn't hit any more.

He sagged against Kirby. He thought that Kirby was holding him up. When he figured that he could stand on his own, he backed off and saw that he had been holding Kirby up. Kirby slid down to the floor and sat with his back against the wall. His jaw hung open and his eyes were closed and he made strange sounds trying to breathe.

Nate was swaying back and forth and knew that he would fall if he didn't get some support. He went over to the wall and leaned against it. He thought that he was going to be sick. He wished he could stop breathing because it hurt so much when he breathed. His hands felt swollen and he wondered if he had broken them.

Jayán was standing in the door with his hat in his hands, and, the way he was gaping, Nate figured he'd never seen a fight before. Inez had crossed to Kirby and was kneeling beside him. Nate thought it was a caution how calm she was. He expected most girls her age would go to pieces after such a thing. She was kneeling beside Kirby, washing at his face with a damp rag and saying something over and over in Spanish. Kirby made a groaning sound and pushed her hand off.

She settled back and looked at Nate. She was not crying or making any sound and she did not say anything. He didn't know whether it was hate in her eyes or shock or pity. He didn't want to look at her any more. He thought that he was going to be sick again. He knew that it was useless to ask her again to come with him. She had made her choice. The fight had left him so crippled he couldn't have taken her by force even if Kirby hadn't been there. He realized that he didn't want to take her now. He just wanted to go away.

He went out to his horse and Jayán had to help him get on. Before he rode away, he looked back into the house. Kirby was sitting against the wall with his head in his hands and he wouldn't look at Nate.

150

After Nate left, Inez turned back to Kirby. He was still sitting against the wall with his head in his hands, his long yellow hair hanging through his fingers, his face hidden from her. She touched him gently, wanting to help somehow, to soothe. She tried to pull his hands away from his face and he groaned miserably, and pushed her off.

"I wish you would let me do something," she said. "I could rub tallow into the cuts and you would not have so much pain."

"I never had a fight with him before," he said. "I never even hit him before. In seven years I never hit him."

His lips were so cut and swollen that the words were hard to understand. She wet the cloth again and pressed it to his mouth. She could see the misery in his eyes and knew that it came more from hurting Nate than from his own pain. He got up and walked to the door. He stood, looking out in the direction Nate had ridden, and finally he walked away from the house. She went to the door but she saw that he wasn't walking toward the road. He was walking up the hill into the twisted piñon trees. She realized that he wanted to be alone.

She went back inside and busied herself at meaningless jobs around the room. She remembered the curious way he had watched her and she tried to decide what had been in his mind. She wondered if he was surprised that she had not been more shocked. It was hard for her to understand. When the fight had

151

started, she had thought that she was going to act very badly or hysterically. But that had passed quickly and now she wondered why. She wondered if there was something wrong with her. For some reason it made her think of the Apache ears Governor Armijo had collected and she had seen hanging on a rawhide string every time she went to the palace. She thought of the dead bodies of peasants she had seen lying in a field after an Indian raid and the *penitentes* whipping themselves on Good Friday till their backs ran with blood. She had always thought of her life as sheltered and yet she realized how close pain and death and violence had always been. As close as the agonized Christ hanging on his cross in every household. Her mother had once said that was very Spanish. Inez wondered if people who inflicted pain upon themselves felt differently about pain.

In several hours she began worrying about Kirby and went hunting him and found him high on the hill, sitting on a rock and staring emptily off toward the south. She persuaded him to come back to the house. She washed the dried blood from his face and heated tallow and rubbed it into his bruises and cuts. He was over the worst effect of the fight and was able to eat the food she made. It seemed to revive him but he still sat looking emptily out the door. Inez glanced at the statue of *Santa* Rita she had brought with her. She had put it in one of the wall niches that all the houses had for saints.

"We could pray," she said. "We can pray that Nate can forgive you and that you can forgive Nate. I know

152

you have forgotten much, but it will not take long to learn again. You can follow me." She turned to the image. "Oh, heavenly patron, in whose name I glory, pray ever to God for me, strengthen me in . . ."

She realized that Kirby was making no attempt to join her. She turned to see him, watching her intently. There was an expression on his face — she could not define it. For a moment he seemed very young and vulnerable. She had the sense of a conflict in him.

"Inez," he muttered. "I don't deserve you."

"Kirby . . ." She hesitated. The name still sounded strange on her lips. All men had been señor. "Kirby . . . you must not blame yourself. Nate . . ."

"I'm not talking about that." He ran his hand through his yellow hair. "You're too good for me, Inez."

She crossed to him and knelt before him, her hands on his arms. He pulled free and rose and walked to the door. He stood with his head bent, scowling. Then he cursed softly.

"Kirby," she said, "the fight . . . what was it about? I could not hear what you were saying to Nate outside . . . and then . . . why did Nate want to take me home?"

"I can't explain it. The fight . . . something between me and Nate . . . you wouldn't understand. I wasn't against taking you back, exactly, I just wasn't a-going to give you up."

"Give me up? Kirby, there are certain words for which I do not have the understanding. How is this meant . . . give me up?"

He looked at her sharply. He wiped his hand across his mouth. "Never mind. I didn't mean it that way.

153

What I meant is . . . Nate did have a reason for coming up here. He brought word from your pa. It seems *Don Miguel* ain't a-going to be as hard on us as we expected. Nate said something could be worked out. Maybe we can make your pa see it's better having a *gringo* for a son-in-law than losing his daughter entirely."

For a moment she could not believe it. Her father was inflexible. She had never known him to relent before, not in the smallest thing. Yet Nate wouldn't have come all this way if it hadn't been true. She felt breathless, a little dizzy.

"Then we don't have to run any more?"

"No," Kirby said. "We don't have to run."

She let out a little cry and ran to him. He took her in his arms and she buried her face against his chest. She was laughing but her tears were getting the curly yellow hair on his chest all wet.

"We can go back," she said. "Kirby, we can go back."

"Yes, honey," he said. "We can go back."

They got a ride south in a big two-wheeled cart that belonged to a farmer who was going to Santa Fé. It was hard for Kirby to understand his feelings. He bitterly regretted the fight with Nate. He wished that Nate had understood. He hadn't really meant to take anything from him, to hurt him. He hadn't realized that the girl had meant so much to Nate. He'd thought it was just puppy love. He had seen Nate go through the same pattern with girls back at Marshall, goggle-eyed, lightning-struck, a storm of adolescent emotion, gone as quickly as it came. In a few days Nate would be over it and they could laugh together about the whole thing.

But that still didn't explain what had happened to Kirby. He remembered telling Inez how he didn't deserve her. What had gotten into him? He'd never felt that way with a woman before. And the fight had really been to keep from giving her up. That didn't make sense. It didn't fit in with his original ideas. At the beginning Inez had just been a way to get hold of the wool. Why hadn't he played it that way? Why hadn't he jumped at Doniphan's terms? He could have agreed to hand her back for a price. Ten wagonloads of wool, and *Don* Miguel could have his daughter back, and Kirby would forget that he'd ever had a wife.

Now he was getting as bad as Nate. He felt guilty about using her to make any sort of deal. He felt guilty about deceiving her. But he hadn't really deceived her. All he'd said was that something could be worked out with her father. And he figured that was true. Apparently *Don* Miguel was willing to compromise and forget the whole matter if Inez were returned. *Don* Miguel's pride or his love for Inez — it didn't matter what motivated him — if it meant that much to him, chances were he'd go a step further, chances were, if he saw it could be no other way, he would make a bigger compromise and accept Kirby as a son-in-law. It had happened once. Jim Magoffin had married a distant kin of the Torreóns and had become one of the richest traders in New Mexico.

The possibilities were enormous. They fairly took his breath away. That's what he'd been fighting Nate for.

155

He couldn't lose sight of that. Maybe Inez was a beautiful, soft, white little kitten, something different from anyone he'd ever known before, but they all seemed different at first. He could get a hundred soft white little kittens, but it would be a long month of Sundays before he ever hooked up with another deal big enough to make him as rich as Jim Magoffin.

Kirby didn't want Inez in on his meetings with Doniphan and Torreón until the deal was closed. He left her about five miles outside Santa Fé at the house of a man named Nuño Vádez, who had worked for James Magoffin as a muleskinner and who knew Inez. Kirby convinced her that it would be better this way — until he found out for sure about her father.

She didn't cry when they parted. It struck him that he had never seen her cry, even when he could see how scared she was at La Tules's and later in the coach on the way north. It seemed strange in such a young girl.

He was about 100 feet away from the house when he looked back and saw her standing in the doorway. It made him stop. He had a sense of guilt again, and something else, an impulse so strong he almost started back to her. He would tell her the truth. They would go north together again, they would leave the country together, and the hell with ten percent of Ganoe's profits, the hell with thinking big and with Missouri hooraws, and with all the elegant schemes that never caught fire.

He turned away, cursing his weakness. He should have known better than to get a woman involved in his deals. They always clabbered a man's brains.

156

It was evening when he topped the low northern hills and saw the city spread below him. Flat roofs like a checkerboard in the dusk, streets so narrow a man had to stand against a wall to let the wagons pass, the shadowy quadrangle of the palace with the crumbling towers at the east and west corners. The church bells were ringing Vespers and all the Mexicans were kneeling in the square, the old men with their straw hats in their hands and the women with their heads bowed and their faces hidden by the inevitable shawls.

The torches in front of the palace cast their smoky yellow light over the women selling cheese and soap and tamales in the market at the west end of the palace. The usual mob of soldiers and trappers were gathered around the stalls, ignoring the Vespers bells and talking and cursing in loud voices as they poked at the red cuts of buffalo and pork or haggled over bundles of hay for their horses. Kirby talked with them and got some of the news. Ruff was no longer lieutenant colonel of the 1st Missouri. Two days ago he had received the captain's commission in the regulars for which he had been bucking ever since Leavenworth. He resigned his volunteer commission and prepared to leave Santa Fé. The volunteers were happy to see him go. He had been harder on the men than a West Pointer.

Captain Congreve Jackson of Company G had been elected the new lieutenant colonel. Yesterday he had marched to Indian country with Companies D, F, and G. It seemed that the Navajos were raiding again and Kearny had to keep his promise to protect the Mexicans. It gave Kirby a strange feeling to know that

157

he had missed Nate by only one day and that now Nate was marching without him into a country that neither of them had ever seen before. He stood looking off to the west and didn't want to talk for a spell. Finally Kirby found a Mexican boy who would take a message to Colonel Doniphan. Kirby would meet Doniphan alone at La Fonda.

The inn on the southeast corner of the square was mobbed. Kirby waited near the bar till he saw Doniphan come in, stooping to keep from cracking his head on the low door. Kirby found the manager, pointed to Doniphan, and said how he was the colonel's aide and how the colonel would like a private room. The manager obliged, clearing a group of Mexican traders from one of the private card rooms, and then going to the colonel himself to tell him all was prepared.

Doniphan entered without knocking. He had to stoop again to get through. He shut the door behind him. He took off his hat, set it on the table, unbuttoned his collar, and sprawled into a chair. Only then did he look directly at Kirby.

"Well, Private . . . how's married life?"

Kirby grinned. "Powerful, Colonel. Powerful." He saw that Doniphan was not smiling. Well, Kirby didn't like Doniphan, either. Doniphan was a Whig. Kirby quit smiling and said: "Nate told me the deal you offered."

"That was a mortal beating you gave him," Doniphan said.

Kirby wiped the back of his hand across his mouth. He waited, and, when Doniphan didn't say anything more, Kirby said: "What about my horse?"

Doniphan squinted at him. "You ride a Morgan, don't you? Do you think Morgans are better than Mexican girls?"

"I didn't mean it that way. He's just a good horse and I just wondered what about him."

"I'm sure he's being taken care of. I haven't posted you as a deserter yet. You're on the books as on detached duty. Until you officially return to your regiment, we'll just leave the horse attached to Company D. Now, if that concludes our business, I'd best be going."

"You know it don't. What about Inez?"

"I'm glad you brought up that point." Doniphan leaned back, looking at Kirby with narrow eyes. "Well, Hatcher, the success of this whole thing depends on saving face for *Don* Miguel. Apparently La Tules hasn't talked yet, although I don't know why. Nate seems to think she helped Inez for some kind of revenge."

"Revenge against *Don* Miguel, not Inez," Kirby said. "La Tules promised to give us plenty of time to get clear. And that coachman's so scared of La Tules he won't dast say anything. He only told Nate because Nate already knew what was going on."

"Well, maybe you're right. We haven't heard any talk yet, so apparently the town doesn't know what happened. We've got to move fast to keep it that way."

"Colonel, you're thinking in terms of giving the girl back to her father. There's another way of saving his face."

159

Doniphan put one hand flat on the table, staring at it. "Our agreement didn't cover that. I gave my word you wouldn't be touched only if you brought her back and turned her over to her father."

"Suppose I won't."

"You've already committed a court-martial offense, soldier."

"And if you make that big a stink, what chance will you have of hiding what happened? It'll be spread over all New Mexico." Kirby studied Doniphan shrewdly for some reaction. The colonel's face was expressionless. Kirby said: "Supposing I was willing to turn Catholic. That should soften up Torreón some. Supposing you could talk him into accepting the marriage, and announcing it to the town as if it had been his idea all along, and he was standing behind it foursquare. He could keep his pride then. La Tules wouldn't hurt Inez by talking, and the priest at Taos would certainly keep quiet."

"It can't be," Doniphan said. "*Don* Miguel won't go for it."

"I think he will, when he realizes there ain't no other way."

Doniphan was silent so long Kirby thought that he didn't mean to answer. There was a pale, pinched look to Doniphan's cheeks, and Kirby couldn't tell if the man's eyes were focused on his face or something far behind him. It gave Kirby an eerie feeling. It made him remember what Nate had said about how Doniphan always looked in court, when he was getting ready to shatter a witness.

"You think you've got a real big coon by the tail, don't you?" Doniphan said. "You think you've got one of the richest families in Santa Fé wrapped around your finger, the whole U.S. Army backed into a corner, all the United States fighting a war just for your benefit."

"It'll work out, Colonel," Kirby said. "Just give it a chance."

Doniphan buttoned his collar. He took a long time at it, watching Kirby narrowly. The look in his eyes disturbed Kirby. Kirby wondered why he hated officers so. He hated fathers and schoolteachers and parsons, too. They always seemed to be sitting in judgment on a body.

"Where can I get in touch with you?" Doniphan asked.

"I'll get in touch with you," Kirby said. "I'll be here tomorrow night."

Doniphan rose and put on his hat. He walked to the door. He halted with one hand on the knob, his shoulder to Kirby, not looking at him.

"Hatcher, when Nate spent that six months in my offices at Liberty, he told me a lot about your schemes. He gave me the idea you were the greatest one for hatching up schemes since Aaron Burr. Some of them sounded very ingenious, but some of them sounded almighty harebrained. What kind of a scheme have you hatched up here?"

Kirby wondered if this were the right time to mention the dowry. It might as well be wool as anything else, and it might as well be enough wool to fill Ganoe's wagons. Perhaps it would be easier to get it out of

Torreón now, while Kirby could still use the girl as a lever, than if he waited till after Torreón had recognized the marriage. He saw a little muscle ripple in Doniphan's cheek. Maybe it was what checked him. Or maybe it was his own sense of timing. He had pressed Doniphan pretty hard. He was on shaky ground till Torreón had accepted the deal. Better not try for too big a chaw the first bite. Plenty of time to get wool after he belonged to one of the richest families in Santa Fé.

"No scheme at all, Colonel," he said. "I just fell in love with Inez, that's all."

Doniphan gave him a withering look. "Hatcher, I don't think you give a damn about that girl."

Doniphan left La Fonda alone. He still had the taste of bile in his mouth. There was an aching pressure behind his eyes. There was always a pressure behind his eyes when he wanted to clout a man and had to hold back. He hadn't wanted to clout a man so much in a long time.

When Kirby had first announced that he wouldn't give up the girl, Doniphan had thought of putting the man under arrest and sending a search party for Inez. But he knew that it was impossible. And Kirby had known it, too. Such a search would give the whole story away. Kirby was in the saddle, and there was no denying it.

Despite his anger at the man, Doniphan couldn't help a certain grudging admiration. He didn't think that he'd ever met such a cool customer. Walking into the lion's den, defying the whole U.S. Army, taking a

162

chance on getting court-martialed, shot — and grinning all the time. Doniphan could understand Nate's blind worship for the man.

He was glad that Nate was out of it. Maybe he could keep it that way. Even if Kirby were reinstated, maybe he could keep Nate away until Kirby made another mistake. It would come inevitably. The man couldn't stay out of trouble. Maybe the next time it would be big enough trouble to get him drummed out for good.

Doniphan hesitated at the corner. If he went to Torreón now, he would be late for a meeting at the palace. Kearny wanted to discuss his appointments to the new territorial government. He had already suggested Charles Bent for governor. The Bent brothers had run their fort on the Arkansas River for almost twenty years and were well liked and highly respected by the New Mexicans. Kearny wanted Donaciano Vigil for lieutenant governor. Doniphan had questioned the choice. Vigil had served under Armijo and had too many ties among the Archuleta faction. But Kearny thought that Vigil would be loyal to the United States. He said a completely American slate would be a mistake, only intensifying New Mexican resentment.

Despite their disagreements Doniphan had gained great respect for Kearny. Kearny had a sort of gray and inexorable competence that always got the job done without benefit of bugle and drum. On military matters Doniphan thought that the man's orthodoxy got a bit stuffy at times, but he had to admit that Kearny hadn't made many mistakes. Except with Archuleta.

There were more rumors of a revolt stirring and Kearny had talked about arresting Archuleta. But Bent had convinced him that they did not have enough evidence to make the arrest legal and it would only stir up more trouble. So Kearny planned to march for California in a few days without taking any action against Archuleta. Doniphan felt that it would leave him holding a sackful of snakes. It made him think that the Torreón matter was more pressing than deciding on the rest of the civil officials, and he turned down toward the river. A servant answered his knock on the door. In a moment Doniphan was admitted. *Don* Miguel Torreón received him in the parlor. The *don*'s suit was of black velvet and Cordovan leather. He stood by the image of Christ in the corner. The statue was several feet tall, dressed in a long green robe, and holding its hands out in supplication, or benediction, Doniphan could not tell which. A crown of thorns sat on the head and drops of realistic blood spattered the face.

Magoffin had told Doniphan that such an image in a room was not often displayed too openly. It usually meant that a man in the household belonged to the *penitente* brotherhood, and they were not officially sanctioned and were deplored by the Church. Doniphan could never see *Don* Miguel Torreón without thinking of the scars the man must bear on his back from a lifetime of the penitential Easter rites held every year in the mountains.

"My servant told me you came on behalf of Inez," *Don* Miguel said.

164

"I figure that by now you have an idea of what happened," Doniphan said.

"I got a message from *Padre* Martínez, in Taos. He told me my daughter married a soldier in your command by the name of Kirby Hatcher."

"*Don* Miguel, I realize how humiliating this is for you. But as far as you know, does anyone else in town realize what has happened?"

"Not yet. But it is impossible to keep such a thing quiet."

"Still . . . your daughter might be returned without any public shame being brought on your family name. As for the marriage, there's nothing you can do. It exists . . ."

"It does not exist. This Kirby Hatcher is not a Catholic."

"He's willing to become one. That's my point. If you fight the marriage, the facts will become known. But if you accept it, give it your sanction . . ."

"Impossible. Without dispensation, Inez is living in sin, which makes her, in my eyes, no better than a whore."

"*Don* Miguel . . . we're talking about your own daughter."

"She is my daughter no longer. I saw you only to give you a message for her. Tell her that she has renounced the Torreón name forever. I do not want to see her in this house again. If she meets me on the street, she is not to try to talk with me. I will not hear her. She no longer exists."

"That strikes me as uncommon hard . . ."

"It is my final word. Good night, Colonel."

Outside, Doniphan stood with his back against the door that had been closed behind him. Some kind of reaction had set in. He was trembling. It didn't seem to be rage, exactly, although he was mad enough. It was more like frustration. He had thought that he was beginning to understand these people. He had thought that it was possible to span the gap, to step back through the centuries and meet these people in their own world and understand their world, if a man kept an open mind. Now he didn't know.

As Doniphan started up the street, he thought that he heard a woman crying somewhere inside the house.

CHAPTER
ELEVEN

Nate was glad to be on the march. He would have bought some kind of trouble in Santa Fé. There was too much time to sit around and think in camp. He would have fetched up in a brawl, or a big drunk in town, or gone over the hill, thinking about Kirby. Riding did something for a man. Just riding, hour after hour, day after day, drained off some of the poison.

Jackson was proving to be a different lieutenant colonel than Ruff. He didn't try much for discipline and the way the volunteers straggled along made Nate think of a bunch of schoolboys on a holiday. They had left Santa Fé on September 18th and they were moving through the same country Nate had seen with Kearny on his recent march to the Downriver. Three days out they reached San Felipe. Nate had heard that there were several dozen of these Pueblo villages scattered along the Río Grande between Taos and El Paso. The Pueblos were sedentary Indians, farmers, converted to Catholicism by the Spaniards a century and a half before and living in comparative peace with their conquerors since then. It was a mud town, 400 or 500 people, a central square with a twin-spired church on one side and a scattering of terraced buildings that stood bleakly against the skyline like broken, water-streaked mesas.

San Felipe gave the volunteers their first glimpse of the Navajo trouble. They saw some Pueblo funeral rites for a woman killed by the Navajos. They marched through cornfields destroyed by the raiders and came across dead stock bloating in the pale sun. It was an old war. The Navajos and the Apaches were nomads, living in the desolation to the west; for centuries they had been raiding the Pueblo villages and Spanish towns along the river, coming out of nowhere to pillage and kill. Both the Pueblos and the Mexicans were disillusioned with Kearny's earlier promises to protect them from their old enemies. They felt that the appearance of the three volunteer companies was a little belated, with thousands of sheep gone and half a dozen people dead. It gave a new meaning to the name the Mexicans had given the volunteers. The volunteers cursed so much that the people had started calling them Los Goddamies. Nate had heard the name before in Santa Fé and had thought it was funny, but it was being used more often now and the way the people were saying it didn't make it sound funny any more.

Nate was surprised at how much he missed Jayán. On the day the column marched, Jayán had brought Nate a plug of tobacco. He said that he had gotten it from the Leitensdorfer store for a load of wood. The Indians prized the tobacco, and, if Nate traded shrewdly, he might get one of their fine baskets. Nate had thanked him. After that they hadn't had much to say. Nate had felt that he wanted to say a lot but he couldn't find the right words.

"Well," Jayán had said, "we will see each other again."

"Of course. We will see each other. Sure we will."

"Well, go with God, *compadre*."

"Well, certain . . . good bye, Jayán."

The volunteers reached the Río Grande near Albuquerque. It was here that Lieutenant Colonel Jackson left the company wagons with the tents and all surplus equipment behind. Lieutenant Merritt objected hotly. He thought that it was foolish to face a winter march without adequate clothing or tents, but Jackson thought that the bad weather would hold off, was convinced the campaign would be a short one, and thought it would be better to move as fast as possible without being slowed down by the wagons. They crossed the river and moved west through a land where the red earth stretched out to the red mesas on the skyline and the red sand came up in long blinding hauls before the wind.

Forty-five miles west of the Río Grande they reached a place called Moquino. It was a lonely little village with about 350 Mexicans, the last civilized outpost on the edge of the Navajo country. They had thought that they were going out to fight the Navajos, but Jackson told them his specific orders had been to sound out the Indians about a peace treaty and that he was to make war only as a last resort. He finally got one of the local Mexicans, a man named Chavez, to contact some of the Navajos. In a few days one of the Navajo chiefs came in for a talk. He was a seamed, toothless, grinning old pirate with stringy gray hair that fell below his waist, hung with silver belts and bracelets and rings that must have come from a dozen murdered Mexicans. He said that the other Navajos were willing to talk but they didn't want to come to Moquino for fear of being ambushed.

Jackson had orders that if he could contact the Navajos in no other way, he was to detach a party to meet them in their own country. The Mexicans in camp told Jackson that it was crazy. In their memory no white man had dared go that far into Indian country. Captain Reid volunteered for the duty and Jackson gave him ten men from each of the three companies. Everybody thought that it was a little parcel of men to send on such a job but Jackson explained that there was not enough food in camp to supply any more men. Nate wanted to go just to escape the boredom of the miserable camp, but he wasn't lucky enough to get the detail.

Reid rode out on October 12th and on the same day Jackson moved the whole camp a few miles south to find better graze and water. As usual, their commissary was so poorly supplied that they were soon down to nothing but parched corn. They got up a petition, with Camp Starvation for a title, begging Doniphan either to send them food or march them back to Santa Fé. Their corn ran out, and after four days on nothing but rotten pumpkins three wagons of provisions arrived.

They brought a lot of military news. On September 25th Kearny had left Santa Fé for California with three companies of his dragoons. On October 3rd Colonel Sterling Price, marching from Fort Leavenworth, had arrived at Santa Fé with his regiment, the 2nd Missouri Mounted Volunteers. He was to hold Santa Fé while Doniphan and his 1st Missouri marched south, first to clean up the Navajo campaign, and then to join General Wool in Chihuahua. The day after Price's arrival Doniphan had left Santa Fé with 300 men and was now headed toward Jackson's camp.

On November 4th Doniphan and a few staff officers arrived at camp, riding ahead of the main detachment. One of the first orders Doniphan issued was for an election. Congress had authorized a fourth commissioned officer for all companies over 100 men. Company D unanimously voted in their orderly sergeant, William Hicklin, as a second lieutenant. Nate had the feeling that they had done it as a hooraw. Hicklin had wanted to be a good soldier so badly and was always studying his manuals that he had become a standing joke.

Doniphan saw Nate privately to tell him about Kirby. "*Don* Miguel is still refusing to see his daughter," Doniphan said. "But the *don* hasn't yet declared openly against the Americans. I hoped that time would soften his attitude. If we can only get him to take her back, the danger of his going over to Archuleta will be a lot less. I persuaded your uncle to remain at Santa Fé until the thing is settled. He's temporarily attached to Colonel Price's regiment. He and the girl are living in a house outside of town."

Nate went away from Doniphan in a depressed mood. He had been trying to forget Inez and Kirby, but they had been with him every minute. He was sick about the fight. Whenever he thought about Kirby's taking Inez from him, he knew that he hated his uncle, but when he remembered hitting Kirby, it gave him a sick feeling. Whipping Kirby had surprised him. He had always taken it for granted that Kirby could lick him, and had never stood up to Kirby before. It made Kirby seem different somehow. It made a lot of things different. It seemed that his disillusionment cut the ground out from under everything Kirby had ever represented to him, or everything Kirby had ever told him. It made him think about the war. He realized that he had never really questioned it too deeply. He had accepted Kirby's explanations, and Kirby's reasons for joining up. Back at Marshall everybody had been volunteering and Kirby had told about the hooraws they would have in Santa Fé and the women and the big deals, and it had seemed enough.

Nate remembered the atrocity stories that had fired him up to join. The newspaper accounts of Taylor's first battle down in Texas, a place called Palo Alto, where a Mexican had stuck his lance into a Vermont boy and dragged him around the field, or a dragoon at Resaca de la Palma who had cut off a Maine lieutenant's head and paraded it back and forth in view of the American Army. There had been a hundred such stories and they had sent him to Santa Fé in a sweat to take revenge on the monsters capable of such outrages. But there hadn't been any monsters. Only the little brown people

172

offering them apricots and melons wherever they stopped, and an old man teaching him how to speak a new language, and Inez. Kirby called them greasers. Most of the men in the regiment called them that. It hadn't meant much to Nate. It was the way a man would call an Indian a redskin or a man from Missouri a puke. Now there seemed something wrong with it. He had seen what happened to their faces when a man called them greasers. He couldn't think of Jayán as a greaser, or Inez.

The whole thing got to plaguing Nate so much that at mess call he started an argument. He was standing in line, waiting for his burned meat and half-cooked beans.

"This war doesn't make much sense to me," he said. "It seems a bunch of Mexicans killed a bunch of Texans so they sent a bunch of Missourians out to kill a bunch of Navajos because they killed a bunch of Mexicans."

"On the contrary," Lieutenant Hicklin said. "The sense it makes is eternal. Manifest Destiny, gentlemen. Manifest Destiny. An irresistible impulse in our racial life. From the beginning of settlement in America, from Jamestown onward, it has been our destiny to expand. We are fated by our heritage, our economy, our religion, the very outlines of our national geography to bring the superiority of our institutions and our mode of life to the inferior, less fortunate people of this Western territory."

"Hogwash," Hugh Long said. "This thing has been manipulated from the beginning. Manifest Destiny is just a phrase out of the *Democratic Review* that's

173

supposed to make a crooked horse trade sound divinely sanctioned. Who's been the noisiest agitators in Congress for expansion? All those cotton planters from south of the Mason-Dixon line. Why do you think the South started moving into Texas thirty years ago? The pro-slavers saw all that land filling up above the Missouri Compromise. They knew some free states would be formed mighty soon, they couldn't let the North take away their power, they had to have some slave states to keep the balance in Congress . . . so they moved into Texas and started agitating for annexation."

"If you feel that cynical about the war, what made you volunteer?" Lieutenant Merritt asked. They all turned to look at him. Nate hadn't noticed him moving in while they talked. Hugh gaped at Merritt. Nate didn't know whether Hugh couldn't answer or was just surprised. Merritt had never taken any part in their campfire talk. "Your whole neat little theory," Merritt told Hugh, "is just a myth perpetrated by the Abolitionists. If anybody manipulated this war, it's Polk. One of the planks he got elected on was acquisition of California. Texas merely provided him with an excuse. General Taylor didn't have any justification for moving into that disputed territory south of the Nueces. Polk wanted his incident and he got it."

"I refuse to blame Polk," Hicklin said. "This war was started before he got the Presidency. It was Tyler who signed the resolution to annex Texas, two days before he left office. He knew Mexico had threatened war if the U.S. annexed Texas."

174

"Which gets us right back to the Southern conspiracy," Long said. "Tyler was a Virginian, a Democrat, and a slaveholder."

"There are plenty of Whigs from Virginia who never owned slaves," Merritt said. "I happen to be one of them, and I refuse to believe that my people would conspire to plunge this whole country into a holocaust simply to get two new seats in the Senate."

He turned and walked away from the fire. They all watched him go in silence.

"Well," Nate said, "I can't honestly say that clears the whole thing up."

That evening Captain Reid returned with his thirty men. He had been gone twenty days, had marched 200 miles into Indian territory, and had met with some Navajos at a place called Laguna Colorado. Reid was not authorized to conclude any treaties, but had secured a promise from the Navajos that they would meet with Doniphan at Bear Springs, five days' march to the west. About half of Company D, including the exhausted men who had marched with Reid, were sent back under his command to the Río Grande. Nate was one of the D Company men left behind and attached to Doniphan's command. On November 15th Doniphan started to Bear Springs. He had with him 150 commanded by Lieutenant Colonel Jackson, Captain Parsons, and Lieutenants Merritt and DeCourcy.

Merritt didn't hide the fact that he thought the march was sheer insanity. Nate tried loyally to retain his confidence in Doniphan, but he couldn't help thinking that Merritt was right. It was Merritt who had originally protested so bitterly at the Río Grande when Jackson ordered them to leave their tents and company wagons behind so that they could travel lighter and faster. Now they appreciated Merritt's wisdom. Their horses were in terrible condition, half starved, rachitic, galled, and mangy. Their commissary was still failing them and the supplies they had were so meager that Doniphan had put them on half rations from the beginning. Many of them had replaced worn-out boots with Indian moccasins or were wearing Mexican serapes for overcoats. They were starting into an unknown country, at the beginning of winter, without adequate food or clothing, 150 farm boys meaning to bring peace to thousands of savages who hadn't been conquered since the white man first saw them.

For the first two days they moved through a broad tableland. The graze was fair but there was little wood and what water they could find was brackish and muddy. Nate was so sick the first night from the water he couldn't eat his dinner. The second night, as soon as they made camp, it began to snow. They had to take turns holding their blankets over the fires so the snow wouldn't put them out. Kelly Goff was riding Bristol again.

"I tell you what, Bristol. I admit I made a hooraw with you about La Tules, and I feel bad about it. I want to make it up somehow. I won't try to make out these Indians are beautiful, but they got a way of making love . . . it'll make the hair stand up on your hindquarters."

"And I wager they only hanker after the ugly men," Bristol said bitterly. "They'd do most anything for an ugly man."

"No," Goff said soberly. "This time I'm telling the truth, Bristol. Ugly or not, it don't matter much. These women don't have much say-so what man they git. It's all up to their pa, or their uncle, or whatever male kin you can talk into selling them."

Bristol's mouth began hanging open. "You mean they sell their women . . . like they was a horse or something?"

"All you got to have is the right price," Kelly said. "That jacket of yours now, with them brass buttons. They go for that. A Navajo would give most anything for it. I tell you what . . . if you take my turn holding your blanket over this here fire, I'll introduce you to a chief that'll trade you any one of his four daughters for that jacket."

Dubiously Bristol took Kelly's place at the fire. "Kelly," he said, "if you're hoorawing me again, you won't come back from this march. I put my mother's name to that."

The talk about women had disturbed Charlie Hayes. He went down to the river to wash. He sang the hymns his mother had taught him out of Orange Scott's *New and Improved Camp Meeting Hymn Book*. His father had told him that it would always drive away evil thoughts. His father had been a hard-shell circuit rider. Charlie had been born in Memphis twenty years before. His family had moved to Marshall when he was four. By that time Charlie already knew that God was a man who looked like his father, except that God had a longer beard.

Charlie went back to camp. He spent half an hour currying his horse. Then he polished his shoes and harness. He sat before his half shelter and cleaned the flintlock rifle they had issued him and polished his saber. When he was all finished, he washed at the river again. He sat down for his hour with the Bible. He was reading Exodus when Lieutenant Hicklin came around to tell him that he had drawn first watch. The bugler was sounding tattoo as he went to his post.

The men were in their blankets and camp was growing quiet. The snow was falling more heavily now and he couldn't stop shivering. A coyote howled in the distance. Charlie knew that the Indians sometimes made signals with animal sounds. In a way he was glad not to sleep. Last night he had dreamed of fire. He often dreamed of fire. He dreamed that he was burning in the fire, as his father had so often warned he would, and he woke crying and drenched with sweat. Sometimes he dreamed that his father was in the fire, shouting as he did at camp meeting, and that he had pushed his father there. When he woke, he was filled with shame and he prayed for forgiveness and read his Bible.

Charlie heard the coyote howl, nearer this time. He brushed the wet snow from his eyes, trying to see through the blackness that should have been whiteness. Something happened before his eyes, a movement, a sense of shape. With stiff fingers he fumbled to load his rifle. He cocked it, brushing snow from the flint and

178

flashpan. He heard the coyote howl again and thought he saw movement once more. He fired.

"Alarm!" he shouted. "Alarm!"

When the commotion woke Nate, he thought that he was dead. He was covered by something soft and mushy; it was pressed all over his face, and, when he started to shout, it filled his mouth and he almost choked on it. He thought that he was buried in his grave and he sat up, spitting out the wet mush and coughing and yelling. The uproar of camp brought him back to reality, and he realized that he was sitting a foot deep in snow. The dim shapes of men were running back and forth past him, pulling on their britches and trying to load their guns. Nate could hear Bristol's hysterical voice.

"Enemy in camp, enemy in camp . . ."

A man stumbled on Nate and almost fell across him. Nate saw it was Lieutenant Merritt, holding his Colt in one hand while he pulled his braces on over his shoulders with the other.

"Get up, soldier!" he shouted. "Haven't you heard the alarm?"

He lurched past Nate to where Kelly Goff still lay in his blankets, hidden beneath a pile of snow. Merritt stopped and shouted at Kelly, but Kelly didn't answer. Merritt began kicking at him.

"The alarm's been given!" Merritt shouted. "Get out of there and fall in!"

Goff rolled over to avoid the kicks, pulling his blanket tighter about him. "It's jist a false alarm," he said. "We fellows know that Colonel Jackson is always telling the sentries to do this jist to keep us on our toes."

Merritt shouted: "Soldier, I'm giving you a direct order! Get up and answer the alarm!"

"If there was any Navajos out there, I could smell 'em," Kelly said.

Merritt made a strangled sound and began kicking at him again. Doniphan passed by and saw what Merritt was doing. "Lieutenant," he said, "as you were. What's the matter?"

"This man refuses to answer the alarm."

"It's all right, Lieutenant," Doniphan said. "It was a false alarm."

"What's the difference?" Merritt demanded. "Aren't you going to put this man under arrest? It's as bad as sleeping on sentry duty. If it was Kearny, he'd have this man shot."

Doniphan crossed to Merritt and put a hand on his shoulder. "Taylor, take a little slack. If you shot every man who didn't answer this alarm, you'd lose half of the First Missouri."

He turned to look across camp. In the darkness the long line of mounds was barely visible. As far as Nate could tell, most of them were still unbroken. It looked as though most of the detachment was still huddled in their blankets, hidden under their heaps of snow.

180

CHAPTER
TWELVE

The next day they reached the mountains. They left the Río Puerco and turned northwest. After the empty benchlands and the sand that never stopped blowing, Nate welcomed the timber. Chalk-trunked aspen scarred with the black welts of clawing bears, red-tinged alder standing in the streambeds, the piñons like twisted dwarfs with their feet hidden in yellow heaps of second-season cones. There was a gummy smell in the wet air, and a few piñon jays still fluttered and chattered back in the shadows.

The mountain stood above them in towering granite slabs and iron-colored basalt. Enormous shattered fragments of rock had been tumbled from the heights by past storms, littering the shoulders of the mountain and choking the cañons. The going got so bad that Doniphan ordered the men to dismount and lead their horses. Snow had drifted in the cañons and in some places they sank to their waists.

They were still in the lower timber when Nate heard a sound like cannon fire from the peaks above. It made the horses nervous. Strawberry started lunging at her bit and Nate had to fight to keep from losing her. The

181

booming reverberations continued, seeming to shake the whole mountain.

"What is it?" Nate asked. "What's a-going on up there?"

"It's the wind," Hugh Long said. "We're in for a blizzard, Nate."

Nate had seen blizzards aplenty on the plains, but the high mountains were new to him. He'd never heard the wind make such a racket, crashing and echoing against the unseen sounding boards of distant cañons, gathering a cloud over the peaks and whipping it to a black froth and sweeping it down toward the climbing troops. Lieutenant Merritt came back down the line of the Company D men, telling them to keep their hands and faces covered.

Merritt was hated and distrusted by most of the men, and they paid little heed to any of his orders. But Nate pulled his neckerchief over his face and held his hands under his blanket as much as he could. He thought that Merritt was a cold, pompous, stiff-necked jasper, but he had to own that the man usually seemed to know what he was talking about. Merritt had certainly been right when he'd argued against leaving their tents behind, and now any one of them would have given all the pay coming to him for one night in a half shelter.

In another ten minutes the storm's unworldly night had reached them. The black cloud closed about them and the first blasts of snow were carried stingingly against Nate's face. The wind slammed against Nate, almost carrying him off his feet. He ran into the man ahead of him and had to stop. The whole column was stopped. They stood without moving while the wind hammered them and the sleet cut at their faces and the snow piled up on their shoulders. Nobody seemed to know what was happening till Lieutenant Hicklin came struggling down the line. He said that the officers were undecided whether to turn back. Captain Parsons and the lieutenant colonel wanted to retreat to the benchlands below but Doniphan thought that they would be even more exposed down there. He figured that they were halfway through and they might as well try to push on over the top. Finally the column began to move again, on up the cañon.

The trail climbed a cliff and soon it was no more than a narrow ledge on the face of the precipice. Nate's joints started to ache unbearably with the cold and the feeling was gone from his hands. He began to get spells of nausea and dizziness. He didn't know if it was the altitude or hunger. They had been on half rations since Camp Starvation. He guessed that a hungry man didn't really know how weak he was till he had to get off his horse and walk. The others were feeling it, too. A boy fell to his knees ahead of Nate and couldn't get up. Two others had to lift him by the elbows and half carry him along.

Nate didn't know how much later it was that they lost the mule over the side. He heard it hee-hawing and struggling, and then it was gone, the hysterical braying swallowed suddenly in the storm as the animal plummeted into the chasm. He tried not to think of it as he struggled on up the narrow ledge, bent against the cushiony pressure of the snow.

He lost all track of time. The booming crash of the wind never stopped. He started cursing it aimlessly. He was weaving drunkenly and he began talking to himself. Suddenly he realized that he was laughing, and broke off in the middle of it. He knew how the steady battering of a storm could affect a man's mind. Panic gripped him and he pulled over against the cliff, unable to go on for a moment. Hugh Long came up against Strawberry, shouting something that was lost in the deafening wind.

Struggling against his panic, Nate took up the march again. He was growing sleepy now and he knew that was even more dangerous than the panic or the drunkenness of the storm. He came up against the horse ahead of him and knew that they had stopped again. He went to his knees in the snow. He thought that he would just go to sleep there. When he woke up, the storm would be over . . .

Someone was shaking him. Someone was slapping his face and pulling him to his feet. He heard Doniphan's voice.

"Stand up, soldier. You're not through yet. We're all going to sing a song. We're going to sing 'Blue-Tail Fly'. When you feel yourself getting sleepy, you just swing your arms and shout. If that isn't enough, bite your lips or slap yourself in the face. And keep on singing 'Blue-Tail Fly'." He moved on down the line, accompanied by Lieutenant DeCourcy and another member of his staff, stopping at each man and talking

184

to him. "We're almost over the top now. A fire and a hot meal on the other side. I promise you that. Just keep singing that song."

Nate began swinging his arms. He slapped himself in the face and shook his head savagely. They were beginning to sing now. He joined in. It made a weird, muffled sound in the storm, but it seemed to help. Doniphan passed him again, going back to the front, and finally the column began to move. Whenever the grogginess threatened to overwhelm Nate, he swung his arms and shouted and took up the song again. He sang until he was too hoarse to sing any more. Somebody told him that one of the boys who had lost a horse over the side had fainted from hunger, and that Doniphan was letting the boy ride his own horse.

The trail turned and wound through a heap of icy rocks. A fresh rush of snow came against Nate from above. He realized that it was a slide and threw himself wildly against the face of the cliff. Strawberry panicked, rearing and hauling on the reins in an effort to get free. Her hind hoofs slipped off the trail and she went over the edge. Nate was pulled down to his knees by the violent jerk and he had to let go of the reins to keep from being pulled off after the mare. There was a flurry of kicked snow, a wild scream, and she was gone into the emptiness below.

Nate crouched on his hands and knees, staring into the maw. He couldn't feel anything. He had ridden Strawberry 1,000 miles. She had carried him through the furnace of the Kansas prairies when men were going out of their minds with the heat. She had fought off the wolves with him in Raton Pass and had saved him during the stampede at Bent's Fort and had survived with him through a dozen hells when they ran out of water and the animals and men were dying on every side. There was no explaining what a horse could come to mean to a man during such a march. And now he was too numb to feel anything. He got up and started walking again.

Several other men lost their horses over the cliff before they reached the summit. It was so dark Nate didn't know whether it was day or night. The fury of the storm seemed to fade on the west side. They could hear the wind howling and booming in the ridges behind them but they were descending now underneath a steady fall of snow. The drifts were so deep in some places Nate was struggling through them up to his waist. Nate figured that he was more dead than alive when they finally got off the mountain. They left the snowfall behind and it was night for sure now, probably past midnight, when he saw the yellow blossom of a fire ahead and realized that the advance units had set up a camp. Drunk with exhaustion, he stumbled to the first fire and sat down near its warmth. Half a dozen others were huddled around the flames. They had ignored Merritt's command to keep their faces and hands covered. Their flesh was black with frostbite and they were in agony.

Nate saw Doniphan moving from one fire to the other, issuing orders and seeing to the comfort of his men. Nate thought that he looked bigger than ever, silhouetted against the flickering light. It made Nate remember when he was a kid, scared of the dark, and how everything had seemed safe the minute his father appeared, towering like a giant above him. Doniphan had his Bowie knife out, and, whenever he stopped to talk with a man, he twisted his face into a grimace and scraped a few red bristles off his cheeks. It gave him a casual, easy look, and it was hard to believe that the man had just finished such a grueling march. But when Doniphan got nearer, Nate could see how sunken and haggard his face was.

He stopped close to Nate, looking down at his feet. "Don't thaw those feet out so quick, Nate," he said. "Rub them in snow first and then try to get some lard from the cook. Cut some strips off your blanket and wrap them up good tonight."

Nate looked stupidly at his feet. He could see his own bloody prints in the snow. It was the first time he realized that he had walked the bottoms out of his boots. They were the same boots he'd worn all the way from Missouri, 1,000 miles of desert and mountains, six months of drilling and marching and sentry duty. There hadn't been much left of them anyway and that last march over the mountain, stumbling on the icy rocks and jagged talus, had torn them to shreds. He tried to pull his boots off but they wouldn't come, and finally he had to cut them away from his swollen feet.

He saw Doniphan across camp talking with one of the Indian guides. Doniphan was dangling his watch in front of the Indian and finally the Indian nodded and squatted down to pull some kind of gear from his sack. He handed something to Doniphan and got the watch in exchange. Doniphan crossed to Nate again and tossed on the ground what the Indian had given him. Nate saw that it was a pair of moccasins with knee-length buckskin uppers.

"Wear those tomorrow," Doniphan said. "You'll find them tougher than boots."

"Colonel, I can't do that," Nate said. "That was the watch Turnham gave you when you won his case."

"Turnham didn't march twenty hours through a blizzard for me," Doniphan said.

Some of Captain Parsons's company were still straggling in. One of the men had gotten a chill and was shaking so hard he couldn't keep to his feet without the aid of two others holding him up. They took him to a fire and wrapped him in a blanket but he was still shuddering violently. Lieutenant DeCourcy thought he should be bled immediately.

"Don't take any blood," Doniphan said. "That's an order. I never did believe you gave a man strength to fight the ague by draining the life out of him. These Indians have more sense than we do. They have a kind of sweat house that'll do more in one hour than a whole wagonload of Doctor Sappington's anti-fever pills." Doniphan took off his own topcoat and wrapped it around the man. "You just keep as warm as you can, John, and hang on till we get to that Navajo camp. In the meantime, we'll have the cook fetch you up some hot soup."

When Colonel Doniphan woke up the next morning, the snow had stopped. He hadn't slept much. The itch was keeping him awake again. It was what convinced him that he'd never been meant for a military man. The wool uniforms irritated his skin, and, when he was on the march, he got rashes and sores that wouldn't heal.

He rolled out of his blanket and started to rise. The earth seemed to heave up into the sky and he had to drop back to his hands and knees and crouch there till the dizzy spell passed. He hoped that it was just hunger. He couldn't let the old fever get him. He couldn't fail his men so far from home, out here in the middle of nowhere.

He got himself on his feet before anybody noticed what had happened. The food was so low he had to cut the rations in half again. It was hard to get the men on the move. They were all suffering from frostbite, aching and bruised from the long march, weak with the same hunger that crippled Doniphan. Merritt came with rumors of a plot being hatched against the officers, but Doniphan took no action. He had been hearing the same rumors ever since Leavenworth. The boys had to let their steam out somehow.

For the next two days the ragged, starving column moved through a vast, broken upland. More and more Navajos began to appear, hanging on the flanks. The other officers were content to rely on their interpreter, a man named T. Caldwell, to communicate with the Indians, but Doniphan was trying to learn their language. He didn't know what made him such a curious man. It seemed that he had spent all his life studying some book or asking questions of somebody.

On November 21st they came to mountains again, gray masses of granite and basalt, matted with a timber so green it looked black. They passed herds of sheep like an endless fleece of clouds drifting across the red earth. They came to the edge of a sandy bench and had their first sight of the Navajo camp. In the blue shadows at the base of a towering cliff, hundreds of feet high, stood a gathering of hogans made from brush and logs, their doors so low a man would have to bend double to get through. An ant-like horde of Indians swarmed through the camp, and their sound at this distance echoed against the cliffs with the sullen mutter of thunder. Merritt sat at Doniphan's stirrup, his aristocratic face pinched and hostile.

"Colonel," he said, "I spent five years at Fort Leavenworth. I know the Indians. According to everything we have heard, these particular Indians are the most notorious traitors in this country. I am firmly convinced that, if you go down there, you are asking for a massacre."

Doniphan smiled bleakly. "I hate to remind you, Taylor, but you said the same thing when we started this march, and when we saw the first Indians, and they haven't touched us yet. Now, if they wanted to massacre us, they could have done it long before this."

Merritt shook his narrow head. "I think we're traveling under suspended sentence of death. The very audacity of this campaign is the only thing that has stayed their hand. They can't conceive of anybody but crazy men coming into their country with such a small force."

"Whatever it is, it's too late to turn back now." Doniphan raised his hand. "Forward, at the trot."

Doniphan wasn't looking at Merritt as they rode down off the bench. He knew only too well the pinched, bloodless expression that had settled in Merritt's face, giving him the look of an outraged marble statue. Doniphan had to concede the man's abilities as a soldier, but he had always been sorry that the boys had elected Merritt second lieutenant of Company D. Doniphan had known that in volunteering for service in the 1st Missouri, Merritt had hoped it would be a steppingstone to a commission in the regulars again. Doniphan had warned him that Polk wasn't likely to hand out any commissions to a Whig.

That had been May, when the Mounted Rifles was being created. Merritt had been one of over a hundred army officers to send in their applications for a commission in the new regiment. In Santa Fé word had reached them that Polk had filled every one of the Mounted Rifles' forty-four vacancies with civilians, and forty of them had been Democrats. Merritt was doomed to spend the duration with the yokels and farmers and tavern bullies he despised. Doniphan had a bad feeling about it. He could see how the hooraws and the frontier insolence infuriated Merritt. There was a poison building up in Merritt, pus in a wound, and it was going to break loose sooner or later. Doniphan just hoped that it didn't happen at the wrong time.

Somebody was talking in the ranks. Doniphan recognized Kelly Goff's voice. "You want to watch these Indians and their knives, Nate. They're even worse than the spicks and their knives. If you go to turn your back, they'll stick a knife in it quicker'n you kin say kinnikinnick."

"Goff," Merritt said acidly, "as you were."

As the column approached the camp, the Indians began to gather around them. The Navajo men wore britches of red baize or buckskin. If they weren't naked to the waist, they wore blankets with a hole in the center for their heads. The women wore buckskin squaw dresses and some of them wore white cotton leg wrappings. Aside from their costume they didn't look any different to Doniphan from the Cheyennes or the Arapahoes or the Kiowas he had seen while at Leavenworth. They had the same wild stench, the same matted, dirty black hair, the same coppery cheeks, some of them so flat and Oriental they could have been taken for Chinese. From a distance their eyes looked startlingly white in their dark faces; closer up they were tinged yellow in the corners or bloodshot and filmed with trachoma.

In the center of camp the Indians were building an enormous corral. They had chopped down dozens of cedar trees, eight or ten feet tall, and had dragged them in from the hills to plant them again in the ground, their branches laced together, forming a circular fence about 100 feet in diameter. There was only one gate, facing the east. Doniphan had to know about it. He asked Caldwell.

"I don't know whether we're in good luck or bad," the interpreter told him, "but it looks as though we've come in on their Mountain Chant. Not many white men have seen it. The chief tells me they want us inside."

"I don't like that corral," Merritt said. "We'll be trapped in there."

"We might be worse off if we insult them by refusing to go," Doniphan said.

Caldwell nodded agreement. "You would, Colonel. You've come this far. You might as well go whole hog. This is probably the ninth day of the ceremony. I understand that's when they go into the corral. The whole chant is to chase out the spirit of the bear. They consider the bear evil."

"Superstitious rot," Merritt said.

"I'll bet they'd feel the same way about Jonah and the whale," Doniphan said.

"When an Indian kills a bear its spirit goes to his stomach," Caldwell said. "He's got to go through the whole hooraw to get it out. For eight days he's been taking a pounding from them medicine men and going through all kinds of purges and a-sweating in one of them medicine hogans."

"Speaking of sweat baths," Doniphan said, "see if you can get some for those boys of ours with the fever."

Caldwell made some arrangement with a head man and the sick volunteers were told that they could fall out and follow him across camp to the medicine hogans. The remaining men unsaddled their animals and set up rope lines to picket them. The Indians were already bringing in grass for feed. When the horses were tended to, Doniphan got the men into ragged ranks and marched them to the big corral. Caldwell told them to turn right once they were through the gate. It was a religious thing with the Navajos.

Hundreds of Indians had gathered inside the corral. They stood in dense ranks against the fence or squatted around small campfires. Doniphan saw brown-cheeked babies lying among piles of gaudy blankets, watermelons, and heaps of food. The smell of roasting mutton and corn mixed with the pungent scent of cedar smoke. The men seemed armored in silver, belts made with silver bosses as big as teacups, silver bow guards and silver rings and silver bracelets up to the elbows, all giving off a barbaric glitter in the firelight. The women were draped with necklaces of turquoise and clam shell and cannel coal, their black hair smelling of bear grease and their eyes bright as beads. The whole crowd held back against the fence, leaving a big space in the center of the corral where a huge pyre of wood had been piled, eight or ten feet high.

Blankets were spread for the volunteers and they were fed on roasted corn and greasy mutton that had probably been stolen from some Mexican. There was a lot of preliminary talk, with Caldwell interpreting. Navajo seemed a weird language to Doniphan, a string of grunts, wheezes, puffs of air, sighs, whirs, and attempts to swallow every other word. He wondered if English sounded as strange to the Indians. While they ate, the chiefs were presented to Doniphan. The first one was a very old man with a blue band around his forehead to hold his long white hair. The brown spots of great age covered his face and he was so stiff with rheumatism that a pair of young men had to help lower him to a blanket. Caldwell said that he was Narbona, the greatest chief of all the Navajos. After a dozen others had been presented, and had seated themselves, Narbona held up one hand. Doniphan saw that the fingernails were very long and filed to points.

"*Haish anti?*" Narbona said.

"Narbona asks who you are?" Caldwell said.

Doniphan said: "Tell Narbona we are representatives of a people a thousand times more numerous than the Mexicans. Tell him our President is a hundred times more powerful than the governor who ruled Santa Fé, and that, if all of our armies were to come into his country, they would make a solid line, ten men wide, from here to the Río Grande."

The translation went back to Narbona. The old chief listened impassively. Then he said: "*Ha at iish biniigheyniya?*"

Caldwell said: "Narbona asks what you have come for."

"Tell him we have come to make a treaty of peace. We are the enemies of the Mexicans, which should make us allies of the Navajos."

The talk was stopped by a crackling roar from the center of the corral. Doniphan grabbed at the Colt holstered against his leg, almost lunging to his feet. He settled back when he saw what had caused the sound, realizing for the first time what a tension he had been under. They had lighted the pyre in the center of the corral. It made a frightening blaze. A column of smoke and flame shot 100 feet into the night. A chorus of startled yells came from the volunteers as the first

195

shower of sparks descended upon them. The heat became so great that Doniphan and the others in the front ranks had to pull their blankets back a dozen feet. Even at such a distance the heat beat against him in a great blinding pulse and he had to shield his face with both hands.

There was a shrill whistling from outside the corral and a dozen weird white figures ran in through the gate. Doniphan saw that they were naked Indians, painted all over with white clay. Leaping and gyrating, howling like lost souls, they made a circuit of the fire.

"How can they do it?" Doniphan asked. "I couldn't stand it any nearer."

"That's a secret I doubt we'll ever discover," Caldwell said.

"Rubbish," Merritt told them. "That clay is a non-conductor. They take some kind of dope."

"I saw a white man try it once," Caldwell said. "He got within twenty feet of the fire before he fainted."

Each of the weird white dancers held a sumac wand in his right hand, tipped with a delicate white down. Still whooping and yelling, the leader ran in close to the towering blaze. He threw himself on the ground, groveling forward until he could thrust his wand into the flames. He let out a shriek and jumped back, holding up the wand to reveal that the down had been burned away. One by one the others repeated the act. When they were finished, they all circled the fire again, doing something with their wands, and new puffs of down flared mysteriously at the end of each stick.

196

Doniphan's cheeks felt seared, and he had to look away to ease his burning eyes.

"By the everlasting," he murmured. "This is one tale Beth and the boys will never believe."

The dancers were trooping back out the gate now, and the conference resumed. There was a chief named Sarcillo Largo, a young man with a fierce, shining face who showed more hostility than Narbona.

"Why should the Navajos stop fighting the Mexicans while the Americans go on fighting the Mexican?" he asked, through Caldwell. "The Mexican has been our enemy much longer than he has been your enemy. Why should the Navajos be punished for fighting with the Mexicans on the west when the Americans are doing the same thing on the east?"

It stumped Doniphan for a moment. He almost grinned at the irony. He guessed his trouble was that he couldn't decide whether he was pleading for the prosecution or the defense.

"The fact is that New Mexico now belongs to the Americans," he said. "When the Navajos steal from a New Mexican, they are stealing from an American citizen. When they kill a New Mexican, they are killing an American citizen. The Navajos have no direct cause for war with Americans and it must stop."

Another ceremony had started out by the roaring pyre. A chorus had come in through the gate, led by a medicine man, singing and wailing, apparently oblivious of the intense heat. One of their number sat down on a blanket on the west side. Caldwell said that was the patient, who wanted to get rid of the spirit of the bear. A pair of young men came dancing through the gate. They each held a long plumed arrow. After posturing and dancing before the patient, they held up their arrows, placed them against their lips, and jammed the whole length of the shaft down their throats. Doniphan heard the volunteers nearby gasp in surprise.

"It's a trick," Merritt said. "A cheap magician's trick."

A lot of *tiswin* had been passed out to the soldiers. It was the Navajo version of corn liquor and just as potent. Some of the men were drinking too much. It made them bolder and they had begun to wander among the Indians. Doniphan saw Kelly Goff grab a young girl and try to pull her toward the gate. Doniphan spoke in a low voice to DeCourcy, who sat next to him.

"Stop Goff. Get a couple of men and stop him quick. Don't make a scene of it."

DeCourcy got up quickly, calling to Lieutenant Hicklin and two other Company D men. A couple of Navajos were already heading toward Goff, their faces dark and menacing. DeCourcy and his men surrounded Goff and pried him loose from the squaw before there was any real trouble.

"You've got to do more than that," Merritt said. "You've got to make these men realize the danger we're in. You should issue an order before the whole detachment. Any officer who sees a man laying a hand on these Indian women is to shoot him."

Doniphan shook his head. "Taylor, I will never issue an order like that."

"Colonel, you leave your officers in a hopeless position."

"I don't mean to. You know I'll stand behind my officers if there's trouble. I've left it up to your discretion before, Taylor. Just don't make any mistakes."

Doniphan turned to Caldwell, telling the interpreter that he wanted to leave the conference for a moment, and asking the man to make an excuse for him to the Indians. Doniphan always unbuckled his belt when he sat down and he had to fasten it as he rose. He looked around at the hundreds of Indians, blanketed in barbaric colors, glittering with silver, a sea of dark and savage faces. He wondered how many of them had ever been seen by a white man. He wondered what they were thinking. From the beginning he had not been blind to the audacity of the campaign. Now he suddenly thought that Merritt had been right — it was sheer folly. The responsibility of command became an unbearable pressure in his chest. What right did he have to lead 150 men into a trap like this, an unknown land, an unknown people, a horde of murderers?

He wasn't a soldier. He was a country lawyer. Two terms in the Missouri Legislature were the biggest thing he'd ever done. He must have been crazy to accept the commission.

He looked up at the sky. The Indians called their god by a different name. *Yeibitchai*. What did the name matter? He wanted to pray. He felt the overwhelming need to get down on his knees alone somewhere and pray for help.

He looked at his ragged Missourians, their gaunt faces smeared with mutton grease, their bellies full for the first time in weeks. He realized that, if he hadn't brought them into this, some other officer would have. Maybe an officer like General Taylor who couldn't control them, who would let them turn into a gang of thieves and drunkards and rapists. Or a man like Merritt who would shoot them for the sake of discipline.

He took a deep breath and began moving across in front of his men. Most of them were still seated on blankets, stuffing themselves with mutton and corn cakes. The heat of the great fire burned against Doniphan's back.

"Boys," he told his men, "if we were all back in Missouri, and we'd invited these Navajos to be our guests at a hoe-down or a husking bee, and they started getting familiar with our women, we'd naturally feel ornery, and it would end up with a few bottles of good corn busted over a few heads, and some blacked eyes, and then everybody would be friends again and go back to the dancing. But these Indians take their brawling more seriously. There's probably over a thousand of them in this camp, and less than a hundred and fifty of us. If a fight started, I doubt me that many of us would get out alive." He nodded at a Company F man. "Harry, your Cole County folks would be almighty proud should they hear you died on the field of battle fighting for them, but they'd be everlasting ashamed if

200

it came back that you and a hundred and fifty of your regiment had been massacred away off in some Indian camp that nobody ever heard of, just because you couldn't keep your hands off of a woman." He moved on down the line, snapping his gallus. "I tell you what I'm going to do. I'm going to put you all on your honor. I'm going to make each of you responsible for his mate. Because we all know that whoever touches a woman first is going to be the man responsible for getting us all killed."

Nate thought that it was a caution how much effect Doniphan's little talks always had on the boys. Maybe it was the personal touch he gave it, singling out a man here or there and talking to him. It gave a body the idea that Doniphan really cared for each one of them. Nate remembered the sick boy who had ridden Doniphan's horse over the mountain, and the soldier with the ague who had been wrapped in Doniphan's overcoat. Maybe that's why they'd do so much for Doniphan.

The Indians were doing some kind of magic act out by the fire now. A little boy about ten years old, stripped and painted, feathers in his cropped hair, a red sash around his middle, was dancing before a basket in which lay a single eagle feather. A long sigh rose from the crowd as the feather began to rise. It stood straight up. It began to dance in time with the boy, turning right when he turned right, turning left, whirling when he whirled, never losing a beat. Nate realized that his mouth was hanging open.

He saw Bristol Graham over by the gate. Bristol still had a few buttons left on his jacket. An old buck was bargaining with Bristol, tugging on the jacket and pointing at a squaw in a red blanket near the gate. Maybe Bristol hadn't heard Doniphan's talk, or maybe he was too drunk on the *tiswin* to care. He was laughing too loudly and his eyes were getting filmed. He let the buck lead him toward the squaw. They went out the gate, with the buck still tugging on the jacket.

Lieutenant Merritt stood up, moving through the crowd toward the gate. Nate realized that he had seen Bristol. Nate had been near enough to hear what Merritt had told Doniphan about shooting any man who touched a woman. He was afraid that it was still in Merritt's mind. He didn't want to see Bristol get killed. He didn't want to see them all massacred because Bristol wanted a woman, either. He didn't know what to do. He had the impulse to tell Doniphan, but the colonel was busy talking again with the head men. He thought about what Doniphan had said, making each man responsible for his mate. He'd never actually shared a tent with Bristol but he guessed it was up to him, since nobody else seemed to know what was going on.

He hated to leave the fire. He hadn't been really warm enough since the Río Grande. He didn't want to leave the food. He was just beginning to feel full, the first time in two months. He took a last big chunk of greasy mutton and rose, moving through the crowd toward the gate. The heat of the great fire was so intense that he had to keep his face turned away.

He reached the gate and saw Merritt's shadowy figure outside the corral, crossing camp toward the line

202

of hogans. He couldn't see Bristol or the Indians and figured that they had gone in among the hogans. There was a bunch of young bucks gathered just outside the gate passing around a bottle made of woven reeds pitched with gum. They all looked drunk, and, when Nate went by, one of them said something. "*Juthla hago ni!*"

The Indian spat on the ground as he said it, and the others laughed. It had a nasty sound. A couple of them had already started wandering toward the hogans. Nate couldn't tell whether they were just moving idly across camp, or deliberately following Merritt. As Nate started after the lieutenant, more of the Indians started drifting after him. It struck Nate that a shooting might be just as dangerous as trouble with their women — even if the one Merritt shot were Bristol. If these young bucks were anything like the jaspers who hung around the Missouri taverns, any excitement could start a brawl.

The fire made a bright glow high against the sky but its heat didn't reach outside the big corral. A cold wind whined against Nate and seemed to blow through his bones. The rocky ground was icing over and he began to shiver uncontrollably. He was wearing the moccasins Doniphan had given him but his feet were still so swollen and tender that each step made him cringe.

He followed Merritt in among the hogans. They were little houses, some not higher than his head, cedar logs chinked with brush, mud plastered over the roof with a smoke hole in the center. He was in darkness now, beyond the reach of the fire glow. He had lost sight of Merritt ahead of him, and the Indians behind, although he could still hear them talking in husky voices and laughing. He moved quicker, trying to lose them, to catch up with Merritt. He heard the whicker of a horse, the distant shouts of the crowd in the big corral. Then, startlingly close, Merritt's voice.

"Let her go, soldier. Let her go or I'll fire."

Nate rounded the corner of a house and saw Merritt's shadowy form directly ahead of him. About twenty feet beyond Merritt, by a log pen, two shadows were struggling.

"I ain't letting nobody go." It was Bristol's voice. "I paid me a good jacket for this squaw and she ain't running out now."

The squaw was cursing him and fighting to get free. Merritt was going toward them with his Colt out and Nate heard the hammer *click*.

"Soldier, one more warning . . . let her go!"

The squaw made a screeching sound and tore free, lunging around the pen. Bristol stumbled after her, disappearing before Merritt could shoot. Merritt cursed and plunged after him. Nate followed, looking back for the other Indians. He couldn't see any sign of them, but he knew that they must have heard the woman caterwauling. He lost Merritt in another scattering of hogans. Then he heard the sound of running feet ahead of him, and the squaw's shrill voice.

He headed toward the sound. It led him back toward the glow of the great fire. He was able to see things again when he rounded a hogan and ran head-on into the squaw. It knocked the wind out of her. She made a sound like the safety valve on a steamboat engine, falling heavily against him. He grabbed her and was trying to hold her up when Bristol came around the hogan after her.

"Bristol," Nate said, "you got to git out of here. It's Nate. You got to leave her alone."

"I ain't gitting out." Bristol grabbed her by the long hair. "I gimme a jacket for this woman and she's mine."

The woman started screeching and clawing, and Nate said: "Certain, Bristol, you go ahead and take her."

He pulled away from Bristol. The squaw was still struggling and Bristol's back got turned. Nate felt around on the ground and found a rock. He hit Bristol on the back of the head.

As Bristol went down, Lieutenant Merritt came running around the hogan.

"Don't shoot!" Nate called. "A bunch of drunk ones following us . . . a shooting would set them off for sure."

For a moment Nate thought that it hadn't done any good. Merritt had stopped five feet away, his cocked gun leveled at Nate. The lieutenant was gasping for air, and his face was visible in the fire glow — the same expression Nate had seen so many times before when the volunteers had driven him to the breaking point, the spastic twitch of muscle in his cheek, the feverish shine to his narrowed eyes.

Merritt looked down at Nate's feet. The squaw had gotten caught under Bristol's falling body and was wailing and screeching as she tried to drag herself from underneath the unconscious man.

"We got to do something about her," Nate said. "We can't let her git back to camp in this shape."

"I ought to shoot her," Merritt said. "I ought to shoot all three of you."

Nate could hear the young bucks coming, calling to each other as they ran through the hogans. Nate remembered what Jayán had told him about Indians and tobacco. He had been saving the plug Jayán had given him to make a trade, and he pulled it out and quickly bit off a chaw. The plug was cased with licorice and molasses, and biting into it released the syrupy smell. The squaw had just gotten out from beneath Bristol's unconscious body when the scent reached her. Nate held the plug out to her. She stared at him, breathing in hoarse, rasping gusts, her black hair hanging in front of her face. Finally she reached out and took the plug. She lowered her face, staring at Nate, like a kid with stolen candy. Finally she tried a bite. The suspicion and the rage in her dark face faded away. She swallowed the bite, making a cooing sound. She took another bite. About that time the Indians started arriving. For a minute Nate thought there was going to be trouble, but one of them saw what the squaw had and took it from her and tried a bite. He grunted, passing it around to the others. By the time they all had a bite the plug was gone and they stood around, chewing and grunting and swallowing and grinning at each other like a bunch of hard-shell deacons at a church social.

CHAPTER
THIRTEEN

On the day after Doniphan reached Bear Springs, Inez and Kirby arrived at Padillas. It was a village of several hundred people on the Río Grande, seventy-two miles south of Santa Fé. Kirby had heard that the paymaster was in Padillas, issuing the Missouri volunteers the first pay they had received in six months, and had persuaded Inez to go south with him to get his money.

The road was choked with traffic. The scattered units of Doniphan's regiment were moving downriver to a rendezvous at Valverde, almost 100 miles beyond Padillas. The companies straggled for miles along the sluggish yellow river, half of them without mounts or leading sick horses, making no attempt to keep ranks, wandering through the fields or stopping to nap in the sun. With them crawled the endless lines of wagons, the rumbling freighters that carried army supplies, the white-topped Conestogas of the Santa Fé traders, over 300 of them belonging to the Magoffin brothers, Samuel Owens, Ed Glasgow, and a dozen other big firms that had been dissatisfied with prices in Santa Fé or that had planned from the beginning to take their goods to Chihuahua City. Kirby had gotten a ride for himself and Inez in one of them, an outfit belonging to a Spaniard named Manuel X. Harmony.

The Conestoga was a big wagon, sixteen feet long, carrying a payload of two tons, its boat-shaped bed sagging in the belly so the cargo would shift toward the middle and not break out the end gates. For five days it had been Inez's world — the grinding complaint of sour-gum hubs, the rattle of linchpins straining to hold on the great dished wheels, the windy flap of Osnaburg sheeting against the rusty arch of wagon bows overhead. It hadn't been an unpleasant trip. There were other women in the wagon trains, the New Mexican wives of some of the traders, and Inez gratefully accepted their casual friendship.

The evening air was thick with the pungent smell of piñon smoke around Padillas. In the fields on either side of the road, men were working with wooden mauls to crush the sweet sap from the corn stocks for molasses and the pounding echoed in a steady rhythm against the mud walls of the small village. The wagons pulled into the fields outside town and the muleskinners began unhooking their teams. Although the army still used mules on its wagons, Charles Bent had introduced oxen to the Santa Fé trade fifteen years before, and since then most of the freight was hauled by plodding double-yoked ox teams.

As soon as Harmony's wagons came to a halt, Kirby left for town to find the paymaster. Inez tried to stifle the loneliness she always felt when he left her. At Santa Fé he had been gone almost every night. He told her that he had to make a living for them somehow. La

Tules had let him work as a relief dealer at one of her faro tables for a while, and, when he wasn't there, he was sitting in on the short card games at La Fonda. Inez knew that he must be good with the cards because he usually came home with money. It allowed them to live well on what the town could provide, and the time they had together made up for her nights of loneliness.

Sometimes she had the sense of a restlessness in Kirby, a shadowy conflict going on inside him. The same brooding spell she had seen at Taos would sweep over him, and he would declare that he wasn't worthy of her. She thought that it was the circumstances of their marriage, or the trouble he'd had with Nate, although she still didn't understand the reasons for the fight between Nate and Kirby. Then, after the spell, as though trying to expiate some sense of guilt, Kirby would show her an excess of passionate attention. His love was a never-ending marvel to her. He was always bringing her bright clothes and trinkets from Santa Fé, going into outrageous antics to make her laugh when she was depressed, matching his every mood to hers, passionate, savage, teasing, tender, whatever she seemed to need. As long as he was with her, she had no doubts about what she had done. But when he was gone, she could not help her periods of torment.

She had gone to the Torreón house half a dozen times but the servants would not admit her. There had been chance encounters with her mother or her aunt in the plaza and the church, brief, tearful meetings that upset them all and accomplished nothing. Inez still cherished Doniphan's hope that time would soften her father's attitude, but as the weeks had worn on the hope had faded.

It was several hours before Kirby returned from Padillas. He had tied the four ends of his neckerchief together to carry the coins, clinking them as he walked, but he was in a bleak mood. He said that they hadn't gotten their pay at all, just $42 commutation that they'd been allowed for bringing their own horse and clothes.

"It ain't half what I expected," he said. "They owe me seven dollars a month for six months, and eighteen cents a day extra for all those days I spent a-building Fort Marcy. The only way I can make this add up into something is some kind of deal. I seen Jim Ganoe in town and I think I've got an idea."

He told her how Doniphan had ordered all the Chihuahua bound traders to gather at Valverde and wait till the regiment was ready to march. But it was known that Dr. Connelly and half a dozen others had gone ahead to El Paso with their goods. There were many others at Valverde champing at the bit — Mexican traders who knew that they would be safe and some others representing English firms or traveling under foreign passports that they thought would give them immunity.

"Now Ganoe says that this Englishman has come up the trail with a proposition from the governor of Chihuahua," Kirby told Inez. "All a trader has to do is fire his American teamsters, take on Mexicans, pay thirteen cents a pound at the custom house in El Paso, and he's cleared for Chihuahua City."

"It will do the traders no good," she said. "*Señor* Harmony told me that since Doctor Connelly and the others went against Doniphan's orders, a guard has been posted on the trail to keep any traders from going farther than Valverde."

"That's just where I come in," Kirby told her. "If I can rig it so the guard don't stop Jim Ganoe, he'll let me use this commutation money to buy some of his shoes. Ganoe figures a thousand-per-cent profit, Inez. Just calculate on that . . . forty-two dollars times a thousand."

She wondered why he always looked so young when he was talking about one of his deals, like a little boy, with his eager smile, his squinted eyes.

"But how can you make it so the guard does not stop Jim Ganoe?" she asked.

"Nate will help me out, certain for sure. His pa was Doniphan's best friend, you know. Nate studied law with Doniphan. Nate always claimed it didn't make any difference, but I know he's got the inside track with Doniphan. Nate could pull all kinds of hooraws and Doniphan wouldn't touch him. There was some trouble in Las Vegas, something about sabers and such. If Doniphan hadn't reared up on his hind legs, Merritt would've court-martialed Nate. If Nate handles it right, I know he can git Doniphan to let Ganoe through."

"After what happened at Taos?" she asked.

"That's all over. Nate ain't the kind to hold a grudge about that fight. I saw some Company D boys lined up at the paymaster. They just pulled in from Camp Starvation with Captain Reid. They say Nate and all the others will be marching for Valverde as soon as Doniphan finishes with the treaty at Bear Springs."

"You cannot go there," Inez said. "You told me you were attached to Colonel Price's regiment in Santa Fé."

"I know, I know, but Valverde's only a little piece downriver from here, and, as soon as Colonel Doniphan gets there, he can switch me back to the First Missouri."

"And then we will never have to go back to Santa Fé?"

"I didn't say that."

"You said we would go back as soon as we got the money here. How can you go back from Valverde if you have all your money invested in Ganoe's shoes? You will have to go with him."

He scratched his head. "Maybe you're right. I hadn't thought of that."

"Hadn't you? Maybe you hadn't thought of keeping your promise to Colonel Doniphan, either."

"I told him . . ."

"You told him you would stay in Santa Fé."

"Dammit, Inez, what right have you got being so uppity? I'm doing this for you, ain't I? Coming down here, trying to git some money so you can live high on the hog, taking a chance on getting shot . . ."

"Who would shoot you?"

"Nobody. Nothing."

"Maybe because you are a deserter."

"I ain't no deserter."

"Then why should they shoot you?"

"Nobody's a-going to shoot me."

212

"You said they might. Kirby, I do not care that much about living . . . living high on the hog. If it means you break your promise to Colonel Doniphan . . . if it means some kind of trouble . . . you have what we came for now. Let us go back to Santa Fé."

"I can't," he said. "I got a big deal a-going. You're as bad as Nate. Every time I get a big deal a-going, you want to back out on me. This is the kind of thing I been waiting a long time for. The shoe king, they'll call me. I'll sell shoes to every man in Mexico. I'll take my pay in wool and they'll call me the shoe king here and the wool king back in Missouri. I'll take back so much wool it'll be coming out the governor's ears. I got to find Ganoe now and give him this money."

She caught at his arm. "Kirby . . . please . . . I think you are making the mistake."

"My mistake was talking it over with a damn woman!"

He pulled free of her, a savage look to his face, and stalked away. She put her hand to her mouth, watching him go. She wondered what had made her act in such a way. All her life she had been taught complete submission. She had never seen her mother question her father or defy him or stand up to him. If she had married *Don* Fecundo, she would not have dared speak to him in such a way. She wondered why the thought of Kirby's being a deserter should disturb her so deeply. She had always thought of a deserter as a bad soldier. Why should she care if he was a good soldier or a bad soldier? In a way she was a deserter. She had rebelled against the same kind of thing. The army made her think of the austere, disciplined, rigidly prescribed life of her own people, the walls, the rules, the chains of a dozen centuries. Escape from it was one of the most precious things Kirby offered her. He had reminded her of a wild horse, leaping all fences, destroying all rules. Why should his rebellion bother her now? She wondered if she had escaped her world as completely as she had thought. The rules did not seem so terrible now. The codes did not seem so absurd.

She had married an enemy. The thought came out of nowhere, abruptly, shockingly. It had occurred to her before, but it had never seemed so final, so frightening. It was as though some door in her mind had stubbornly remained closed on it. Perhaps she had been afraid to dwell on it. Or perhaps it had been held back by the first glowing wonder of their love. But now the wonder was marred — their first real clash — and she could not hide from the truth any longer.

She looked around at the bearded traders, the dusty bullwhackers, the ragged soldiers camped beyond the wagons. She hated to see them descending upon the land like a horde of locusts — trampling through the cornfields, stripping the fruit orchards, fondling the women, shouting drunkenly in the streets. They had done her no personal harm, but the war was not over. There would be fighting in the south. Mexican bodies lying in the fields and Mexican widows huddled in the little houses. And she would be a part of it. She had joined the enemy.

She shook her head miserably. She could not condemn herself so simply. She was not the only woman who had married a *gringo* soldier. There were dozens. And how many New Mexicans were doing business with the *gringos?* Inviting them to their houses as honored guests? La Tules had loaned the *gringos* $1,000 for military supplies. Donaciano Vigil had agreed to serve as lieutenant governor. Half the people in Santa Fé had joined the *gringos*, in one way or another. Most of the *gringo* soldiers didn't seem as much of an enemy as Armijo's corrupt circle had been. She couldn't think of Kirby as an enemy. Or Nate. Why must she still try to think like her father? General Kearny had said that they were all one people now.

Her head seemed to swim with a bitter confusion. She wanted to see her mother. She had always turned to her in trouble. She wanted to sit in the little white-walled room with her mother and Leonor and Aunt Maximiliana and her 709th Lady of Guadalupe. It had seemed such a prison then. It seemed such a sanctuary now. Kirby's world had suddenly become a chaotic desolation, devoid of guideposts, no rules, no standards, no right or wrong, sin or virtue. She felt lost, achingly alone. She needed someone.

It made her think of a priest. It made her realize how long it was since she had seen a priest. There would be one in Padillas. She started through the wagons, toward town. She wanted to confess.

CHAPTER
FOURTEEN

On November 23rd, Nate left Bear Springs with a detachment of men commanded by Captain Parsons and started the long march back to the Río Grande. Doniphan remained behind with a second detachment, intending a separate march to the Zuñi villages southwest of Bear Springs. He had concluded the treaty of peace between the Americans and the Navajos and now hoped to negotiate a second treaty between the Navajos and their traditional enemies, the Zuñis. Lieutenant Merritt and some of the other officers who had experience with the Indians felt that both treaties would be worthless pieces of paper.

Nate couldn't seem to worry much about it. When a man's feet hurt him all the time, it didn't seem that he could think about much else. He had been afoot since losing Strawberry. What horses were left were doing so poorly that they couldn't pack double and there wasn't anything to do but walk. The moccasins Doniphan had gotten him were about worn out. His feet were bruised and swollen and frostbitten so badly that every step hurt, and now he was getting the splints. It was the same thing a plow horse got when it was worked too long. He had heard the infantry companies complaining about it as far back as Bent's Fort. His shins burned till he thought he was walking through a fire, and, when his calf muscles took to cramping so much, he had to sit down and rub them a while before he could walk some more.

They reached the Río Grande on December 4th and turned south, passing a town called Padillas. They learned that the paymaster had been there but had left three days before, and they had to go on without their money.

The grasses by the river were rusty and dead and in the morning the cottonwoods were white with frost. At the Indian pueblo of Isleta, Nate saw blocks of ice floating in the river. At Belen he woke up in the morning with six inches of snow on him. Nate had only one tattered blanket and he never could get warm enough. He had been trying to keep shaving with his Bowie knife, but his cheeks got so scabby with frostbite that he was afraid he would scrape them all away and he finally gave up and started growing a beard. It was quite a bramble by the time he reached Valverde. It was a large camp in the timbered bottoms and got its name from the ruins of an old town nearby. Captain Walton and three companies had been there since late November. There were over 400 wagons with him, mostly belonging to the traders.

Camp was full of the usual rumors. An Englishman named Ruxton had passed through from El Paso a few days before Nate arrived. He said that there was a big Mexican force at El Paso getting ready to attack.

General Wool had been ordered to abandon his march to Chihuahua City, and James Magoffin had been captured near El Paso. He would probably be shot as a spy. Nate remembered that James Magoffin was Inez's uncle.

The tents and brush shelters of the volunteers were scattered haphazardly through the bottoms. The ground was littered with droppings and cast-off clothes and used, paper cartridges and the bones of animals slaughtered for food and other refuse. Horses and mules that had strayed from the herds wandered untended through the shelters. Most of the men had long beards and their clothes were in rags. If they didn't have typhoid, they had Blumberg's sign or scurvy. The doctors could do little for them and they sat listlessly before the makeshift shelters, yellow-faced and shivering in the winter cold. The officers couldn't get them to police the camp and half of them wouldn't show up for roll call and no amount of threats would produce enough sentries for guard duty. The officers couldn't enforce the orders against wasting ammunition. The men strong enough to lift a rifle spent their days firing at rabbits or birds or making up shooting matches by the river. Nate didn't think that he had ever seen their morale so low.

The second night he was there Nate got guard duty. Gaines was corporal of the guard and he argued Nate and Kelly Goff into relieving the sentries by the river. They found Isaac Hayes sleeping under a big cottonwood tree and had to yell to Bristol till he came from the willows where he had been collecting bark to

218

shred for tobacco. Corporal Gaines said that they might as well not bother with sentry duty if they were going to act that way. Kelly Goff thought that it was a good idea.

"Ain't no use walking up and down out here," he said. "We been hearing about the Mexican army for six months and ain't seen a sign of it yet. If I had a dollar for every hour I wasted on sentry duty, I could go back to Missouri a rich man. What about a game of all fours?"

Gaines tried to argue them out of it but Goff got out a pack of cards. Nate wouldn't join them. He didn't know why, exactly. Before they had reached Santa Fé, he had left his sentry post more than once with Kirby to take a swim in some river or carry on a hooraw in the traders' camp. Now he got a guilty feeling about it. His feeling about a lot of things seemed to be changing.

When Gaines saw that he had one sentry left, he took Nate to a post by the river. Nate had to pace about 100 yards between the water and the grove. It was a lonely spot after Gaines left. It was bitterly cold and Nate's teeth got to chattering so loudly he knew that it would give him away if there was a Mexican within a mile. Moonlight made a pale yellow haze in the grove and the cottonwoods towered silently all around him, looking 100 feet high. Their bark was white and glaring as naked flesh and their enormous mottled trunks were riddled with woodpecker holes and covered with a sickly green beard of mistletoe. Nate had been alone about fifteen minutes when he heard a sound in the willows by the river, and somebody called his name softly. Nate swung his rifle down off his shoulder.

"Who goes there? You better give me the password."

A man pushed through the willows and stepped into the open, grinning broadly. It was Kirby.

"I been trying to get in touch with you," he said. "I saw Hugh Long over by the traders' camp and he said you got sentry duty."

For a moment Nate was so surprised he couldn't answer. Kirby looked different. He had shed his volunteer rags for a black slouch hat and a fancy blue fustian with coattails to the knees and sassafras-yellow jeans. After the first surprise a rush of bitterness swept Nate, so strong it almost gagged him. He thought that he would begin to shake the way he had for so long after their fight, whenever he thought about Kirby, but he couldn't hold onto it. The feeling faded, leaving him empty, confused. He wanted to hate Kirby. He couldn't hate Kirby. He shifted around, fingering his cold face, feeling awkward the way a body would with a stranger. He didn't know what to say.

"Uh . . . looks as how you been having some luck with the cards."

Kirby seemed to feel a little awkward, too. His grin looked sheepish, and he glanced down almost apologetically at the handsome clothes.

"I did all right in Santa Fé. And then the boys got paid in Padillas, you know. If I didn't win it from them, somebody else would."

"Looks like they gave you the scurvy along with it. Your face is yellow as tickseed."

"Not the scurvy," Kirby said quickly. "A little ague, maybe. I get to aching at night. It's that time of

220

year . . ." He trailed off, looking helplessly at Nate, and the stepped closer, impulsively putting a hand on Nate's shoulder. "Nate, Nate . . . you and me . . . I mean, that's all over now, ain't it? You understand things better now, don't you?"

"I understand things," Nate said.

"And you don't blame me so much. I mean, it was something I couldn't help. I didn't know it was a-going to hurt you so much, believe me . . . you'd only seen her once . . . I never dreamed it meant all that to you . . ."

"You explained all that before. I thought Doniphan ordered you to stay in Santa Fé."

"Well, I guess Doniphan's afraid that, if we don't smooth this over somehow, old man Torreón will join Archuleta in some kind of revolt. I tried to fix things up with old *Don* Miguel, Nate, but I tell you, he ain't a-going to take no ragtag volunteer without a cent to his name into his house. He wants a man of substance for his daughter's husband. Do you know, he turned down one young jasper just because his family hadn't been in Santa Fé for more than a hundred years?"

Nate shifted uncomfortably, guessing what was coming. He had listened to a hundred of Kirby's schemes before.

"I've got a deal," Kirby said, "that'll set me and Inez up in high style. It'll give me enough to support Inez in the way she's used to . . . a big house, servants, silver on the table, the whole works. I'll come out of this the kind of man *Don* Miguel wants for his daughter. But I need your help."

He told Nate about investing his commutation money with Ganoe, and asked Nate to approach Doniphan about letting Ganoe through.

"Doniphan won't do it," Nate said.

"He's got to," Kirby said. "He wants *Don* Miguel to take Inez back, don't he? This is the only way it can be done. I've got to convince *Don* Miguel he ain't got no backwoods tobacco roller for a son-in-law."

"Why don't you go to Doniphan yourself?"

"He won't listen to me. You got the inside track with him. You can make him see the sense of this."

"If it makes sense, it wouldn't matter who told him," Nate said. "Are you a deserter, Kirby? Is that why you're afraid to see him?"

"Nate, you know I ain't."

"Doniphan said he attached you to Colonel Price's regiment at Santa Fé."

"I got permission to leave."

"Then you must have a pass."

"I don't need a pass. This whole deal was a private agreement between me and Doniphan."

Nate wondered why he was asking so many questions. He had accepted so much of what Kirby always said without any questions. "What you're asking me to do is tell Colonel Doniphan some lies, so Doniphan will let a deserter through his lines, so this deserter can swing a deal that will make him rich, so he can come back to Santa Fé and live in high style while the rest of us're getting killed down in Mexico."

"Nate, what's got into you? You never talked that way before. It ain't like that at all. This is for Inez. Forget about me. All I'm trying to do is for her. You want her back with her family, don't you? Think what it is, a gal like that, cut off from everybody she loved, living with a bunch of strangers, never knowing where she'll light next. This ain't no life for her, Nate, and I know it. She's pining away. I'm afraid she'll get sick if it keeps on much longer. All you got to do is see her. Why don't you come over to the traders' camp? Me and Inez are staying there. She's sold on this, certain for sure. She's convinced it's the only way to swing her pa around."

Nate felt himself weakening. The thought of seeing Inez again gave him an ache in his throat. He began to feel guilty. Maybe Kirby was right. He was letting them down. He thought of all Kirby had done for him. Up at Taos it had seemed that he had fallen in love with a girl and Kirby had stolen her. Now he wondered. It was like Kirby had said at Taos. Inez had made the choice. She had picked Kirby instead of Nate and what Nate might have felt about her, once he had come to know her better, didn't matter much. Maybe, if he helped them just once, if he went along with one of Kirby's deals this one, last time . . .

A sound back in the grove startled Nate — the crackle of feet in the harvest of fallen leaves. "You better light a shuck," Nate said. "It's about time for inspection. Lieutenant Merritt's the officer of the day."

Kirby caught his arm. "You'll come to the traders' camp?"

Nate hesitated, frowning, and then said dubiously: "If I can."

Kirby grinned, squeezed his arm, and turned to disappear in the willows. Nate hurried back toward the grove to warn the card players. He burst into the clearing where Kelly and Bristol and Hayes had built a fire and were huddled beside it with their cards, but, before he could say anything, Lieutenant Merritt appeared at the edge of the trees beyond the game. He stopped there, staring blankly at the men. He spoke to Nate first.

"Soldier, is this your post?"

"No, sir," Nate said. "I just . . ."

"We done took a vote," Kelly said. "Ain't no use for guard duty. Majority rules, Lieutenant."

"A vote?" Merritt's voice sounded strained. "You're in the army, Goff, not back at some Saline County election."

Bristol said: "We vote our officers in, don't we?"

"That had nothing to do with it."

"Damn it, Lieutenant, why don't you light a shuck?" Kelly said. "How can we concentrate on our cards with you scrounging around?"

Merritt couldn't seem to speak for a moment. Finally he said: "Goff, I'm not going to take any more of your insubordination. We're in enemy territory. If you don't get back to your posts immediately, you'll go on report. There isn't anything in the book that would keep you from being shot."

"Us volunteers never read that book," Kelly said. "You won't be able to collect enough men to make up a firing squad."

Nate saw a spastic twitch start in Merritt's face. His hands began to tremble so visibly that he had to grip his sword belt to hide it. The man had changed in the last eight months. When Nate had first met Merritt, he had been an icy, austere, marble statue of a man, a book with all the answers. He had lost thirty pounds since then and it was hard to tell if it had been the marching, the short rations, or just living with the volunteers. He had a stooped, emaciated, rather desperate look. He had made a pathetic attempt to maintain his uniform but most of the yellow trim was shredded away, the blue tunic was sweat-stained and faded by the sun to a chalky color, and a greasy buckskin patch was plastered like an ignominious brand across the seat of his trousers. His eyes were cavernous, glittering feverishly, and his cheeks had a look of shrunken parchment. Merritt tried to say something, but all that came out was a strangled, mewing sound. He wheeled and rushed off toward camp.

Kelly and the other two went on playing, thinking that Merritt had given up, and Nate went back to his post, but in a short time Merritt returned with a whole squad from Company D and put all the sentries under arrest. Nate protested that he hadn't been in on the card game, but Merritt wouldn't listen. They were disarmed and taken to the guard tent, where they were held till a court-martial could be convened. Major Gilpin had arrived from upriver with two companies and he sat on the court with Captain Walton and Captain Reid. Lieutenant Merritt charged the sentries with deserting their posts and mutiny and recommended that they be shot. Nate pleaded not guilty and the other sentries testified on his behalf, but the fact that he had been at the scene during the card game was too damaging. The final decision was that they should lose a month's pay and spend four hours a day, until the regiment left Valverde, marching before the guard tent, carrying forty-pound packs.

Nate heard a lot of plots hatched against Lieutenant Merritt that night. About an hour after tattoo somebody threw the entrails of a slaughtered sheep in on Merritt. It left such a smell that he had to burn his shelter and wash his uniform three times in the river. He accused the four sentries who had stood court-martial but he couldn't prove anything, and Major Gilpin wouldn't take any action. Merritt got a new tent, but Nate knew that his trials weren't over. The following night Nate came awake with the ground shaking under him. All he could think of was a Mexican cavalry raid and he grabbed his rifle and squirmed out from under his half shelter.

He was almost trampled by a pair of mules running past him. By the pale moonlight he could see that somebody was running behind them and whacking their rumps with a doubled rope. They were stampeding directly toward Lieutenant Merritt's tent at the end of the company street.

If the noise had waked Merritt, he started moving too late. As the mules reached his tent, they were running ten feet apart so that one of the animals passed on either side of the half shelter. Nate didn't realize that they had the long rope tied between them till he saw it strike the tent, catching in the rigging and lifting the half shelter and dragging it across the ground like an enormous, flapping bat, with Merritt tangled up in it. Nate started running after him.

"Cut him loose!" he shouted. "Somebody cut him out of that tent! They're dragging Lieutenant Merritt!"

The whole camp was aroused by then, a horde of half-dressed men lunging from the long lines of shelters. They all began shouting at once and Nate saw a sentry running in from one of the posts by the river.

"Halt!" the sentry yelled. "Who goes there?"

"It's the Mexican dragoons!" somebody shouted hysterically. "It's the whole damn' Mexican cavalry!"

The confused sentry took a shot at the mules and other sentries began firing wildly from their posts.

"Hold your fire!" Nate shouted. "You're shooting at Lieutenant Merritt, that's Lieutenant Merritt!"

Something broke free of the flapping tent and rolled to a stop. Nate saw that it was Merritt, and ran toward him. The mules galloped on through camp, upsetting more tents, the men scattering from in front of them to escape their charge. The animals finally disappeared into the cottonwood grove with half a dozen sentries in pursuit.

Nate was one of the first men to reach Merritt. The lieutenant's britches had been torn completely away and his bare white legs were mottled all over with blood and bruises and dirt. His tunic was shredded and his face was covered with black patches of blood and dirt mixed together and ground into the flesh. He was groaning dazedly and trying to get up on one elbow. Nate put his rifle down and helped the man to a sitting position. Merritt's head swung around and the first man his dazed eyes focused on was Nate.

He cursed and pulled his arm from Nate's hand. He tried to lunge up and almost pitched onto his face, catching himself by going to one knee. Somebody else tried to help him and he tore loose from him, finally gaining his feet, swaying heavily. He wiped his hand across his face and looked around the crowd till he saw Major Gilpin.

"I want you to put Nate Hatcher under arrest," Merritt said hoarsely. "He tried to kill me."

"He didn't do no such thing," Corporal Gaines said. "I saw Nate rolling out of his tent after those mules went by."

"That's the truth," Hicklin said. "It was Nate stopped the sentries from shooting at the lieutenant."

Major Gilpin stirred uncertainly, fingering his jaws, staring at the rank upon rank of sullen, unsmiling faces that surrounded him in a dense mob. Nate had always thought that Gilpin was young to be a major. He was only twenty-four and had cultivated an opulent beard to give him added dignity. He had a brilliant background, educated in England and at the University of Pennsylvania, tutored by Nathaniel Hawthorne, graduated from West Point. He had seen service in the Seminole War and afterward had resigned his commission to practice law in Independence, Missouri. He hadn't been as harsh with the men as Lieutenant

Merritt or the other officers with regular military backgrounds.

"I am going to make formal charges against this man," Merritt said. "I insist you place him under arrest."

Reluctantly Gilpin ordered a sentry to disarm Nate, and he was marched through the crowd to the guard tent. It seemed that nobody slept in camp that night. Whenever he looked out of the guard tent, Nate could see the men sitting in little bunches in front of their tents, or drifting aimlessly around the fires they had built. Their voices made a sullen sound, like the buzzing from a bee tree. In the morning Nate found out what it was all about. Captain Reid told him that the feeling was so bad over the treatment of the four sentries that Gilpin feared that another court-martial would cause a general mutiny. He had withdrawn the punishment of the other three men and had ordered Nate confined to the guard tent and its immediate vicinity. Captain Reid seemed to think that the confinement was as much for protection as punishment. Lieutenant Merritt was swelled up like a poison pup with his hate and they were afraid of what would happen if he locked horns with Nate again.

It kept Nate from seeing Kirby and Inez as he had planned. He knew that if Kirby was a deserter, he would be afraid to enter the army camp without an assurance of amnesty from Doniphan. The traders' camp was three miles downriver and off limits, but a few volunteers were sneaking down there every day and Nate finally got a message through to Kirby. Kirby sent word back that Ganoe was getting impatient and that, if Nate couldn't do something soon, Ganoe would probably try to get through to El Paso without Doniphan's permission. Gilpin's decision to ease things up had at least stopped the volunteers from hoorawing Lieutenant Merritt, and everything hung fire till December 12th, when Colonel Doniphan arrived. Shortly after he showed up, Doniphan wandered through camp in a pair of jeans and an old coat, greeting the men.

"Bill," he told Sergeant Lewis, "why don't you shake out your platoon and make a company street out of this jack-rabbit trail? I met an Englishman in Albuquerque that had passed through here recently. Seemed he thought you were the traders and the traders were the army. It would be a mortal shame to get home after all this and find out they were giving those bullwhackers the credit for winning the war."

The shelters were aligned. Company streets appeared in the mess. The volunteers couldn't bear to think of the traders hogging their glory.

"Gaines, why don't you fetch a detail and sort of gather up some of these bones. I've got a requisition of Taos Lightning coming from Santa Fé and I'll issue an extra ration a day to every man found policing camp when the wagons pull in."

Camp was policed. The refuse disappeared. A whiskey issue hadn't been in the regulations for twenty years but they knew that the colonel could wink at a lot of rules when it came to his boys. The Mexicans didn't call them Los Goddamies for nothing. In a few hours

Doniphan accomplished what Gilpin and Merritt and the other officers had failed to do in weeks with all their ranting and threatening. The stray animals were rounded up and sent out to the herds where the guard was doubled. Sentries stood at their posts. The shooting matches stopped. Nate thought that it was notable how Doniphan could strike just the right note, all casual and friendly-like, volunteer style.

Doniphan spent a week reorganizing the regiment. He had asked Price to send the artillery from Santa Fé but the only unit that arrived was 103 men calling themselves the Chihuahua Rangers. They had been formed from the companies of Price's 2nd Missouri Volunteers and were commanded by Lieutenant Colonel Mitchell and Captain Hudson of that regiment.

The traders were impatient to get under way and were giving Doniphan a lot of trouble. On the 16th he sent Lieutenant Colonel Jackson and 200 men farther south to guard the trail. Two days later Nate heard that Jackson had caught Jim Ganoe and some other traders trying to slip through and was holding them till the main command caught up. There was no mention of Inez and Kirby, and Nate hoped that they had escaped.

The regiment left Valverde on the 19th. They soon entered a ninety-mile desert the Mexicans called the Dead Man's March. There was only one watering place in the whole stretch, no wood for fires, and not enough graze for the animals. The only way to get through was to push as hard as they could and most of the time they were marching till midnight. Nate had been unable to get any shoes and his moccasins wore through the second day. When he reached the point where he couldn't walk any longer, Hugh Long let Nate ride his horse. He kept worrying about Kirby and Inez, and blaming himself for not seeing them, but he could find out nothing from the traders about them. At the south end of the desert they came to the river again. Nate was standing sentry duty when camp was approached by a stranger with half a dozen Indians. He told the sentries his name was James Kirker. He wore buckskins, a glazed Mexican sombrero, and the biggest cartwheel spurs Nate had ever seen. He said that he and his Delawares were scalp hunters. The Apaches were so bad in Chihuahua that the Mexican government had a price on their heads. Kirker had been there for years making a handsome living by selling Indian scalps. He said that the Mexican governor owed him $30,000 and had denied the claim and threatened to throw Kirker and his Delawares in jail if they didn't leave. Kirker wanted to join the American Army. He didn't make it clear whether he was a patriot or just figured that he could get his $30,000 if the Americans won. Nate called the captain of the guard and Kirker was taken to Doniphan.

CHAPTER
FIFTEEN

Hugh Long had been sharing a half shelter with Nate. On the evening Kirker arrived, Hugh didn't sleep very well. He thought about the big Mexican army they were coming up against and he began to feel shaky. He wasn't afraid of being killed himself. It was that he couldn't help retching at the sight of blood. Whenever there was a brawl in the street, he had to walk away because, if he stood and watched men fighting, he got to shaking all over. The thought of killing worried him more than the thought of being killed. When they had heard they were going to have a battle at Apache Pass, he had almost deserted to keep from killing.

Hugh's great grandfather had been with Washington at Trenton and Valley Forge. Hugh's grandfather had attended West Point when the cadets were still quartered in the Long Barrack and had commanded Stephen Watts Kearny during the War of 1812 when Kearny was only a lieutenant in the 13th Infantry. Hugh's father had studied at West Point under Sylvanus Thayer and had commanded a company of 6th Infantry in the Black Hawk War. Hugh was born at Jefferson Barracks and grew up in a succession of army posts. He could never get over jumping when a gun went off. The sound of bugles hurt his ears. When his father took him hunting for the first time, he had cried over a dead rabbit his father had shot. But there was never any doubt in the family as to what Hugh's profession would be. He ran away from West Point during his first year there. He was ashamed to return to his family and drifted West. He got a schoolmaster's job in a string of frontier settlements and had been the schoolmaster at Marshall for a year when the war broke out.

He knew that he shouldn't have volunteered. He hadn't believed the atrocity stories and he thought that the Southern expansionists had manipulated the war and he would rather desert than shoot a Mexican. He felt closer to Nate than anybody else in the squad and several times had been on the point of telling Nate why he had really joined. But he was glad that he had held back. It was bad enough to be a coward. There was no use making it public.

Hugh shared his horse with Nate again during the following days, riding two hours, walking two. On the night of December 24th they were issued fifteen cartridges apiece and a strict order was issued to keep camp quiet. On Christmas Day they marched twelve miles through a brushy country and made an early camp near a sandy island that created a fork in the river. The smaller branch of the river that went around the east side of the island was called by the Mexicans a *brazito*. Captain Waldo said that *brazito* meant "little arm".

Thickets of thorny chaparral covered the marshy land and the hummocks of sand between the road and

234

the river. The wood details scattered through the brush. Hugh unsaddled his claybank and turned it over to the herders to water at the river. The wagons had begun to arrive, although the majority of traders were still straggling along the road miles to the rear. Doniphan had kept scouts and advance parties out all day for protection. Hugh was getting ready for mess call when a squad of the advance rode into camp leading a riderless white stallion.

The officer in charge, a lieutenant from Company G, said that he had sighted a half a dozen Mexican soldiers about three miles south of the *brazito*. The Mexicans had escaped, but only after the white horse had pitched his rider. There was some contention as to whom the horse belonged. Colonel Doniphan suggested that he would settle it with a game of cards. That appealed to them all, so they sat down to play three trick loo, winner take the horse.

They were still playing when somebody noticed the dust forming over the flat land to the south. Doniphan squinted at it.

"Does look suspicious," he said. "Dave, why don't you send a squad of Company A out and see what's up." He threw a card down. "Now, Lieutenant, play to that."

Captain Waldo got a squad together and rode out. But the cloud got bigger and bigger. Finally Doniphan put his cards down.

"I had a silver-plated hand," he said disgustedly, "but that cloud of dust looks just about army size to me. We better finish this game after the fight."

Hicklin was near Hugh and he turned and began shouting without waiting for an order from Doniphan. "Nick," Hicklin yelled, "sound 'Boots and Saddles'!"

Nick Snyder got his bugle and began the call. The blare of it made Hugh squint his eyes. Everybody started running back and forth. Hicklin was yelling at the other company buglers.

"Sound 'Boots and Saddles', sound 'Boots and Saddles'!"

Doniphan had to bawl at the top of his voice to be heard over the confusion: "Hicklin, will you shut up? The horses are at the river. We'll have to fall in on foot here. Bugler . . . blow assembly, make it general assembly, damn you!"

The bugler finally heard Doniphan and changed his call. Some of the men heading toward the river stopped and looked back for some point to rally on. A lot of them paid no attention to the call and kept on running.

Corporal Gaines ran past, still carrying a load of wood, and Doniphan called to him: "Jim, find your company flag! All you corporals, get your company flags!"

Gaines stopped and looked blankly at the wood in his arms. He let it fall and turned to run toward the Company D guidon. Hugh got his gun out of his tent. He had been issued one of the Yager muzzle-loaders. He had never learned to load on the run, and, after he spilled his powder and lost three patches, he gave it up as a bad job. He ran past Charlie Hayes sitting before his half shelter and reading his Bible.

"Charlie," he yelled, "didn't you hear the call?"

Charlie didn't look up from his Bible. "I'll be right along. I've got four verses left."

Nate joined Hugh and they ran toward the other Saline County men gathering around the Company D guidon. The traders were forming to guard the wagon park, most of them within their forted Conestogas. They were doing it quietly and without much fuss and Hugh thought that they looked a lot closer to being soldiers than the volunteers did.

The dust cloud was enormous now. The Mexicans emerged from it and formed a front. Hugh saw the blue pantaloons and red coats. Somebody said that they were the Vera Cruz dragoons. They wore tall brass-plated caps topped with buffalo-tail plumes, and, as they emerged from the dust, the sun glittered against the long line of lance tips. They came on steadily, spreading across the horizon till the line stretched as far as Hugh could see on either side.

"I haven't ever killed a man, you know," Hugh said.

Nate looked at him curiously. "Well, ain't no man ever killed you, neither. I guess today you gotta decide which it'll be."

Nate didn't feel too booming himself. He didn't blame Hugh for being a little scared. He figured that they were all a little scared. The ground began to vibrate as the Mexican cavalry came on, and Nate's palms got sticky. He kind of wished that Kirby was there. Kirby was always good in a fight.

Nate saw that Charlie Hayes had started to load his gun without waiting for any orders. Charlie did it methodically, the way he did everything. He got a paper cartridge out and tore it open with his teeth and poured the powder in and seated the ball. He hadn't even looked at the Mexicans yet.

Captain Reid came up and told the company that Colonel Doniphan wanted them to form two ranks and count off. Number Ones would stand and Number Twos would kneel.

"Do you want a horse holder, sir?" Hicklin called.

"What for?" Reid asked.

"The order was to dismount."

"The hell with that," Reid said. "I volunteered for the cavalry."

The companies counted off. Nate was a Number Two. They formed a kneeling line in front of the Number Ones. The officers were finally getting some order out of the mess. There were men ranked before all the company flags and they formed a ragged front extending roughly north and south across the road, with the regiment's rear toward the river. Only about half the regiment was assembled and men were still running from camp or straggling in from the water and wood details. The Mexican front was coming steadily closer.

"What about them knives?" Kelly Goff said. "You suppose they'll come in close enough to use them knives?"

"Will you shut up?" Nate said. "If there's anything makes my skin crawl, it's knives."

"They got long ones and short ones and curved ones," Kelly said. "Them curved ones is the worst.

238

They can stick you in the belly and cut out your Adam's apple all in one motion."

"Sergeant," Hicklin called, "load arms!"

"All right, boys," the sergeant said. "Load your guns."

"Damn it, Staples," Hicklin called, "do it right!"

"I never read that part of the manual, Lieutenant," Staples said. "This is infantry stuff."

Hicklin cursed and turned to the company. "Present arms," he called. "Load arms. Get your cartridge box around front, Nate. Handle cartridges. Tear . . . cartridges . . ."

"I can't do that," Kelly said. "I left my false teeth in my tent."

Everybody started laughing. Doniphan rode past on his chestnut and called to Hicklin: "Bill, what's going on here? That Mexican front doesn't look to be such a mortal joke to me."

They stopped laughing, and Hicklin shouted: "All I'm trying to do is get them to load their guns! A body'd think we never had any drill!"

"Maybe you'd do better if you forgot that book," Doniphan said. "After all, we didn't get much dismounted training. Now, boys, after you get your guns loaded, I want you to reserve your fire. Those Mexicans are going to look powerful big, after a while. They'll keep coming on till they look about the size of elephants, and you'll be in a sweat to start the shooting match. But I want you to hold your fire till I give the order."

Nate thought that it was remarkable the way the little talk calmed them down. Hicklin walked back and forth, fooling with his pistol and looking red in the face. Nate felt sorry for him.

About 300 yards off, the Mexican front came to a halt and a single rider detached himself and galloped toward the Missouri regiment. He was carrying a black flag. On one side it had a white skull and crossbones. On the other were the words **Libertad o muerte**.

"What's that mean?" Bristol asked.

"Liberty or death," Nate said.

The rider halted about fifty yards away. The man named Caldwell, who had been interpreting for Doniphan, rode out with Doniphan's adjutant to meet the Mexican. There was some talk, the Mexican waved his flag angrily, turned, and galloped back toward his lines. Caldwell came back, and after a while the news of what had happened was passed through the companies. The rider with the flag had come with a summons for Colonel Doniphan to appear before the Mexican commander, General Ponce de Leon. Doniphan's adjutant had refused the summons.

"We shall break your ranks, then, and take him to General Ponce de Leon," the Mexican said.

"Come and try it," the Missourian said.

Bugles began to call from the Mexican line and they started moving forward again. The Vera Cruz dragoons were on the Missouri left. A long line of infantry flanked them, moving toward the Missouri center. Nate started looking for their knives. He knew that the cavalry carried sabers but that didn't bother him so

240

much. He kept looking for the curved knives the infantry carried.

Skirmishers began to move from the Mexican line into the chaparral and hummocks of sand. There was a rattling sound. Nate didn't realize that it was the Mexicans opening fire till Kelly Goff said something. Nate looked at him and saw that Kelly was staring down at his arm. It was covered with blood.

"I've been hit," Kelly said.

"Take it easy," Gaines said. "If you hadn't looked, you wouldn't know it."

"I've been hit," Kelly said. His mouth was loose and there was a blank look in his eyes. He dropped his rifle and stood up, staring at his bloody arm. Lieutenant Hicklin shouted at him to get back down. "I've been hit," Kelly said. He turned and pushed his way through the rear rank and ran toward the river. Nate could hear him shouting over and over again that he'd been hit.

"When are we gonna shoot, Hicklin?" somebody yelled. "I've taken the rag off the bush at twice this distance."

Captain Reid had gathered fifteen or sixteen mounted men behind the infantry ranks, and Nate could hear him calling: "Hold your fire! Reserve your fire till you get the order!"

The Mexican line fired another volley. About fifty feet on Nate's right a volunteer stood up, holding his chest with both hands, and then pitched onto his face. The black powder smoke drifted across the Mexican front. They were so close now Nate could see that most of the infantry were barefoot.

The Mexicans had a single howitzer somewhere. Nate could not see it but he could hear its coughing sound every now and then. He had almost lost sight of the Vera Cruz dragoons in the drifting smoke and thick mesquite on the left. Lieutenant DeCourcy rode up behind D Company. He had been Doniphan's adjutant since the death of George Butler at Cubero. DeCourcy shouted an order at Hicklin, and Hicklin turned to the men and began yelling.

"Shoulder arms!" Hicklin said. "Left dress! By platoons . . . left into line . . . wheel!"

The men got all tangled up trying to execute the orders and DeCourcy shouted at Hicklin: "You're just confusing the hell out of them, Lieutenant! All we want to do is get them bent around in an elbow facing those dragoons! The dragoons are trying to move in on our rear and we've got to stop them!"

When the men understood the movement, they began a rough wheeling motion toward the *brazito*. Nate saw the Mexican dragoons then, moving through the thick chaparral along the arm of the river. When they first saw the movement of the American line, the Mexicans must have thought that it was a retreat, because they began shouting and Nate was near enough to hear them calling: "*¡Bueno . . . los goddamies . . . bueno, bueno!*"

They stopped shouting when the Missouri maneuver was completed, because they could see then that it blocked their flanking movement. There was a pause in the battle. The Mexican infantry quit firing. In the hush

Nate could hear one of the wounded Missourians groaning.

"They're going to charge," Hugh said.

A trumpet sounded from the Mexican line. Nate heard the crash of thick brush as the dragoons broke into a gallop through the chaparral. They presented a solid front of red coats and brass-plated helmets.

"Come on, Hicklin, let's fire," Nate said.

All along the line the men began to shout at Hicklin. The lieutenant looked helplessly back toward Captain Reid. The captain was checking his Colt. Major Gilpin came back from farther along the line.

"Hold your fire," he said. "The colonel says to reserve your fire."

Nate saw a silvery flicker along the Mexican front. The lances were down.

Nate got thirsty. He did not think that he had ever wanted a drink so badly. His mouth was dry and his throat closed up till he could hardly breathe. Then he got an itch on his back where he couldn't reach. He thought it was a hell of a time to get an itch. The Mexicans were so close now Nate could see their white teeth in their dark faces. There was a young Mexican officer in the lead who had a little mustache and a golden cross on the chest of his red coat. Nate was trembling and he didn't know whether it was he or the ground. All along the Missouri line men were shouting for Reid to give the order.

"Hugh," Nate said, "will you scratch my back up there by the shoulder blade. I got an itch I can't stand no longer."

"Fire!" somebody said. "Number Ones fire!"

It came from far down the line. It was repeated three or four times by nearer officers, and then their voices were drowned in the roar of guns. Nate saw that Hugh's gun was pointed at the sky when it went off. Everybody else was aiming at the Mexicans, but Hugh's gun was pointed up at the sky.

Nate was blinded by the black powder smoke. It had a greasy smell and it got in his lungs and made him cough.

"Number Twos!" Hicklin shouted. "Fire!"

Nate tried to get a target and squeezed his trigger. Nothing happened. He thought the gun had snapped and looked disgustedly down at the hammer. He saw the piece of paper caught in the breech and the smoke still coming out. He realized that he had fired with the Number Ones. He had fired without even realizing it. He couldn't even remember shooting. Everybody else in the Number Two rank must have done the same thing, because they were all looking sheepishly at their guns or hurriedly trying to reload. Hicklin looked fit to have apoplexy.

But it had accounted for the complete shattering of the Mexican dragoons. The smoke was clearing now and Nate could see the Mexican line. Horses were down everywhere, kicking and squealing, and the bodies of the men littered the marshy field. The Mexican officer with the mustache lay on his back twenty feet from the Company D line. His mouth was open and he was staring at the sky. Nearby another dragoon sat on the ground looking at his bloody stomach. Farther away a Mexican with his hands over his eyes was stumbling toward the Missouri regiment.

The dragoons had fallen back and were trying to re-form. They started wheeling toward the right for a charge on the forted wagons. The teamsters gave them a volley. Nate saw more Mexicans go down.

At the same time Reid and his squad of mounted men galloped from behind the Missouri lines. He struck the Mexicans before they were re-formed. His charge and the fire from the wagons completely broke the Mexican line.

Nate saw Reid gallop past a Mexican whose horse had been shot from under him. The Mexican fired at Reid and Nate thought that Reid was hit for sure. But the captain chopped the Mexican down with his saber as he galloped by. After that all Nate could see were the red backs of the dragoons dodging back and forth through the thickets as they disappeared.

Nate looked up toward the center and couldn't see the infantry. They had pulled back, too, leaving their dead and wounded littering the field. Nate couldn't begin to count the bodies. He could see some of them moving feebly and one man was crawling into the bushes. Nate looked back at the bodies of the dragoons sprawled in front of Company D. He wondered if he had hit one of them. He wondered if he had killed one of them.

He began to feel sick. He thought that it was the smell. The greasy smell of black powder was mingling with the hot smell of blood. There was no wind to carry it away or to break up the dark mist of powder that drifted across the scene.

The Missourians were getting restless and beginning to shout and yell. The officers had a hard time holding them in ranks. After a while a rider came back from Reid and reported to Doniphan. The word spread through the ranks that the Mexicans were in full retreat.

"I thought it was different than this," Nate told Hugh. "I thought it lasted longer or something."

Hugh didn't answer. He was staring out at the bodies on the field. His face was white and he kept moistening his lips and clearing his throat.

Because he spoke a little Spanish, Nate got on a detail to gather in the wounded. Charlie Hayes and Bristol and several others were with him. Some company wagons were driven from camp to carry the wounded Mexicans who couldn't walk. There were a lot of Mexican horses running around loose and Nate caught one and carved his initials in the fancy cactus-tree saddle and hitched the horse to the Company D wagon.

They came to a dragoon who had been wounded in the stomach. Nate called Jim Garrett over to help get the man into the wagon. As they lifted up the half-conscious Mexican, Nate saw Charlie Hayes farther out in the field.

Charlie was bent over the dead officer with the mustache. Charlie was taking the golden cross off the dragoon's coat. Charlie put the cross in his pocket and moved on to another officer. He went to one knee

246

beside the corpse and took two rings off the man's hand. He broke the chain that held the silver crucifix around the Mexican's neck and took that, too. Then he got up again and moved off, looking from side to side at the other bodies.

CHAPTER
SIXTEEN

At roll call next morning Nate heard the official casualty list for the Battle of Brazito. Hicklin announced that the 1st Missouri only had eight wounded and none killed. A count of the Mexican dead had come to over seventy and more than twice that wounded. Kelly Goff didn't report for roll and he was put on the books as a deserter.

They marched about ten that morning. Nate rode the Mexican mare he had caught on the battlefield the day before. She was hard-mouthed, the way many Mexican horses were, but was a middling good single-footer. They expected to meet the Mexicans in battle again and Doniphan ordered them to march with loaded guns. The following day, about six miles north of El Paso, they reached the pass where the river flowed between the shoulders of two barren mountains. Some Mexicans with a white flag crossed the ford and Nate sat at rest with 1,000 ragged Missourians while Doniphan negotiated.

Captain Reid was in on the talk, and, when he came back to Company D, he told some of the men what had happened. Apparently the Battle of Brazito had broken the Mexican morale. The Vera Cruz dragoons had been withdrawn to Chihuahua City and the militia infantry had been disbanded. After the truce talk the 1st Missouri crossed the river and marched into El Paso.

A broad valley spread out ahead of them. Nate had heard that there were 4,000 people in the El Paso district. The column passed through miles of cornfields and orchards and vineyards where little heaps of earth stood in long lines covering the grapevines to protect them from the frost. The gridiron of irrigation ditches cut up the land as far as Nate could see. They finally reached the town, a church and a handful of buildings scattered around the plaza.

The Mexicans stood in doorways or in lines against the mud walls, watching the Americans pass. Among them Nate saw men wearing bloody bandages — casualties of the Battle of Brazito. It gave him a prickly feeling to be so close to men who had just been shooting at him.

The regiment went into camp on the flats south of the plaza. Nate got sentry duty till retreat. At his post he could see the traders puffing in. The Conestogas were parked three deep about the plaza. Their long lines stretched through the crooked streets and out into the cornfields beyond the buildings. The traders set up shop immediately. Crowds of Mexicans surrounded the wagons and their haggling voices turned Nate nervous. The war made less sense to him all the time. These were the people who had been trying to kill the Americans two days ago. They still hated the Americans. Nate had seen it in their faces when he passed them. Yet they were falling over themselves to buy from the Americans, paying three and four times more than they knew they should, and whooping it up fit to deafen a man.

In spite of the good showing at the *brazito*, their maneuvering had been so miserable that Doniphan put the regiment to drilling again every day. Bill Hicklin left it all up to the sergeants. They had made such a joke of his performance at the *brazito* that he had burned all his manuals and declared that he would never conduct another drill.

Nate knew that Doniphan was waiting for the artillery to come from Santa Fé and was trying to find out what had happened to General Wool. Nate was glad for the rest. He'd had his fill of marching. He had given his only plug of tobacco to the Indians back at Bear Springs and he'd been hankering after a decent chaw for so long that he was beginning to taste it in his sleep. He finally made a deal with one of the Company D men who had been paid at Padillas to stand a month of his sentry duty for a dollar. He found a trader who sold him a pigtail called Crown of Virginia. It was five times the Missouri price and the lump makers had got more stem than leaf in it and the casing was so heavy with rum and sugar that he got a toothache at the first bite. While he was idling in the plaza enjoying it, Hugh Long brought an old Mexican to him. The man said that his name was Josélito Otero. There were brown spots on his waxy face and he held his hands together to keep them from shaking. He said that he had been hunting Nate for a long time. At his house, he said, was a man with yellow hair who was very sick, and a woman named Inez.

Nate got an empty feeling in his stomach, almost a sickness, and he wondered if it was the shock or the thought of seeing Inez again. He went with Otero out of town. They followed the river up toward the falls. They crossed fields where the wind was a gale whipping through the little trees and scattering the mounds of earth that protected the grapevines. Beyond the crumbling riverbanks rose sand hills, freckled with mesquite, and the gray skeletons of bare winter trees, and the dusty, violet haze of the mountains that formed the pass. Near the dam of rocks and brush they reached the mud house hidden back among the willows in the bottoms. A candle burning in a niche lighted the room. Its feeble glow revealed the three people — a shriveled old woman crouched in one corner, Kirby lying under a ragged blanket on the floor, and Inez kneeling beside him. She rose as Nate entered, turning toward him. Nate stopped just within the door, staring at her. The candle flame wavered in the wind and the black shadows crawled across the walls. The door creaked softly as Josélito shut it behind him.

Inez had her black hair pulled tightly against her head and tied in a bun at the back. It made her face look exotic, older. She held a shawl tightly about her shoulders, black *crêpe de Chine* splashed with flame-colored flowers. The hem of her heavy skirt was frayed and dusty and he saw that her little shoes were broken and tied together with rawhide.

"I've been wondering about you," he said. His voice shook a little. "You don't know how I been wondering about you."

She touched her throat with one hand. She moistened her lips. "Nate," she said. "Nate . . ."

She broke off, looking at Kirby. The man's head was tilted back so that his eye sockets and his cheeks looked sunken and skull-like. His whole face was as yellow as his long matted beard and he was sweating so much that his clothes were soaked. Nate walked to him and knelt down.

"Is he conscious?"

"He has been sleeping," she said. "Such a heavy sleep."

"It's the scurvy," Nate said. "I guess I've seen enough of it in camp. I'll get the surgeon."

"No," Inez said sharply. "I mean . . . not yet. Not until you see Colonel Doniphan. You must tell Doniphan that Kirby tried to keep his part of the agreement. He did everything he could . . . he cannot be shot simply because my father is a stubborn, blind old man . . ."

She broke off, putting her hand to her mouth, and he said: "Never mind. I guess I've known Kirby was a deserter."

She bowed her head, looking at her tightly gripped hands. "It can be changed, Nate. You can make the arrangement with Doniphan. He can make Kirby a soldier again . . . then it will be safe for the surgeon to come."

252

Nate paced the room, massaging the end of his nose. "It ain't that easy. I have to know what Kirby's got into. I heard Ganoe was caught at Fray Cristóbal by Lieutenant Colonel Jackson. How come they didn't get you?"

She told him that they had left Valverde with Ganoe on December 15th, when it became obvious that Kirby couldn't make arrangements with Doniphan to let Ganoe through ahead of the army. Ganoe had been disgusted with Kirby and hadn't wanted to take them but Kirby had threatened to warn Doniphan of Ganoe's attempt unless he let them go with him. Inez had realized by then what a trap Kirby was in. He had left Santa Fé illegally and Price had undoubtedly already posted him as a deserter.

"I pleaded with him to throw himself on the mercy of Colonel Doniphan," she said. "But he was afraid . . . and he had this investment with Ganoe, this . . . this . . . what is the word?"

"Deal," Nate said bitterly. "This big deal."

She nodded miserably. She told him that Ganoe almost got away, but the day after they left Valverde, Doniphan had dispatched Lieutenant Colonel Jackson and 300 men south along the trail to block any attempt on the part of the traders to get ahead of the army. From the heights of the Fray Cristóbal Mountains the scouts for the wagon train had sighted the dust raised by the pursuing cavalry, and it had given Kirby and Inez time to escape by horseback before Ganoe was overtaken.

The trip through the Dead Man's March had been a desperate ride. Kirby was already coming down with the scurvy. By the time they reached the crossing above El Paso, he could hardly stay in the saddle. He had collapsed near the dam and the old couple had taken them in. When Inez stopped talking, it was utterly silent in the room. Nate couldn't even hear Kirby breathing.

"Well," he said awkwardly, "I'll do what I can." He didn't want to go but he didn't want to stay, either. He felt suddenly shy, ill at ease. He scratched his head. He didn't know what to do with his hands. He pulled the pigtail of tobacco from his pocket and started to take a bite. He saw her frowning at it.

"It's just a habit I got when I git nervous or something, I guess," he said. "When I git nervous, I just natcherly pull out a plug and take a chaw. You don't favor it?"

"The smell. Maybe it is the smell. Maybe it is too sweet or something. It is one of the things that I could never get used to. About Kirby, I mean."

"Well, I don't blame you. It is sort of a dirty habit." He put the pigtail away. He wiped his hands on his britches. "Well, I guess I better go. I'll let you know about Doniphan as soon as I can."

CHAPTER
SEVENTEEN

Inez stood in the doorway a long time after Nate was out of sight. It comforted her to think of his being so near. She had the feeling of a change in him. He had still seemed shy with her, awkward, but she had sensed a new manhood behind it. He had gone through the Navajo campaign and had fought at the Battle of Brazito. He was truly a soldier now. A good soldier. The thought added to her comfort, but she was surprised that it should come to her in such terms. Then she realized how closely it was connected with what had disturbed her so about Kirby these last weeks.

It was an insidious thing, a doubt of Kirby, a disillusionment she hated. But she could not deny the fact. Kirby was a deserter. It seemed to violate everything she had ever believed in. She was beginning to realize how incomplete her escape had been, how impossible it was to shed the values of a lifetime. Despite the stubborn blindness she hated in her father, it seemed to her now that there was a certain grim honesty about his inflexibility. He had remained true to himself and his people. When the governor and the army were fleeing, when the rich were fawning on the *gringos* and the poor were kneeling to them, her father had possessed the courage to stand for what he believed. He had not deserted. In his world a deserter was a man who ran from the enemy, a man who left his post when his comrades needed him most. A deserter was a coward.

She recoiled from the word. Kirby was not a coward. Whatever he was, he was not a coward. Kirby had simply made a mistake. Everything he had done had been for her, an attempt to prove his worthiness to her father.

She went back inside to help Josélito's wife fix their meager dinner. The old woman's name was Antonia and she was almost blind from a lifetime of wood smoke and windblown sand. Josélito was a woodcutter. He had grown too old for the arduous work of chopping and was forced to spend the day with his wife scavenging along the river for driftwood.

On the morning after Nate had come, the two old people were gone shortly after sunup, leaving Inez alone with Kirby in the house. Kirby had been delirious during the night and was in a heavy sleep when Inez started the morning chores. She took a bull-hide bucket to the dam and had to break through the thin crust of ice for water. Josélito had told her that some winters the ice was so thick a heavy wagon could be driven across the river at the pass. When she returned to the house through the mesquite thickets, she saw a red mare hitched near the door. The initials N.H. had been carved in the ornate cactus-tree saddle, and she guessed that it was Nate's horse. She opened the door and saw Nate kneeling beside Kirby with his back to her. Kirby was in a delirium, thrashing and talking in such a loud, wild voice that Nate hadn't heard the door open.

"She's left me, ain't she?" Kirby said. "She's gone back to her pa . . ."

"She wouldn't run out on you, Kirby," Nate said.

"Don't lie to me. Nate . . . tell that old man to bank the fire, will you, my backsides is plumb burnt off. Well, I don't blame her, Nate. I wasn't good enough for her. You know that? Certain for sure. That's the first time I ever admitted it about anybody, but I know I wasn't good enough. I tried, Nate, believe me I tried . . ."

"Don't talk that way."

"It's the truth. I didn't do right by her. Something about her . . . I never felt this way before. She scares me . . . that's crazy, ain't it? A woman don't do that to a man . . . scared of dying maybe, or walking past a graveyard after dark . . . but not a woman. What is it, Nate? These people . . . they're different from our girls. They look the same on top but down underneath there's something . . . you ever gambled? When you know you're losing and you go back anyway, something keeps pulling you back. I never seen her cry. Why don't she ever cry, Nate? When I first met her, she thought a kiss would give her a baby and she got the shakes when I touched her. I thought she was just a child, a girl not yet a woman. I thought a man could learn all about her in a few hours. I don't think I'll ever really learn about her. Close the door, will you? They're trying to freeze me. They took all my blankets away so's I'll freeze myself to death."

257

Nate turned toward the door and saw Inez. She stepped inside, setting the pail of water down, and closed the door behind her. Kirby was thrashing from side to side, his voice rising to a hysterical babble.

"I married her for the wool. Did you know that, Nate? I didn't really mean to hurt you, but I thought, if I could marry her, maybe she could get her pa to give us a dowry of some sheep and I could trade the wool to Ganoe . . ."

"Kirby, stop talking like that. You're out of your head."

"It's the gospel." Kirby didn't seem to see Inez. His head was thrown back, his eyes closed, and he was dripping sweat. He turned from side to side like a man in agony. "You might as well know, now that she's gone. At Taos . . . when you come to get her . . . when you told me Doniphan's offer, I thought maybe I could make a deal with the old man, let him have her back and forget the marriage if he'd give me ten wagonloads of wool . . ."

"Kirby!" Nate almost shouted it, putting his hand over Kirby's mouth. He turned to look at Inez, a tortured expression on his young face. She was staring emptily at her husband, trying not to understand what she had heard. She felt nauseated. She put her hands to her cheeks. They were cold as wax.

Kirby started thrashing again, tearing Nate's hand off his mouth. "I got to tell somebody, Nate. It's been festering in me like a boil. Why does she make me feel ashamed? I never felt ashamed with any other woman. I

258

was a-going to sell her back to her pa, Nate. My own wife. All she meant was another deal . . ."

"Kirby, for God's sake, will you shut up!"

"She was a *verónica*, Nate, did you know that?" Kirby fought with Nate, trying to lunge up. "These brothers, they march up a hill on Easter Sunday . . . whip themselves with cactus thorns till they're all covered with blood, and then these *verónicas* . . . these *verónicas* walk beside them and wipe the blood off." Kirby laughed crazily, his face dripping sweat. "None of our girls was ever *verónicas* when they were fifteen, Nate. Did you ever think of that? None of our girls ever got sold back to their pas for ten wagonloads of wool."

Inez turned her back on them. She closed her eyes. She crossed herself.

Hail Mary, full of grace; the Lord is with thee; blessed art thou among women . . . .She didn't know whether she said it aloud or to herself, in Spanish or in English, asking help, asking strength. She did not know how long she prayed. Finally she stopped. She could no longer hear Kirby's voice behind her. She opened her eyes. The nausea was gone. She wanted to cry but she could not cry. She felt spent, numbed, drained of feeling. She turned slowly and saw that Kirby had stopped thrashing. His eyes were closed in his sunken face and he was shuddering violently. Nate had taken his serape off and was spreading it over Kirby. Inez crossed to the coals of the fire, putting precious wood on for more heat. She got the only other blanket in the room and knelt beside Kirby and spread the blanket over him on top of the serape. Nate met her eyes, looked away quickly, and rose to pace restlessly around the little room. Kirby's breathing settled down, his mouth sagged open, and he fell into a deep and troubled sleep. Inez rose, her hands in her skirt, her head bowed. She did not want to look into Nate's eyes again. She felt ashamed and could not understand why. Nate cleared his throat.

"He didn't mean that, Inez . . . what he said about the wool . . . I mean . . . he was out of his head."

She did not answer. She wondered why she was so calm. She wondered why she had not cried when she first heard it, or acted hysterically, or why she had not run out of the house. There were things about herself she could not understand. It made her think of what Kirby had said about her — a child, a woman, it was hard to tell where one left off and the other began.

"He must love you," Nate said. "He wouldn't've stuck with you this long. Certain for sure. He never stuck with any woman this long. He . . ." A blank look crossed his face. He wiped his hand ruefully across his mouth and looked at the floor, shaking his head. "That beats all, don't it? Me arguing his case."

"Why not?" she said. She was surprised that there was no bitterness in her voice. "You are *compadres*."

"Yeah . . ." Nate looked past her. "Jayán told me that meant something like co-godfathers. He said you couldn't git no closer than *compadres*."

She moved closer to him. "Kirby is fortunate to have such a *compadre*. He does not know how fortunate.

Never stop being that way, Nate. He needs you. We both need you."

A strange look came to his eyes, something close to pain. Nate moistened his lips. "Inez . . . I . . . I'll try to help you, but maybe I ain't so good a *compadre* as you think. I come here today to tell you that I went to Colonel Doniphan. I was afraid to tell him right out that Kirby was here. I sort of sounded him out. Things look pretty bad. Rumors have been coming down from up north that there's some kind of trouble in Santa Fé. Doniphan hasn't got any definite word yet, just what he hears from the Mexicans, but he says, if there was an uprising, and your pa was involved, and any of Colonel Price's men were killed, Kirby will have blood on his hands."

The news shook her. It was something she had dreaded for a long time. "Kirby cannot be blamed," she said desperately. "He did what he could."

Nate said: "Doniphan told me he ordered Kirby to stay in Santa Fé. He said, if Kirby showed up here, he'd have to arrest him as a deserter. We've got to keep Kirby here. I'm afraid to tell the surgeon. I don't know how much good that would do anyway. All they have in their medicine chests is some Sappington's Fever Pills and some zinc sulphate that was supposed to help the eye trouble the men got from having the sand blown at them all the time. The fever pills sure didn't cure the scurvy all of us were getting at Valverde, and, whenever I used the sulphate, it just made me blinder. About all the surgeon would do is purge Kirby and tell him to rest."

261

She didn't answer. She felt her hands knot hopelessly in her skirt. She had counted so much on Doniphan.

"Perhaps if we wait," she said. "Perhaps if these rumors are not true about the trouble in the north. Then maybe Doniphan would make Kirby a soldier again."

"There's a chance," he said. He didn't sound too convinced. He pulled at his nose. "Well . . . uh . . . I got to git back before morning parade."

He opened the door and she followed him outside. As Nate unhitched his mare, she saw that he was shivering in the wind.

"I will get your serape," she said.

"Kirby'll need it more than me," he said.

"I cannot send you back so cold," she said.

She threw her shawl across his shoulders. He wasn't shivering any more. For a moment he was completely still, looking at her. His black hair was long and tangled and made curly mats above his ears. He kept his beard hacked off to a spade shape with his Bowie. It made him look gaunt, older. The pale light seemed to draw out the ague color she had become so used to in the Missourians. It gave the ridges of his cheeks a sallow shine. He turned to mount his horse. He didn't look at her again. He lifted the mare to a canter across the fields toward the road.

She watched him go. Despite the change in him, the new manhood, he still seemed so nervous and self-conscious when he was with her. She was surprised that she should feel so close to Nate. She had seen him only a few brief times, but Kirby had talked so much about him, and she knew how close the two of them had been. Perhaps that was it. She felt a part of that closeness now. The fight at Taos had been forgotten and they were together again.

Reluctantly she went back inside and stood looking down at her sleeping husband. He looked so sick, so helpless. She didn't want to remember what he had said in his delirium. She didn't want to think about it.

Nate must be right. Kirby must love her. He wouldn't have stayed with her, gone through so much with her. Perhaps he hadn't loved her when he married her — she could think of it now without the sick shock that had come when she first heard him say it — but he must love her now. The tenderness he had shown her, the passion, the understanding — it was the one thing she'd had to cling to in all the trouble they'd had since they were married. He had made a mistake in the beginning, but now it was over, and she could forgive him. The women of Mexico were good at that.

Kirby didn't think that he'd ever hurt so much. The backs of his legs were covered with mulberry spots and bruises so big a body would think somebody had been pounding on him with a wagon tongue. His mouth was sore, and once, when he'd raised up on an elbow to spit, he'd seen a tooth come out, his gums were that rotten and spongy. He had fever and chills and his whole body was so touchy that he had trouble sometimes not tearing off his clothes. He wondered if he was going to die.

He hated depending so much on Inez. He hated being beholden to anybody. Antonía had taught Inez about the medicine. She showed Inez how to prepare the *contra yerba* that would stop his diarrhea. She went out with Inez to gather the leathery leaves from the blood of the dragon for his diseased gums. Inez mixed osha roots and brown sugar into a thick syrup and gave it to him when he coughed. Every two or three hours she mixed some cornmeal with water and fed it to Kirby with a wooden spoon.

He didn't think that anybody had ever done so much for him, or shown him so much kindness or love, even Nate. It made him feel guilty. It made him remember again what had been on his mind when he first married her. It made him think of all the lies he had told her. He wanted to make it up somehow. He had told her that he was Catholic but he had always been too impatient even to make a pretense of learning the prayers she wanted to teach him. Now he settled down to memorizing the catechism. He let her pick a namesake for him. He had always been embarrassed by his middle name and hadn't told anybody in years, but, when he admitted that it was Michael, she said that of course his namesake must be St. Michael, the archangel who weighed the souls on a scale and rescued them from the devil in the hour of death. He admitted that was probably it, and his mother had stopped raising him in the faith so young that he had forgotten, and was disgusted with himself for the lie.

Nate came when he could, bringing the dried peaches and limes and apricots the surgeons had been

264

prescribing for other scurvy patients. He had no more news about the uprising in the north, and thought that the best thing Kirby could do was lie low till he had recovered. Nate never mentioned the fight they'd had at Taos, but Kirby never felt comfortable with him. Something lay between them, a gulf, a shadow. He had the same feeling, less tangibly, with Inez. It seemed connected with his desertion. He realized that she knew the truth now, but, when he tried to explain things, she refused to discuss it. He saw an expression in her eyes, her face — he couldn't understand it. He wasn't really a deserter. It was just a technicality. And why should she care anyway? A woman didn't know anything about war. They were the ones who were always trying to hold onto their men and not wanting them to go marching off and pleading with them not to go away and get killed.

Recovery came slowly. The purple bruises faded on his legs and he was able to bend his knees without grimacing in pain. The fever was gone and the gums were healing. His strength was returning and he began taking walks in the mesquite thickets along the river.

Almost every day the old people went out along the river to gather wood and sell it in town. One afternoon toward the end of January, when they were alone in the house, Inez showed Kirby some knitting needles the old woman had given her.

"I will need them now," she said. "I was afraid to tell you. I know that was foolish . . . but it has such newness . . . I mean it has never happened to me before. I know that it happens to all women, and it is not really so new, but it is new to me, anyway. It is not that I am not happy. I do not want you to think that I am not happy. A person can be frightened and happy at the same time, I think . . ."

"Honey, what are you jabbering about?"

"I am trying to tell you, Kirby. I have had these feelings, certain things have happened, and I told them to Antonía, and she knew immediately. What I mean is . . . we . . . we are going to have a baby."

She stood before him with her hands in the fold of her skirt. She had been looking at him, but, when their eyes met, she blushed deeply and lowered her face.

"You are angry?" she asked.

"Angry?" he said. He touched his face. "Do I look angry? It's just . . . well, I never gave it any thought. I don't know how I feel. Yes, I do. Some kind of shock . . . I guess I feel like the first man in history that got kicked in the belly by a mule and felt happy about it."

She made a choked sound and came into his arms. She pressed her face against his chest and he held her tightly. Her body was trembling against his and he couldn't tell if she was crying or laughing, or both.

"I think I would desire it to be a girl," she said. "Unless you want a boy. Of course, you would probably wish a boy. A man always wishes a boy. If you wish a boy, I wish a boy."

"Not unless you want a girl," he said. "But if it is a boy, I tell you, back in Missouri there's a power of hunting to be done. I'll give him a gun all his own, and show him the best fishing holes, and teach him about raising stock. That's something I really know. Nate'll be his cousin. Don't that beat all. Nate'll be his cousin."

"I am so happy you are happy," she said. "I was afraid . . . I mean . . . the way you might feel . . ."

"I feel happy," he said. He grimaced. "But I guess I feel worried now, too." He disengaged himself and walked across the room, his head bowed, tugging thoughtfully at his yellow beard. "It's a powerful responsibility. We got to do something about money. We're plumb broke."

"You always got enough before."

"Gambling. How can I play cards now? How can I even go into town?"

"Colonel Doniphan will do something. If we only have patience . . . he will make you a soldier again."

"What good'll that do us? The army ain't had a cent of pay since November. I'm through counting on Doniphan. He let us down too many times already. We got to do it ourselves, Inez. I'll go to Ganoe. He's still got that money we invested with him."

"Kirby, not Ganoe. You always get into trouble with Ganoe."

"I got to git some money. I'll make some kind of a deal with Ganoe. Maybe I can help him give Doniphan the slip again. Nate says some traders have already done it. We can get a ride with Ganoe to Chihuahua City. There's all kinds of deals down there."

"Kirby, why must it always be some kind of deal? Why can't you do something honest for once?"

"Honey, just because it's a deal don't make it dishonest."

267

"What about the sabers?"

"The sabers?"

"Yes, the army sabers you were going to sell. What about the woman you married because you thought you could use her to sell some wool."

"Inez . . . I never . . . who told you that?"

"You were out of your head for two weeks. You'd be surprised what you talked about."

"Inez, you can't believe all I said, you're upset . . ."

"Yes, I am upset. I thought I could forgive you, Kirby. I thought I could forget all that I'd heard. You loved me. That was all that mattered. Maybe you didn't love me in the beginning, but after a while you loved me . . . that's why you couldn't make the deal in Santa Fé, that's why you couldn't trade me back to my father for some wool . . ."

"No, Inez, no . . ."

"I thought I loved you enough to understand. But not if you don't quit now. Not if you go back to Ganoe and start this all over again."

He grabbed her by the shoulders. "Honey, maybe you're right, maybe I did have some crazy notion about making a deal with your pa, but that wasn't the only reason I married you. You got to believe that. I loved you from the first. I love you now."

"Then stay with me now. Don't go to Ganoe."

"I've got to. It's the only thing we got left. Why is it always this thing we fight about? A man's got to make his way."

"By deserting his army and selling things that belong to his government."

"I didn't desert, dammit. I did all I could do to get back in.

"I wanted to believe that," she said. "I tried to believe it. I tried to believe all the things you told me."

"Then believe me now. We can't just sit around and wait for some money. We've got to do something."

"We can pray. There is always an answer in prayer."

She crossed to the niche in the wall where her statue of *Santa* Rita stood. She knelt down and began to pray in Spanish.

"Don't jabber that monkey talk in front of me," he said.

She crossed herself. "I am praying for you. I am asking *Santa* Rita to intercede for us and make you see that you are wrong."

"Is it wrong to want my kid to grow up decent? Is it wrong to want to support my wife, to . . . will you listen to me? Will you stop talking to that little statue? Every time we git in trouble, you talk to that little statue. It ain't helped you out yet, has it? It ain't put the clothes on your back or put the food in your mouth. Every time you don't want to talk to me, you talk with that little statue. Inez, will you listen . . . I'm sick of seeing you down on your knees, jabbering a lot of gibberish that don't mean a damn' thing. We've got to settle this once and for all."

She bowed her head more deeply, crossing herself, and the murmur of her voice did not stop. He let out a frustrated curse and stepped in front of her, sweeping the image out of its niche. He saw it break into pieces against the floor. Inez put her hands to her face. All the blood had left her cheeks and her eyes were enormous and black. She made a low, groaning sound, staring dazedly at the broken image, and began to rock back and forth.

"Inez . . ." He held out his hand. "Inez, I didn't mean . . ."

She didn't seem to hear him. She kept rocking back and forth and making the groaning sound, and she had put her hands over her eyes now. He cursed helplessly and whirled to cross the room, yanking open the door and going outside. He didn't know why he should feel so ornery. He didn't know why he should feel so guilty for breaking the statue. It was just a little statue; there were hundreds of them in this country. He'd get her another one. He was through trying to figure out the whims of a woman. Couldn't she see that Ganoe was their only way out? He was going to Ganoe.

CHAPTER
EIGHTEEN

That night Colonel Doniphan was in his quarters. He had kept a fire going all afternoon but he still could not get warm enough. Most of the officers had long ago forgotten regulations and were wearing whatever extra clothes they could put their hands on. Over his uniform coat Doniphan wore a Saltillo serape. His head was poked through the hole in the middle and the corners of the tightly woven blanket fell below his waist. It was still not enough. He couldn't get close enough to the fire to stop the shivering that shook his body. His palms were clammy and he had a bile taste in his mouth and his head had ached for a week. He had a hard time hiding his chills from the staff. The surgeon had felt the heat of his face yesterday and had wanted to put him to bed. But he knew that once he gave in to the fever he was lost. When he had collapsed after the Turnham case, he hadn't been able to get out of bed for weeks.

He was afraid of what it would do to morale. He had seen the way the regiment went to pieces whenever he let go of the reins. When he had arrived at Valverde, conditions had been appalling. The other officers didn't seem to have any control over the men. If the Mexicans had attacked then, the 1st Missouri would have been wiped out.

Doniphan had often wondered what qualities gave him such influence over the volunteers. He thought that maybe it was his courtroom training. Half his life had been spent swaying men in large groups. Or maybe his personal feelings got through to them. They knew that a man wasn't just a name on the roster to him. He could never believe in the barrier the regular officers erected between themselves and their men. Maybe that's why he would never really make a good soldier. He was still disturbed about the two men found sleeping on sentry duty. Merritt and Gilpin and the other officers with regular military backgrounds had been insisting that the two men be court-martialed and shot. It would have been automatic in the regulars. But Doniphan couldn't do it. He had come 1,000 miles beside those boys. He had seen them going crazy for water south of the Arkansas. He had frozen with them at Bear Springs. He had watched them march their feet bloody down the Río Grande and suffer the agonies of scurvy at Valverde.

There was a knock on his door. When he answered it, he found the corporal of the guard with Major Meriwether Lewis Clark. Doniphan had been expecting Clark for days and drew him eagerly inside. After the first greetings Clark dumped a pair of saddlebags on the table and crossed to the fire, stamping the numbness out of his feet.

"We've been up to our necks in snow," he said. "My battery's about three days behind, a hundred and seventeen men and six guns."

Doniphan couldn't hide his disappointment. "I asked for the whole battalion."

"Colonel Price wouldn't send it. You can't blame him . . . the way things were threatening up there."

"We've heard nothing but a lot of wild rumors."

"They couldn't be much wilder than the truth," Clark said. "Colonel Price was already worried about an uprising when I left on January Second. That's why he would give me only one battery. On the Nineteenth the whole thing blew up in Price's face. We got the news by courier. A mob of Pueblo Indians and New Mexicans massacred Governor Bent and five other Americans at Taos. The revolt is spreading all through the territory."

Doniphan couldn't hide what it did to him. His whole face felt pinched, sunken. "What are Price's chances?"

"Hard to say. He marched to Taos immediately, but he couldn't gather his whole regiment. Not more than three hundred and fifty men. The enemy is estimated at anywhere between a thousand and three thousand. You'll find Price's communications to me in there."

Clark motioned at the saddlebags. Doniphan poured Clark a glass of Pass brandy and then crossed to open the saddlebags. There were some orders, a list of the known ringleaders among the insurgents. One of the names was Agustín Torreón, Inez's brother. Another was *Don* Miguel Torreón.

Doniphan's fist closed involuntarily on the paper. "This Torreón . . . this *Don* Miguel . . . ?"

"*Don* Miguel had openly declared for Archuleta even before I left," Clark said. "Archuleta has so far escaped but both *Don* Miguel and his son were put under arrest the day after Governor Bent was murdered in Taos. There will be a court-martial. I'm sure the Torreóns will be among the ringleaders executed for this."

Doniphan couldn't remain still. Pacing across the room, he wondered if he wasn't more responsible than anybody for Governor Bent's murder at Taos. If he had just handled it a little differently. If he hadn't been fool enough to try to make a deal with a man of Kirby's stripe. Or would it simply have forced *Don* Miguel's hand sooner? He realized that Clark was asking him something.

"Have you heard anything from General Wool?"

Doniphan was slow in answering. At last he said: "Not ... not from Wool directly. But plenty of indications. From all I can gather, Major, I think Wool's campaign has been abandoned."

"They wouldn't do that. Chihuahua's too important. If it's not taken, Taylor will be threatened on his rear by all of northern Mexico."

"Nonetheless, I don't think we can count on Wool. It looked pretty easy on the map, a march from San Antonio to Chihuahua City. But then Wool got into the country with a brigade of green volunteers. I have a scout with me, James Kirker. He knows that part of Mexico. He doesn't think Wool can possibly get through those Coahuila Mountains. If Wool were in striking distance of Chihuahua, we'd know it. If he hasn't been wiped out, it's my bet he'll have to abandon the whole campaign and join General Taylor on the coast."

"That puts us in an impossible position," Clark said. "If Price can't put down that revolt in New Mexico, we'll be caught in the middle here. Cut off at our rear and outnumbered at our front."

Clark scowled and stamped his feet. Doniphan could see how the news had shaken the man. Why did it always take so much longer for the orthodox mind to adjust to a new idea? Major Meriwether Lewis Clark was a West Point man, brother-in-law of Kearny, a veteran of the Black Hawk War, named after the man who had been his father's companion in the great exploration. With such a tradition behind him he didn't bother to hide his doubts about the volunteer officers. He had never shown Doniphan any direct antagonism but Doniphan always had the feeling of an uneasy truce.

"I admit I feel sort of trapped," Doniphan said. "All I can do is follow my orders. General Kearny gave me our destination, Major. If Chihuahua City is to be taken, I guess the First Missouri will have to do it alone . . ."

He trailed off at the sound of a hard-ridden horse coming down the street and pulling to a halt in front of his quarters. The sentry at his door called out a challenge, there was an answer, and finally a knock on the door. Doniphan opened it to find a dusty volunteer standing beside the sentry, his lathered horse blowing and stamping in the street behind. The man didn't salute.

"The patrol caught another deserter over by the traders' camp, Colonel. The O.D. sent me ahead to find out if you wanted him brought here or straight to the guardhouse."

"I'll see him here. Lieutenant Merritt's the officer of the day, isn't he?"

"Yes, sir."

"Do you know the prisoner?"

"Lieutenant Merritt said it was Kirby Hatcher."

Doniphan made a soft sound of surprise. Yet he knew he shouldn't be surprised. He remembered Nate's coming to him several weeks ago, questioning him about Kirby. He wondered if Nate had been sounding him out then — had known that Kirby was here.

The rider turned back to his horse, but before Doniphan could shut the door, he heard a man running down the street from the square. Nate came into view, dodging past the horse and the sentry, stopping a foot away from Doniphan. His bearded young face was flushed and he was panting from the run.

"Colonel, you got to do something . . . it's all over town . . . they've caught Kirby in the traders' camp . . ."

"You knew he was down here, didn't you? What's he doing here, Nate?"

"I don't know. What does it matter? You can't court-martial him, Colonel."

"He's a deserter, Nate."

"You promised he wouldn't be posted. You made a deal with him, when you first sent me to get him at

276

Taos. He kept his part of the bargain. He brought the girl back."

"He had no intention of keeping the bargain. Don't you think I got any dispatches at Valverde? Colonel Price said Kirby left Santa Fé as soon as I was out of sight,"

"It wasn't like that. You left about October Twenty-Sixth. Kirby didn't go to Padillas for his pay till the middle of November. That means he stayed in Santa Fé nigh onto a month after you left."

"And right after Kirby left, *Don* Miguel joined Diego Archuleta. There's been a revolt up there now. Governor Bent and a lot more Americans have been murdered. *Don* Miguel Torreón is going to be executed as one of the ringleaders. I think Kirby's name ought to be right there alongside of Torreón's."

Doniphan saw that the news shook Nate. The young man was slow in answering. He moved his head doggedly. "You can't blame Kirby for all that. There's a thousand Mexicans that would've been in the revolt, whether Kirby run off with Inez or not."

"Maybe so. But maybe Torreón wouldn't. And a lot of the other big families that followed Torreón. Without them, Archuleta's chances would've been cut in half. He might never have gotten the thing going. I'm not fool enough to think anybody can pin down exactly where the scales tip in a thing like this. But for a while Kirby had the balance in his hands. Torreón didn't go over to Archuleta till after Kirby left Santa Fé with the girl. Doesn't that mean anything to you?"

277

Nate began pacing back and forth. "You ain't in a courtroom now. You ain't the famous Alexander W. Doniphan mixing up witnesses and scaring judges and spinning heads on a jury that don't know which end of the mule hee-haws. You made a deal with Kirby to bring the girl back and he did it. What happened afterward ain't his fault. You made a deal, Colonel. If you back out of it over a little technicality, I'll make you wish you were the one that got shot."

"Soldier," Clark said sharply, "you're speaking to your commander."

"Never mind, Major," Doniphan said softly.

"You can't allow this," Clark told him furiously. "You can't allow this kind of insubordination, Colonel."

Doniphan hardly heard him. He was looking at Nate, his eyes creased thoughtfully at the corners. He could see the disillusionment in Nate's face — and knew it was disillusionment in him. He wondered why it had to be so painful to grow up.

"When are you going to shake free, Nate?" he asked. "In all honesty, I don't think Kirby kept his bargain. If Merritt has captured him, he'll stand court-martial. He's twisted this mule's tail just about as far as it will go."

Nate didn't have time to answer. A distant crash of shots came from the center of town. Nate wheeled to look down the street toward the crowded square. By the torchlight Doniphan could see a turmoil in the mob where the main road entered the south side of the plaza; there was more shouting than usual, and Doniphan could see the heads of mounted men above

278

the crowd. There was another single shot, and Nate made an unintelligible sound and started running toward the square.

Doniphan knew what he was afraid of. A Mexican attack couldn't be ruled out. Doniphan turned back inside his quarters long enough to snatch his gun from its holster. It was one of Samuel Colt's first efforts, the same five-shot, cap-and-ball Paterson that Doniphan had used in the Mormon war eight years before. He told the sentry to stay at his post and followed Nate toward the crowded square. He heard Major Clark's accouterments clashing and rattling like a cavalry charge as he followed at the double. Lieutenant Colonel Jackson burst out of the quarters next to Doniphan's, trying to hold his revolver and pull his braces on over his shoulders at the same time.

"We'd better get a company down to the river!" he shouted. "The horses are the first thing they'll go for!"

"I don't know that it's an attack," Doniphan said. "Waldo has A Company at the ready in the barracks. Hold them there till you get further orders."

Nate had disappeared into the horde of troopers and Mexicans that choked the square any time of the day or night. They were all milling around and shouting at each other and trying to get over to the south side of the square to see what had happened. Doniphan elbowed his way through, passing the line of big Conestogas parked in front of the church. Each wagon drew its circle of Mexican customers trying to make a deal. The Missouri traders stood up on the high seats or inside the tail gates, holding bolts of calico or tin-framed mirrors or Bowie knives that they had been trading, all gaping off in the direction of the shots. The volunteers had a card game going on in every open patch of ground in the square. Most of them had quit playing and were trying to see what had happened, but they were still bunched around the layouts and Doniphan couldn't take a straight line in any direction without running through a game. He wasn't in any mood to dodge back and forth, and he pushed through a group of Company B men gathered around a Mexican monte thrower, looking for the source of the shooting. Six feet beyond, a dozen men were squatting or standing around a chuck-a-luck layout. In trying to get through Doniphan tripped on the dice cage and fell on his face. The volunteers made an uproar with their laughter.

"Why didn't you tell us you wanted in on the play, Aleck?" one of the men asked. "We'd've made room for you."

"I put out an order to stop these damned games in the street!" Doniphan shouted. "If you don't clear away, I'll throw all of you in the guardhouse."

He was on his feet again, and he saw a horse holder hanging onto the reins of five horses in the mouth of an alley on the south side of the square. Nate was pushing through the crowd of jabbering Mexicans and shouting soldiers that surrounded the horse holder. Nate said something to the man, got an answer, and turned to disappear down the alley. As soon as the horse holder saw Doniphan elbowing through the excited mob, he shouted: "It's Kirby Hatcher, sir. We were bringin' him in and he got away. Lieutenant Merritt's got the patrol back in them alleys a-hunting him now."

Doniphan squeezed between a pair of nervous horses and plunged into the same alley Nate had taken. It was crooked and winding, too narrow for the horses. He had a breathless feeling. He didn't know if he was winded from the run or just plain scared. He knew how much trouble Nate had had with Merritt. The lieutenant blamed his humiliation at Valverde on Nate, and still thought that it was Nate who had tried to kill him with the mules. If Nate tried to save Kirby now, if Nate got in Merritt's way . . .

Twenty feet from the square the light of the torches faded and all he had to see by was the treacherous patchwork of moonlight. He knew what a maze the alleys formed back of the plaza. He stumbled in refuse, dodged around a corner. He could hear the distant pound of running feet, the patrol calling to one another as they groped through the narrow passages. He lost count of the turns he took, the times he almost pitched on his face. He plunged into the open suddenly and saw a bank of earth ahead of him. He realized that he had coming up against one of the irrigation ditches that girded the outlying sections of town. He heard somebody call farther down the ditch. He could hardly make out the words over the roar of his own breathing.

"Kirby . . . Kirby . . . wait . . . not that way!"

Doniphan ran toward the sound of it, stumbling up the bank to gain height. He heard somebody running heavily behind him and chanced a glance over his shoulder to see Major Clark plunge from the alley, holding his rattling saber against one leg as he struggled up the bank after Doniphan. As soon as Doniphan was on top, he could see the two dark figures crossing the weed-choked ditch about twenty yards away. Moonlight made a pale flash against the long yellow hair of the man in the lead as he clawed his way up the opposite bank of the ditch, halted a moment at the top to look back, and then disappeared down off the other side. The second figure was splashing through the silvery trickle of water in the bottom. Doniphan had no doubt that it was Nate.

Doniphan was still running along the top of the bank when another figure plunged from behind a corral about thirty feet down the ditch and ran up to the top of the same bank Doniphan was on. When the man saw Nate in the bottom, he stopped. Doniphan saw his arm come up, saw moonlight glint against gun metal.

"Hatcher, stop!" It was Lieutenant Merritt's voice. "Halt or I'll fire."

Nate didn't pay any heed. He splashed out of the water and dodged up the bank of the opposite slope. Merritt's shot made a crash that sent its echoes back into the alleys behind them. He must have missed, because Nate didn't break his run.

"Taylor!" Doniphan shouted at Merritt. "Not that boy . . . he was with me . . . not that boy!"

Merritt didn't seem to hear. He was already throwing down for a second shot. Doniphan knew that he couldn't miss Nate now. Nate was plunging over the top of the bank, in sharp silhouette, a perfect target. Doniphan fired at Merritt while he was still running

282

toward the man. He thought that he had missed. Merritt remained with his feet spread wide, his gun held at arm's length, while Nate ran over the top of the far bank. But as Nate disappeared down into the fields, Merritt's arm dropped and he bent at the middle and fell in a heap. Doniphan reached the man and dropped to one knee beside him.

"Taylor," he groaned. "Why did you have to do that?"

There was no sound now except the husky roar of Major Clark's breathing and the metal rattle of his saber as he came running down the bank toward them.

CHAPTER
NINETEEN

Nate ran into the cover of scrawny willows that filled the bottom land beyond the irrigation ditch. Kirby had disappeared into the same cover and Nate couldn't see him now or hear him. Nate didn't know why the last shot had missed him. He realized what a prime target he must have made, silhouetted on top of the bank. He had heard someone yelling at him to halt, and then someone farther away shouting something he couldn't understand, and then the final shot drowning everything else out.

The twisted *tornillo* ripped at his clothes and the mesquite clawed his face as he scrambled through the thick underbrush. When he reached the riverbank, he stopped for a moment, crouched in a thicket of willows, fighting to hold back the noise of his breathing. The river was frozen over and moonlight made a pale glare on the ice and wind swept across the shimmering surface with a doleful whine, cutting through Nate with its freezing chill.

He heard a crackling in the distance and couldn't tell whether it was soldiers following him or Kirby. He was afraid to give himself away by calling for Kirby. He couldn't seem to make a decision. His head was still clouded with rage at Doniphan. Just thinking about it gave him the shakes. Doniphan's talk had confused him for a moment. Doniphan was like Kirby in that respect. While he was talking, he could make a body think that black was white. But now Nate was out from under the man's courtroom spell and the doubt was gone from his mind. All he could see was that Doniphan had made a promise to him and Kirby, and had broken it, and Kirby would die for it if he was caught. It seemed that Nate had looked up to Doniphan most of his life; he had never expected to see the day he would hate him. He was through freezing for Doniphan and starving for Doniphan and getting fever and making his gizzard a target for every knife in Mexico all for a man who gave you preachments about responsibility and honor one day and stuck you in the back the next.

He heard another dim clatter in the underbrush from the direction of town and it started him off upriver toward the Otero house. He kept to the mesquite thickets for cover. His face and hands were soon bloody from the clawing brush, his clothes torn. By the time he reached the house he was exhausted, chilled to the bone. When he knocked on the door, Inez answered. The two old people huddled by the fitful blaze in the cone-shaped mud fireplace in the corner. Neither of them spoke English and they watched uncomprehendingly as Nate told Inez in a breathless rush what had happened.

"I figured Kirby would get here ahead of me. He must've had to double back to give them the slip, or maybe he circled around to get some horses for us. We all got to git out, Inez. As soon as Kirby comes."

She did not answer. She turned and crossed the room and stood with her head bowed. He thought that she was thinking. Then he saw the niche beyond her in the wall. She was not looking at it but he could see the broken image in it. The pieces of wood were piled carefully in the niche. He saw the carved face and the little skull and broken cross that had once been held in the wooden hands of *Santa* Rita. Inez raised her head. She saw him looking at the broken saint. "Kirby is not a Catholic, is he?" she asked.

He couldn't answer immediately. At last he said: "He did that?"

"One of his deals," she said bitterly. "Why is it always one of his deals? They are wrong, Nate, no matter how he makes them seem, there is always something wrong about them. Why can't he see this? I tried to stop him . . ." She trailed off, looking at the broken saint again. The bitterness left her voice. It sounded hollow, lost. "He told me he was a Catholic."

He felt to blame. He should have told her the truth at Taos when it had first come up. So many things had kept him from it then. He should have told her. He felt some need to atone, to comfort. He crossed to her. He touched her. The contact made her tremble. She turned to him, but resisted his embrace.

"Can't you cry?" he said. "Can't you cry, just once?"

"I do not desire to cry," she said. "Nate . . . oh, Nate, when I first met him, when he was coming to the house, and I knew I had love for him, I was so afraid. I thought it was knowing I would have to leave my family, cut myself off from everything I had ever known. But now I do not think it was that so much. I think it was something I saw in him. I told him I had more fear than ever before in my life. What is it, Nate? What is it?"

"You were just a kid. You've grown up a little bit now, but you were just a kid, and maybe you thought you loved him . . ."

"No. I knew. Whatever it was, I did not think. I knew. Maybe it's wrong, maybe I saw it then, but I cannot help it, Nate, it is something . . . I feel this way, and no matter what he does, I cannot help it."

"Love is crazy," he said. "You go blind or something. I guess I know well enough."

He looked at her broken saint. It seemed to embody all the idols that had been broken, for him, since he had left Missouri. He felt as though something had been going on inside him for a long time, something about Kirby, chipped away, piece by piece, until there wasn't anything left. He thought that being a Catholic was probably not the only lie Kirby had told her. Maybe not even the worst lie. He wondered how much of what Kirby had told him, throughout his life, had been lies. He wondered why he hadn't seen it in Doniphan's office. He guessed that he had been too mad at Doniphan to see anything clearly.

"I got to tell you this, Inez," he said. "Doniphan told me loyalty could be a disease. Well, maybe I got the cure now. I can't keep quiet about how I feel any longer. I got to say it. Leave him, Inez. I ain't ashamed to say it. I can't let him hurt you any more. What he said while he was out of his head was true. He married you just so's he could use you in a deal with Ganoe. Maybe he did fall in love with you afterward. But that won't change him. You've seen that. He'll go on trying to swing his shady deals, hurting you, breaking everything you believe in. Leave him before it gets too late."

"I think it is too late now. It is not something one can do with the mind, just say yes, and do. I thought I could when he broke *Santa* Rita. For a while I could not think, I just sat on the floor and looked at her, I do not know how long. Then I thought it was over and I could leave him. But now I know I was wrong."

"I guess I don't worship him any more, either. He just looks different. He looks a lot smaller."

"But you still love him. You love him in a different way than you did before, maybe, but you still love him. I feel is he is my husband. My place must always be with him. Kirby was my choice. I still love him."

Nate felt spent, as though all his emotion had been used up in one outpouring. His muscles ached and it was an effort to breathe. It was a long time before he could speak.

"When I first came here tonight," he said, "I was a-going to desert with Kirby."

She looked up at him. She moistened her lips. "You must not do that."

"No, I guess I can't. Not now. What I worry about is leaving you here."

"I will be all right. You can do nothing more. Kirby will come, and we can go south. I have relatives in Chihuahua. My uncle is there, you know. James Magoffin."

"He was captured. He's a prisoner."

"But he still has many friends, and much influence. I will be all right. If you do not hurry and get back, you will be in trouble."

He didn't tell her how much trouble he was already in. He didn't want to be here when Kirby pulled in, but he didn't want to go, either.

"Well," he said, "I guess I better leave."

"Good bye, Nate. Go with God."

"Yeah," he said. "I like that saying. You know we don't have a saying like that. We say light a shuck, or something plain. Nothing like that. I like it."

"It is a good saying."

"Yeah . . . well, good bye, Inez."

"Good bye, Nate."

Nate didn't have any trouble getting through the sentries. There was a Company D man at the post on the main road and he told Nate about Lieutenant Merritt's getting shot. The sentry said that the surgeon thought Merritt would live, but was too badly wounded for further service and would probably be sent home. The whole town was in a mortal ruckus about it and the sentry told Nate that he had better report to headquarters before he was posted as a deserter.

As soon as Nate appeared before Doniphan's quarters, he was put under guard and marched into a room jammed with officers — Colonel Doniphan, Lieutenant Colonel Jackson, Major Clark, Major Gilpin, and most of the volunteer captains. Nate told them that, when he had heard the shooting and found out that Kirby had escaped from Merritt, he had lost his head — which was substantially true — and he didn't actually know what he intended doing at the time. All he could seem to think about was finding Kirby. That seemed to strike them all as a natural impulse and they didn't pursue it further. He said that he had hunted for Kirby in the brush along the river, and, when he couldn't find him, he had come back.

He still couldn't betray Kirby, and, when they went into what Kirby was doing here, or whether Nate had seen him prior to this evening, or where Kirby might be now, Nate played dumb. The fact that Merritt had tried to kill him without any cause made Nate seem to be the innocent victim in the whole affair, and most of the officers seemed inclined to shut the books on the incident. They all knew of Merritt's bitter, running feud with the volunteers, and it was a general opinion that he had finally cracked under the strain. There would undoubtedly be an inquiry, but Major Clark's testimony would clear Doniphan. Clark had seen the shooting and felt that Doniphan's act was justified. Clark knew that Nate had just come from Doniphan's quarters, and that Merritt had no reason to fire at Nate.

After the meeting broke up, Nate asked to see Doniphan alone for a moment. "I wanted to thank you for saving my life," he said. "I didn't know about it at the time. I guess I would've come back sooner."

Doniphan had aged this last year. Nate knew that he was only thirty-eight. Tonight he looked fifty. There was a haunted look in his eyes and Nate knew that the memory of shooting Merritt would torture him for a long time. His shoulders looked stooped and unutterably weary. Nate realized for the first time what an overwhelming weight of necessary evils a man in Doniphan's position had to tote on his back.

"You were pretty disillusioned in me, just before the shooting," Doniphan said. "When I saw you disappear into that brush by the river, I would have laid a bet you wouldn't come back."

"I'll tell you the truth, Colonel. I didn't aim to."

"What made you change your mind?"

"Well, it's hard to say. You've been trying to tell me something for a long time. Back at Santa Fé . . . what you said about hooraws . . . a set of values . . . I guess it finally started to penetrate."

For the first time Doniphan smiled. It was brief, bleak, a little sad. He put a hand on Nate's shoulder.

"If we ever get out of this, Nate, why don't you come to Liberty and try studying law with me again. I think you'd make it this time."

"I'll think about it," Nate said. "Just so I don't have to read Byron."

The next day was February 1st, and Major Clark's battery arrived in El Paso. The whole town turned out to greet the column. Nate was in no mood to join the mob but his barracks were so near the square he couldn't miss seeing the show from a window. Some

Missourian suggested that a salute should be fired from the brass cannon captured at Brazito. They couldn't find any wadding to make it a blank shot and Bristol Graham donated his socks for the occasion. They gave him the honor of firing the gun and he was so drunk he didn't pay attention to which way it was aimed. The battery was just entering the square when the gun went off. The wedding hit one of Clark's artillerymen in the face. He put up such a howl Nate thought half his head had been blown away.

"What's the matter, Saint Looey?" Bristol shouted. "You just got some wadding between your teeth."

"You ain't had them socks off your feet from the day you left Fort Leavenworth!" the artilleryman yelled. "I'd rather be hit in the face by a twelve-pound ball!"

Nate knew that they would be marching soon. Doniphan would have moved south long ago if he hadn't been forced to wait for his artillery. The barracks were filled with the usual rumors. General Wool had been wiped out and the 1st Missouri would have to take Chihuahua alone. General Taylor had been smashed at Saltillo. With all the other American armies defeated, General Santa Anna and 50,000 Mexicans were marching north to engage the 1st Missouri at Chihuahua City. Nate had learned not to believe anything but it was hard to feel that they were not alone now, cut off from behind and facing the unknown ahead.

Five men died of the typhoid. The regiment spent the mornings in drills and saber exercises and the cavalry charges. Nate knew that it was no use going back to

Otero's house. Kirby and Inez would be gone. On the evening of February 7th Nate heard that they would be marching the next day. Nate was off duty after mess and he went into town for his last evening. There wasn't much to do but hang around the *cantinas* or idle in the square, and after a couple of hours of it he started back toward the barracks. He met Bristol Graham in front of the church. Bristol had a woman with him. She didn't have any shoes and she was clubfooted. She had lost most of her front teeth, her face was scarred by the pox, and her eyes were filmed and mattered with the disease so many of these people seemed to get from the sand blowing at them all the time.

"I got me a woman, Nate," Bristol said. "I'm a-going to desert."

"How you a-going to live?" Nate asked. "You don't even know the language."

"There's ways. Kirby done it, didn't he? This one says she'll marry me for sure. The joke's on the First Missouri now. They can't never make no more hooraws about Bristol Graham not getting a woman."

The next morning Bristol didn't show up for roll call and he was posted. That was the morning they left El Paso. Nate heard that it was 230 miles to Chihuahua City. Doniphan had ordered the traders to form into a military battalion and a man named Sam Owens was made their major. With the traders and the artillery company Doniphan had 924 effectives.

The column marched southwest along the Río Grande for five days, and then turned due south, leaving the river behind. The high northern plains of

Mexico lay before them, a yellow country, a pale buckskin country that stretched southward for 1,000 miles, a waterless country where the wind never stopped blowing and a haze of sand always lay on the horizon in a sulphur-colored mist. Broken mountains made a purple band of smoke at the rim of the world and dry riverbeds twisted in tortured snake tracks across the burned earth. The bench lands were studded with patches of pale green *lecheguilla* and all that would grow in the shallow valleys was the corkscrew *tornillo* and the only sound in the world was the nerve-racking grind of wagon wheels in the gravel and the ceaseless crunch of marching feet.

The day after leaving the river the 1st Missouri entered one of the deserts the Mexicans called a *jornada*. They had filled every barrel in the wagons at the river, but they had never been able to carry enough water to get them across the desert stretches. They had suffered piteously in the furnace of the Kansas prairies and on the Dead Man's March and on a dozen other dry crossings. James Kirker told them that the *jornada* was sixty miles across. It would take them at least two days of marching. Nigh onto a thousand men had to drink enough to keep going, and more than four times that many mules and horses and cattle had to be kept watered, and all Nate could worry about was how long their water would last, and how much longer they would last after it gave out.

Two men died the first day, and before it was over Nate thought that he would be the third. He didn't see how it could be so hot in the middle of winter. The men tied their neckerchiefs over their faces as a protection from the wind-blown sand but it did little good. By mid-morning Nate's neckerchief was torn to shreds and his cheeks were bloody. Every breath he took seemed to suck in the hot wind. His lungs ached and burned and the sun beat on him till it started a pounding in his skull.

The regiment had been inadequately outfitted to begin with and eight months of campaigning, of carelessness and ignorance had reduced their equipment to a deplorable state. Few of them had anything left of the uniforms they had been issued at Fort Leavenworth. They were dressed in clothes bought from the Mexicans or traded from the Indians, flimsy cotton pants or buckskin britches, Saltillo serapes, Navajo blankets, Pueblo moccasins, all turned to filthy rags by the months of snow and rain and dust. Half of them had no canteens and in desperation had unsheathed their sabers and had filled the scabbards with water before leaving the Río Grande. Nate had lost his canteen at the Battle of Brazito but had been lucky enough to get a pair of *morrales* in El Paso. The water bags of woven, gum-pitched reed would have carried enough to see him through if it hadn't been for the other men. Before noon Hugh Long had used up the meager supply of water in his scabbard. He began getting dizzy spells and started raving, and Nate began sharing his water. Later on Hicklin slumped forward in his saddle and it took Nate's water to revive him. Before nightfall Nate's water bags were empty and Nate's own tongue was swelling in his mouth. The regiment marched till midnight and camped in a wind-swept desolation. A horde of thirst-crazed animals whimpered and moaned outside the ragged lines of tents and the volunteers huddled around their fires hatching the inevitable plots against their officers.

"Captain Reid's got a barrel of water hid in the company wagon," Tom Langford said. "He's selling it for fifty cents a drink."

"Captain Reid wouldn't do such a thing," Nate said.

"If I had fifty cents, we could trap him," Langford said. "You fellows could get Colonel Doniphan over there on some pretext or another, and, when Doniphan saw Reid selling the water, he'd have to court-martial Reid and shoot him."

"Do you think Doniphan would bother?" Hugh asked bitterly. "We've never had enough water. In eight months we've never had enough water or enough food or enough clothes. These officers don't give a damn about us. This war is just a stairway to glory for them . . . and, if they have to make the steps out of a thousand dead volunteers, they'll do it. This isn't a war General Taylor is carrying on down in Mexico. It's a Presidential campaign. Alexander Doniphan's selling us out for a seat in the U.S. Senate and every boy that John W. Reid kills in those spectacular skirmishes is just another vote for Reid in the Missouri Legislature."

Nate stood up angrily. "Hugh, you must be crazy from thirst. You saw Doniphan sharing his own water with the boys today. You were on that march to Bear Springs when he walked all day so's a sick boy could ride his horse."

"That'll sound real booming in the campaign speeches," Langford said. "I say we ought to mutiny before it's too late. Them volunteer regiments of Taylor's mutinied and they got sent home."

Nate saw that it was useless to reason with him. He had heard them hatching plots against their officers that never came off all the way from the Missouri River, but he had never seen them so bitter and vindictive. He was restless and wakeful all through the night, waiting for something to happen, but by dawn the worst he heard was that two men had deserted from Company A.

The scouts brought in rumors of the enemy ahead and the march was tightened. The company officers were ordered to dismount any man who straggled or left ranks during the day and to have him finish the march on foot at the rear of his company. The sand drifts deepened and the traders were having a terrible time with their wagons. They had to put three and four teams to a wagon to get it through the heavy sand. Two wagons sank over their hubs and had to be abandoned. As poorly supplied as they were, the quarter-master sergeant was having such a bad time that before the end of the day he had to jettison 8,000 pounds of flour and several dozen barrels of salt and meat in order to get his wagons through. All day long the animals were dying of thirst, and, whenever Nate looked behind him, he could see the line of carcasses stretching out to the horizon.

Nate was so dry that he couldn't even seem to sweat any more. His face was whipped raw and he was half blind from the sand. His tongue had swelled fit to choke him and there was a vicious pounding in his head. He saw strange things on the horizon, castles, lakes that weren't there, monstrous Mexican dragoons, and he got to thinking that Hugh was Kirby, and croaked at him about how they had to get in the tobacco crop. They were all suffering terribly with thirst and two men in Nate's squad went out of their heads and had to be tied down in the company wagon.

It was near noon, and they had marched about ten miles, when Nate saw Colonel Doniphan ride by with Major Clark and Lieutenant Colonel Jackson. It was Doniphan's habit to drop out several times during the day and pass back along the column. Hugh claimed that it was to catch up any slackers but Nate thought that it was more a fatherly concern for his boys.

A few minutes after Doniphan had passed, Nate saw Hugh sway in the saddle. Before Nate could catch him, Hugh pitched off his horse. Nate dismounted quickly and dragged Hugh out of the line of march. Hugh stirred and groaned and tried to sit up.

"We'll run Alexander Doniphan on the Southern expansionist ticket," he said. "He don't need no slaves to pick his cotton, he's got a thousand Missouri volunteers." There was a loose, flushed look to his face and he began thrashing wildly. "I'm no annexationist, I'm a war-mongering Abolitionist, fifty-four forty or fight, manifest gentlemen, destiny, manifest gentlemen . . ."

Struggling with Hugh, trying to quiet him down, Nate saw that Major Clark had left the group of officers with Doniphan and was riding back up the column.

The major's blue jacket was chalked with dust and the brine of dried sweat made a scaly shimmer on his sunburned face. The slings and hooks of his saber set up a metal tinkle as he checked his horse by Nate and Hugh.

"You had your orders," he said. "Any man who breaks ranks marches afoot the rest of the day."

"Hugh fell off his horse," Nate said. "He's out of his head. He can't walk in this shape."

"Then get him in a company wagon. Don't you idiots understand? This order is for your own protection. The enemy might hit us any time. We can't do anything with an army of stragglers." Clark turned to the passing column and called to a Company D man. "Soldier, come and get these two horses."

The rider, a man named Shannon, broke ranks and started toward Hugh's horse. Hugh said something unintelligible and pushed Nate away, lurching to his feet. Swaying drunkenly, he stumbled to his horse before Shannon could reach it, and tried to mount.

"Soldier," Clark said angrily, "turn that horse over to this man."

"The hell with you," Hugh said. "Tippecanoe and Tyler, too."

His foot missed the stirrup and he fell heavily against his horse. Clark pulled his revolver.

"Major," Nate cried, "he's delirious . . . he doesn't know what he's about!"

"He knows what he's about," Clark said furiously. "You all know what you're about. It's time you understood something about this army." He cocked his gun, addressing Hugh: "For the last time, soldier, you will obey my order."

Hugh didn't pay any attention to him. He'd gotten a foot in the stirrup again and was trying to pull himself on the nervously shifting horse. Nate made a frightened sound and lunged across to him, trying to pull him down.

"Hugh, will you listen, you've got to give up your horse."

He pulled Hugh down onto the ground again, but one of the man's wildly flailing arms struck him heavily in the face, knocking him backward. He stumbled and fell. Before he could get up again, he saw another rider coming at a gallop toward them, shouting at Clark.

"Major, as you were."

Nate saw that it was Doniphan, with Lieutenant Colonel Jackson trailing behind him. Major Clark still had his gun pointed at Hugh, and he lowered it reluctantly, turning to face Doniphan as the colonel pulled to a halt.

"What's the trouble?" Doniphan asked.

"Disobeying a marching order," Clark said. "Insubordination, defying an officer, refusing a direct command."

"Major," Doniphan said, "can't you just tell me what the trouble is?"

"These men broke ranks," Clark said. "They refused to give up their horses."

Doniphan looked at Nate, and then at Hugh, who had caught his horse again and was stubbornly trying to get into the saddle, oblivious to everything else.

300

"Hugh," Doniphan said, "I think you better give up that horse."

"The hell with you, President Doniphan," Hugh said. "The hell with Sergeant Kearny and Corporal Polk and all the other manifesting expansionists."

Doniphan spurred his horse across to Hugh and dismounted. Hugh was starting another swing into the saddle when Doniphan caught him and pulled him back. Hugh wheeled around and took a punch at Doniphan. It struck the colonel on the head, rocking him. He caught himself, dodged Hugh's next wild swing, and hit Hugh on the jaw. It took Hugh's shoes clear off the ground and pitched him three feet away from Doniphan on his back. He lay without moving.

Doniphan turned and located Hicklin in the ranks, calling to him. "Bill, will you take command of these two horses? When Hugh gets to feeling better, put him and Nate to walking at the hindquarters of your company."

"Walking?" Clark said. "They should be put in irons."

"Don't get in a sweat, Major," Doniphan said. "It was just a little ruckus."

"Are you crazy, Colonel? The man attacked you!"

"Nobody attacked me. Hugh just stumbled when he was getting off that horse and his chin fell against my fist."

"You can't mean that," Clark said. "The whole thing's inconceivable. This man should be court-martialed."

"Major," Doniphan said, "it just isn't worth all that fuss. Why don't you relax, now, and join the volunteers?"

CHAPTER
TWENTY

All through February, Kirby and Inez managed to keep ahead of Doniphan's regiment. They had left El Paso on the same night that Kirby had escaped Lieutenant Merritt. Kirby had been forced to cross the river that night to evade the patrols hunting him and hadn't reached the Otero house till half an hour after Nate had left. Inez had already saddled the horses, the same animals they had ridden south from Valverde, and they had fled down the trail to Chihuahua.

Sixty miles out of El Paso, just before they left the Río Grande and turned into the first *jornada*, they had come up with forty-five wagons belonging to a pair of traders named Cufford and Gentry. Cufford was an Englishman, counting on the fact that the Mexican government had been giving safe passage to the traders traveling under British passports. He would not say how he had managed to slip through Doniphan's lines. Inez suspected that they had bribed some volunteer corporal on the patrol not to report the missing wagons till it was too late to catch them. Cufford knew Inez's father and was willing to let Kirby and Inez ride with the train for the added protection the Torreón name might give him. Inez was already showing her child, and was happy to exchange the horse for the comparative comfort of a wagon.

As they moved south, the caravan grew bigger. All along the way they picked up Mexicans fleeing before the American Army. Inez was surprised at how much she had missed her people. Most of them were peasants, traveling in the creaking two-wheeled *carretas*, or riding the diminutive burros, but during the evenings she spent more and more time in their camps, finding a strange refuge in the customs and the attitudes she had tried so hard to escape. She heard encouraging news about her uncle. James Magoffin had not been executed but was being held in Chihuahua City. She knew that Magoffin still had many friends there, even though he was a prisoner, and that, if she could only reach him, he would be able to help her and Kirby.

The deep sand of the *jornada* slowed them down so much that by the third week of February they knew that they were only a day ahead of the 1st Missouri. One night, just south of Lake Encinillas, they saw a glow on the horizon, and some Mexicans who had been scouting the rear came in near dawn and said that the campfires of the volunteers had started a conflagration in the dry grass around the lake that almost burned out the whole regiment.

They crossed the vast grasslands belonging to Angel Trias, the governor of Chihuahua, who was in Chihuahua City raising an army to meet the Americans, and on February 27th made a halt at a Mexican fort called Sanz. It was 200 miles south of El

Paso, and thirty north of Chihuahua City, a dismal collection of rain-streaked mud buildings strung along a creek emptying into the lake. There was a company of Mexican dragoons in camp, handsome, swaggering, arrogant young men in all the glittering brass and fluttering plumes of a grand opera. Inez knew that six months ago she would have compared them to the ragged Missourians and would have thought that they were the first real soldiers she had seen since Armijo's dragoons fled Santa Fé. Now she wondered.

Kirby had become increasingly nervous about showing himself. He was afraid that the soldiers would take him into custody if they found out that he was a deserter. While he stayed with the bullwhackers among the wagons, Inez mingled with the Mexicans in camp to find out what she could. She learned that the dragoons belonged to the cavalry of General Conde, who held a fortified position on the heights above the Sacramento River about fifteen miles south of Sanz. With Conde was a large force of infantry under a general named Heredia, and about twenty pieces of artillery. When Inez returned to the wagons, she found Kirby standing by a lowered end gate, apprehensively watching the activity around the fort. Their eyes met for a moment and then, suddenly, both of them looked at the ground. She wondered why it had grown so disturbing to look directly at each other. Before El Paso, before Valverde, a long time ago, she had been able to see so much in his eyes — love, tenderness, understanding. Why should she be afraid of what she might see there now?

"They checking everybody?" he asked stiffly.

"Just the *guías*."

"The what?"

"It is hard to explain . . . a paper of clearance, the passport of a merchant. The *guía* of Cufford seems to be in order and covers all his drivers. The dragoons have not asked about you. But we might have trouble tomorrow. The Mexican army apparently means to meet the *gringos* about fifteen miles to the south. I am sure they will ask more questions there."

"The Mexican army," he said. He was looking beyond her, and she could only guess what was on his mind. "A pretty big parcel?" he asked.

"It is said to be over four thousand men," she said.

"And the First Missouri ain't got a thousand," he murmured. He was still looking beyond her. "Doniphan's bit off a big chaw of hell," he said softly. The pensive, brooding expression on his yellow-bearded face disturbed her. He was looking toward the north, toward the 1st Missouri, and finally he said: "Inez, do things seem different to you?"

"Many things, they have changed."

"I mean with us. You and me. Ever since El Paso I've felt it. When I used to talk to you, when I used to make love . . . I could reach you, Inez. We was together. Is it the statue? Do you still hate me for breaking your statue?"

"I never hated you. It was something else . . . but it is gone now. *Santa* Rita has forgiven you. I have prayed to her many times and I know she has forgiven you."

"What is it, then? What's between us?"

She bowed her head. She didn't want to talk about it. She had thought that she was getting over it. She had prayed for the time to come when she would no longer doubt him, when she would believe everything he told her again.

"Is it me being a deserter?" he asked.

She clutched the folds of her heavy skirt, her head still bowed, and could not answer.

He said beseechingly: "I ain't really a deserter, Inez. I would've gone back. Any time. You know that. All Doniphan had to do was say the word. You believe that, don't you?"

She closed her eyes, moving her head miserably from side to side. "Kirby, it is not necessary that we talk about it."

"Because you don't believe me, is that it?" His voice was growing bitter. "You think I'm a deserter. You and Nate, you both think I'm a deserter."

"Kirby, how can I say? I do not know . . . why should it bother me so much that you are a deserter? I do not want that . . . it is too much like my father. I thought I had run away from all that, all the things in my world. But maybe I was wrong. Maybe there are things in my world I cannot escape."

"Maybe in my world, too," he said.

"When I first met you," she said, "when I very first met you, there was something about you . . . you were whole, you were a complete man. Now there is something gone from you. A little more of it seems to go all the time. Ask yourself . . . why is there this shame

306

in you? This doubt of yourself? Maybe what stands between us is not only in me. Maybe it is in you, too."

He turned away, rubbing the back of his neck, and took three savage steps away from her. She expected an angry outburst. He paused, his back to her, his head bowed. When his voice finally came, it was barely audible. "It's curious. I guess you and Nate are the only two people I've ever loved . . . and I let you both down."

She crossed to him, grasping his arm. "It is not that bad . . ."

"Don't alibi for me. Let me be honest, Inez. For once in my life, let me be honest. I don't know why I should see it so clear now. Maybe the thought of Nate a-going into battle, Four-to-one. Those are pretty ugly odds. I should be there to keep him out of trouble. A man shouldn't run out on his people. I took you away from yours, and I run out on mine. Will we ever be able to forget that? Will you ever be able to love me again, knowing that?"

She pressed her head against his arm. "Kirby, would I be here if I did not love you?"

"But it ain't the same. When I look at you, it ain't the same, and, when I kiss you, it ain't the same, and in bed it ain't the same. I see it in your eyes, a sort of shame, and I can't stand looking at it any more. Something's gone from between us, Inez, the same as it's gone from me. I want it back. I want it back from you and from Nate, too. What if I went out there now? Doniphan is a-going to need every man he can git. What if I fought beside Nate? Maybe that would take the stink off me.

307

Maybe it would mean just being drummed out of the service instead of being shot. That's what you want, ain't it? You want me to go back."

She did not want to look at him. Her face was pressed against him and her eyes were closed and her hands clung to him in a growing desperation.

"Kirby, you are asking me if I want you to fight my own people."

"What did you think I was a-going to do when you first married me?"

"It had the difference then . . . the war, it was so far away, I was such a child, so afraid, the way you came into my world, the way you talked . . ."

"I hoodwinked you from the very start, didn't I? Inez, I know something now . . . what we had those first weeks, the way it was, we can't never have it again, not the way things stand now, not with this between us. What can I do, Inez, what can I do?"

Inez had always wondered why there were so many women in church, why it was always the women, at any time of day, the women kneeling on the floor with their shawls over their heads, praying.

She pulled away from Kirby, unable to look at him. "You must do the thing that you think is right."

CHAPTER
TWENTY-ONE

On the afternoon of Saturday, February 27th, the 1st Missouri reached the crumbling, deserted fort at Sanz, and Colonel Doniphan talked with a couple of frightened Mexicans picked up by the advance patrols. They told him that a body of Mexican dragoons had been there but had retreated to a position about fifteen miles to the south. James Kirker and his Delawares had scouted with the advance parties a long way ahead of the regiment and had already brought Doniphan word of the fortifications on the heights above the Sacramento. Doniphan knew that tomorrow he would have a fight.

He sat alone in his tent making his plans. He knew the approximate size of the enemy force facing him, and, if the odds seemed frightening, at least he could gain some consolation from the knowledge that he was no longer cut off from the rear. A few days before a courier had gotten through from Santa Fé with the news that Colonel Price had broken the rebellion in New Mexico. Most of the revolting Indians had taken refuge in the village church at Taos, and Price had been forced to blow it down with his howitzers. Over 100 Indians had died in the church and now the military trials were being held. Diego Archuleta had not yet been caught but it was fairly certain that the ringleaders, with *Don* Miguel Torreón among them, would be hanged.

Doniphan slept poorly that night at Sanz, and immediately after "Reveille" on Sunday morning he assembled his staff and gave them the order to march. So many horses had been lost since Santa Fé that a great portion of the regiment was now dismounted. At El Paso, Doniphan had formed three picked companies of cavalry from among the men still ahorse. Captain Hudson commanded the 103 men from Santa Fé who had joined the regiment at Valverde. They were called the Chihuahua Rangers. Captain Parsons had a company called the Missouri Dragoons, and Captain Reid's company was the Missouri Horse Guards. There were over 200 men in the three companies and they made up the advance guard.

Behind them were to roll the 400 wagons. They were formed in four parallel files, with intervals between each file. In the center interval were the artillerymen with six-guns. In the interval on the right marched the 1st Battalion — the dismounted companies A, B, C, and a platoon of D, commanded by the two lieutenant colonels, Jackson and Mitchell. In the interval on the left was the rest of the infantry, the 2nd Battalion, with Major Gilpin commanding. His force included the two teamster companies of 150 men, under Major Owens of Independence.

The column got under way soon after sunup. They had not marched for long when a big eagle appeared in the sky above them. The bird banked and swooped and circled along the whole line of march for most of the morning.

"What did I tell you, gentlemen?" Reid said. "Manifest Destiny. An omen. The American Eagle embracing all of Mexico. Fate has this day written down in the book."

"All he's got to do now is scream," Doniphan said.

Shortly after noon the Mexican position became visible, although it was still four miles distant. The Americans were moving south on the road to the Sacramento River that followed an open valley bounded on either side by ranges of naked brown mountains. As the road approached the Sacramento River, the mountains moved in until the valley was little more than a mile wide. Across this narrow neck from east to west ran two miniature cañons that the Mexicans called Arroyo Seco and Arroyo Sacramento. Between the arroyos was a peninsula of land that formed a rocky bench, several hundred feet high at some points. The Mexicans had taken their position on the bench. The road ran across the center of the bench and directly through their fortifications.

About a mile and a half from the Mexican position James Kirker joined Doniphan. Kirker and his Delawares had been ahead of the main column all morning. They had surveyed the Mexican position from the mountains, and with the aid of Mitchell's glass Kirker pointed out the various redoubts to Doniphan.

"They have one battery of four guns ... two nine-pounders and two sixes, I think ... on that point of the hill to our right. Also three entrenchments of six-pounders. On the brow, near the center, another battery of two, six, and four. And what looks to be six culverins on carriages. On the crest of the hill between the batteries we counted twenty-seven redoubts dug and thrown up, extending across the whole ground. The infantry is there, entirely protected."

"That's a considerable body of cavalry drawn up in front of the redoubts," Doniphan said.

"About a thousand of them, as far as I can figure, in ranks four deep," Kirker said. "It probably represents the majority of General Conde's dragoons, and the cream of the whole force facing us."

The Mexican guns on the heights commanded the narrow valley that passed to the east of the bench. To block the valley further, a stone abatis had been built across its mouth. The rocky breastworks bristled with guns.

"It would be suicide to charge that abatis," Doniphan said. "And just about as foolish to storm them by the road. I think turning their right flank is best. Their weakest batteries are on that side. Once we gain the hill, we'll only be contending with a fraction of their redoubts instead of the whole front."

"Are you ignoring the cavalry?" Major Clark asked. "They'll hit us just about the time we cross that arroyo. If they catch your infantry in that ditch, you'll be wiped out."

"You're overlooking the same thing they are," Doniphan said. "The wagons."

Clark's lips tightened angrily. They had already argued several times about the wagons. It had been Doniphan's idea to hold the caravan in four columns with the troops in the center intervals masked by the long lines of wagons. It was a strategy that had protected traders on the Santa Fé trail for twenty years.

"Colonel," Clark said, "by Kirker's estimate the Mexicans have over four thousand men on those heights, and we haven't got a thousand. Odds of four to one are bad enough without risking the fate of your whole command on a frontier trick."

"Major," Doniphan asked, "would you respect my orders if I were an officer of the regular service?"

Major Clark flushed. He started to speak. Then he reined his horse around and galloped back toward his artillery.

Nate was at the head of the column with Captain Reid and his Horse Guards. Nate saw Lieutenant DeCourcy gallop up to Captain Reid and say something. Reid turned around and waved at his men.

"The colonel wants us to turn right here and cross that gully," he said.

The gully was one of the dry arroyos. Nate's little mare was sure-footed but she almost went on her face getting down the steep bank. There was a lot of scrambling and cursing and fighting with the horses to get them through the deep sand at the bottom. Nate wondered how they would ever get the wagons across in time. Reid's Horse Guards were the advance company and about half of them had gained the high ground on the other side of the gully when Nate saw the Mexican dragoons begin to advance. It made Nate think of Brazito all over again, only this time there seemed about triple the number of shakos and pompons and plumes and buckles and aiguillettes and saber sashes and lances all glittering and shining in the sun. Reid said that it must be two regiments at least. Nate unsheathed his saber and tied it to his wrist with his neckerchief the way Ruff had instructed them at Apache Cañon. He got out a paper cartridge and jammed it into the breech of his Jenks.

"We're in it now, boys," Reid said. "Spread out and form two ranks, will you? We've got to mask this gully till the infantry gets across. If those dragoons break through us and catch the infantry down there, it'll be hell to pay."

They got all tangled up trying to break from the column and form a company front. The officers were shouting a lot of orders they had used in drills but none of the men had tried very hard to learn and now everybody was mixed up and didn't seem to know which way to turn. Parsons only made it worse by leading his Missouri Dragoons out of the gully from behind and riding into Reid's company. Doniphan appeared at the edge of the gully and Nate could hear him shouting at Clark.

"Major, will you get your guns into action. Parsons, clear your men out of the way so Clark can get his guns out of the gully."

The Mexicans were still coming. Nate thought that he hadn't ever heard anything to match the sound their horses made. It seemed to make the whole mountain

314

shake. Their lance tips made a long shimmering line above their black shakos. Nate began to sweat.

"That's about a thousand yards," Corporal Gaines said.

"They're going to cut us down," Hugh said. "They're going to cut us down before those wagons ever get out of the gully."

"Why don't you run, then?" Nate said.

"I'm a coward, Nate. That's why I joined up. Do you want to know why I joined up?"

"I don't want to know why you joined up, Hugh. That's your own business."

"You're always asking me. Everybody's always asking me why I joined up. Well, I'll tell you why I joined up. I joined up because I was afraid to stay home. I don't even have the courage of my own convictions. That's how much of a coward I am. Sometimes I thought I'd desert for fear I'd have to kill a man. Ever since I joined up I've been afraid I'd have to kill a man, but I didn't have the courage to be the only one who stayed at home. You see how much of a coward I am?"

"You ain't a coward, Hugh."

"Yes, I am. I want to run, Nate. But I can't run. I don't even have the courage to run when I want to run."

The Mexicans opened fire with their small arms while they were still too far away to hit anything. There was a scattered answer from the volunteers. Then the whole long front of advancing Mexican cavalry pulled to a halt.

Nate couldn't understand it at first. Clark was getting his guns into position but they hadn't opened fire yet. Then Nate saw some of the volunteers looking back at the gully and he turned to look. The wagons were appearing. Some of them had bogged down in the deep sand at the bottom of the gully but most of them were rolling out onto the high plateau now and moving into formation. Their long line faced the Mexican dragoons at an oblique angle, masking all of the American column except the cavalry.

"They don't know what to make of it," Reid said. "They're just like a bunch of Indians when they don't know what to make of something."

It was all Nate could figure. He supposed that it had come as something of a shock to think that you were charging down on a bunch of infantry trapped in a gully and suddenly be looking at a blank wall of wagons. A lance wouldn't do much damage to a wagon certainly, and that seemed to be most of what the Mexicans were toting. While the Mexicans were halted and still hesitating, the artillery bugler sounded his call, and one of Clark's twelve-pound howitzers fired. Nate saw the bomb land among the enemy cavalry and explode with a bright flash. It tore a hole in their ranks, and, when the smoke blew away, he could see half a dozen horses down and kicking, and three more running away without riders. Clark's six-pounders began their volley, and Nate saw the shells cut more holes in the Mexican ranks. The Mexicans stood up to it for a few minutes, and then broke and retreated back up the hill. The movement unmasked their center battery. It opened fire.

The first shell made a roaring sound going overhead. Nate heard it land among the wagons still in the arroyo. He heard a crash of breaking wood. A mule screamed. He didn't want to look back at it.

Doniphan appeared along their front, paying no attention to a shell that landed near him and bounced along on the ground. "I figure it's going to be an artillery duel now for a while, boys," he said. "Why don't you dismount and spread out. You won't present such a solid target that way."

Another Mexican battery had started now. Nate got off his mare and moved away from Hugh Long, who stood dismounted on his left. The Mexicans couldn't seem to get the range. Either the balls would fly overhead or they would fall short and roll along the ground. By watching where they hit and the direction they bounced, the volunteers could move out of the way in time and let the cannon balls roll harmlessly through their ranks. It got to be sort of a game.

"Watch out, Nate!" Gaines shouted. "There's one sneaking up behind you!"

Nate jumped so hard he almost lost his grip on his reins, but when he turned around there wasn't anything there. Then a sergeant in the Missouri Dragoons didn't jump quickly enough and a ball cut his legs out from under him, and he went down. The surgeon came to him and said that both his legs were broken. They took him away on a stretcher and Gaines quit making jokes.

Nate got to thinking about the knives. He remembered how thinking about the Mexican knives had bothered him so much at Apache Cañon and Brazito. It didn't seem to bother him so much now.

The woolly shreds of smoke stirred and thickened against the pale glare of the sky, eclipsing the sun, spreading a dark shroud over the Mexican cavalry where they still stood in deep ranks behind their artillery, a peacock-colored mass of black leather shakos, blue coats, scarlet turnbacks, yellow sashes, glittering brass buttons, whole segments of the mass seeming to erupt and disappear in the blinding flash of exploding shells. Nate could see that the artillery was cutting them to pieces. They didn't seem to have the sense to deploy into open order. The volcanic explosions flung up the broken black confetti of men and horses and earth in prodigious handfuls. It gave Nate a sick feeling. He didn't want to watch it any more. He didn't even want to fight them. He thought about Inez and Jayán and he didn't want to fight them at all. He wished that he had deserted with Kirby.

The whole mountain seemed to rock and tremble and crash with the pounding of the guns. The volunteers stood up the better part of an hour while the artillery duel went on, dodging the Mexican cannon balls. There were a lot of Mexican horses running around without riders and causing confusion. A man came leading one out of the gully to the rear and Nate saw that it was his uncle.

It was such a shock that Nate couldn't speak. Kirby led the horse up to him, grinning. Over one arm Kirby had slung a belt with a pair of holstered pistols that he must have gotten from a wounded volunteer.

"Hello, button," he said. "You didn't think I'd let you hog all the glory, did you?"

"Kirby," Nate said helplessly, "they'll shoot you. If the Mexicans don't shoot you, the army will."

"Not till after this fight is over," Kirby said. "And then maybe Doniphan will see things different."

"Inez . . . ?"

"She's safe," Kirby said. "An Englishman named Cufford is taking her to her uncle in Chihuahua City. It's something I had to do. Can you understand that, Nate? It's something I had to do."

Kirby's voice was almost drowned in the roar of cannon fire and Nate hardly heard the words. But he could see the expression in Kirby's face, a lost, pleading look that he hadn't ever seen there before. It gave Nate a strange feeling, like a hand in his innards, knotting them up till they hurt.

"Sure, Kirby," he said, "I understand."

A bugle blew about the same time he spoke, making such a racket that he wasn't sure Kirby heard him. He realized that the batteries had quit firing. The powder smoke was so thick that Lieutenant Hicklin seemed little more than a shadow drifting past them. He was shouting at them to mount. Hadn't they heard the bugles blowing the advance?

Nate's mare was skittish as a schoolmarm in a thunderstorm from all the gunfire and he had a battle to get aboard her. When Hicklin's section was finally in the saddle, Nate saw that Captain Reid and the rest of the Horse Guards were already moving out. They were on the right flank of the cavalry screen. Hudson and his Chihuahua Rangers occupied the center, and Parsons and his Missouri Dragoons were on the left. Nate thought that he had never seen such a mess. There wasn't any attempt to hold ranks. Everybody was shouting and yelling and making jokes. Lieutenant Hicklin didn't seem to care. He had wasted the better part of a year trying to train the damned fools. Since his fiasco at Brazito he had given up trying to be a good soldier. He didn't use any regular orders on them but just shouted at them the way Jackson and Reid and all the rest did.

"Follow me!" he called. "If you get your heads shot off, it's your own damn' fault!"

The whole regiment was moving to the right of the enemy position to turn the Mexican flank. Nate could see the lines of white-topped wagons rolling in the wake of the cavalry. They masked the two infantry battalions and the enemy fire was having no effect on the bulk of the regiment. It was the cavalry that began to feel it. Nate saw a man in Hudson's company scream and pitch from the saddle.

Lieutenant DeCourcy galloped past, calling to Hicklin: "Prepare for a charge! The three cavalry companies are to charge that center battery!"

DeCourcy gave the order to Reid and crossed toward the other two cavalry companies. Nate saw Reid lift his sword and call to his company bugler, and the bugler blew the charge. The volunteers responded raggedly but finally the whole line got into motion. It was then that

320

Nate saw that Parsons and Hudson had not charged. They were still holding their companies back with the main command. Captain Reid's Horse Guards were galloping away from the regiment and the only unit charging with them was Captain Weightman and a pair of twelve-pound howitzers.

"Isaac!" Hicklin shouted. "Get up to Captain Reid! Tell him something's gone wrong and we're alone up here!"

Captain Reid was apparently unaware of what had happened. Nate could see him galloping at the head of the company waving his saber and shouting. Before Isaac Hayes could get to Reid, the whole company had reached a gully at the foot of the ridge. The Mexicans began to pour a fire on them from the redoubts above. Nate saw horses go down, squealing and kicking. The noise deafened him. The company was milling around in the gully and Reid couldn't get them up the hill in the face of the fire. DeCourcy galloped up from the rear. Nate was near enough to hear what he shouted at Hicklin.

"I have orders to halt you here!" DeCourcy demanded.

"What the hell?" Hicklin yelled. "We can't do that. Either move us back or move us ahead. If we stay here, we'll all be dead in five minutes."

"Something went wrong!" DeCourcy bawled. "Hudson says he didn't understand my order to charge and he didn't relay it to Parsons. You've got to halt here till they can bring their companies up."

Nate saw that Reid had started up the hill alone. Either he thought that his company was following or he had decided to provide an example. The only two men who followed him were Major Campbell and Major Owens of the traders' battalion. Nate couldn't understand how Owens had got there. He was dressed all in white.

The company was a complete mess now. All of them were milling around in the gully with gunfire constantly pouring in on them from above. It was impossible to rally them and get any of them to charge after Reid. They were all fighting their horses and the horses were rearing and squealing and the fire from above made such a racket that Nate could hardly hear any of the other noise. Lieutenant Miller was vainly trying to rally his section.

"Hicklin!" Miller yelled. "Can't you do something? I can't seem to make them understand . . ."

Hicklin looked around him. He stood in his stirrups and cupped his hands and shouted as loudly as he could: "Prepare to dismount! Prepare to dismount!"

Nate saw some of them reacting as Hicklin rode through the tangle yelling at them. "Prepare to fight on foot! Dismount! Dismount, damn you!" Half a dozen of them closest to Nate swung out of their saddles and they provided the example for some others. "Horse holders in!" Hicklin yelled. Every seventh man took the reins of his six companions and moved to the rear with the excited animals. The fire was still being poured on them from above and a man went down at Nate's side.

322

"Fall in! Fall in and close up! Prepare to load! Prepare to load at will! Load!"

Nate was surprised to see some of them starting to react to Hicklin's orders. Maybe some of the training had finally made an impression. Or maybe they just had to be scared enough. They hadn't really been scared enough back at Brazito. They hadn't really needed anybody badly enough. "Fire by squads!" Hicklin shouted. "Squad . . . ready, aim . . . fire!"

After that it was just a matter of Hicklin's moving down the line and repeating the order. The sergeants took over by squads and the crash of rifle fire became so regular that it drowned out the sound of the enemy's shooting. On the extreme flank Captain Weightman had just pulled two howitzers into position. The first twelve-pound gun crashed. As Hicklin rode past, Nate saw Weightman turn and heard him ask where Captain Reid was. Hicklin said that Reid had charged the hill alone but they couldn't see Reid up there and thought that he had probably been killed. Captain Weightman looked down the line of firing volunteers.

"Well, he left the company in good hands. You should be in the regulars, Hicklin."

Hicklin rode on down the trench and Nate lost sight of him in the ragged mists of powder smoke. Lieutenant Moss came stumbling through the tangle of men crouched in the ditch, trying to get a section mounted to lead up the hill in support of Captain Reid.

Nate got his mare from the horse holder and joined Moss. Kirby appeared beside him, the pistol holsters belted around his middle now, fighting to control his plunging horse. Nate saw Hugh Long mounting, too, all his struggle against fear and panic stamped into the twisted grimace of his white face. There were about twenty-five men in the section that Moss led out, a ragged surf of hoarsely shouting volunteers and whinnying horses that broke out of the gully and surged up the steep, rocky slope. They were raked by a heavy fire from above. Nate was drowned in the sounds of yelling men, the roar of guns, the squealing, hoarse grunts of his mare as she struggled up the hill.

They came upon Captain Reid about seventy yards below the Mexican redoubts, sprawled in a hollow and protected from the fire above. Those closest to him halted momentarily, milling around in the hollow, and Nate heard Reid shout that his horse had been hit and had pitched him. A volunteer offered the captain his horse, and Reid mounted it.

Nate couldn't understand why more of them weren't hit. He could only guess that it was because of the fire from their own company below. He could hear the regular volleys from the riflemen and the howl of howitzer shells passing overhead and the crash of them exploding in the enemy trenches. The Mexican infantrymen were apparently afraid to poke their heads out for fear of getting hit. All Nate could see were the rifles leveled across the breastworks. The Mexicans were crouched below the rifles and firing them blindly without aiming them.

Reid's sword made a quicksilver flash in the air as he swung it around his head, leading the section out of the hollow and up the remaining incline. There was a last deafening crash of gunfire; Nate had a meaningless glimpse of Major Owens dressed all in white lying dead across the first parapet, and then Nate was one of a dozen plunging over the breastworks.

The trench was choked with Mexican infantry, a wild tangle of barefoot men in white cotton rags still trying to fire or reload their guns or bring their bayonets into play or scramble up the rear and escape the American attack. Nate plunged into their screaming mass, a man going down under his mare, and chopping with his saber at another one who tried to bayonet him. His horse, snorting and rearing, was buffeted back and forth by other horses and by the shifting mass of infantry. He saw a volunteer shot out of his saddle, saw two more pulled off their horses. They got to their feet and stood back to back fighting off the Mexicans with their clubbed guns.

Kirby plunged into view from somewhere, his face smeared with blood, shouting as he fired one of his pistols point-blank into the bearded face of a Mexican. Nate's horse wheeled and he lost sight of Kirby. A barefoot Mexican came at Nate with a machete. As Nate wheeled to meet the man, Hugh Long got in between them somehow, blocking the machete with his saber, and then thrusting at the man. Hugh had his sword tied to his wrist with his neckerchief, and, when the Mexican fell back, the sword wouldn't come out of him, and it pulled Hugh out of the saddle on top of him.

It was suddenly quiet around Nate. He realized that the fighting had passed on into the next redoubt. The trench was choked with bodies as far as he could see, some of them still stirring feebly or groaning, and Nate didn't know if the stench in the air came from the blood or the powder smoke or just the general smell of death. He saw Hugh pulling himself off the Mexican he had killed. Hugh's saber was still buried in the man and Hugh had to tear his wrist out of the neckerchief to get free. He stared down at his bloody victim with glassy eyes, and then turned to lean against the side of the trench and vomit.

CHAPTER
TWENTY-TWO

Colonel Doniphan was nearing the base of the slope with the main column when he saw Reid enter the trenches. Doniphan saw that Weightman had gone up in support of Reid and had unlimbered his single howitzer fifty yards from the redoubt and was raking the Mexicans with grape. The charge had taken the pressure off the rest of the Missouri Horse Guards trapped in the gully below and Lieutenant Hicklin had rallied them and was now leading them up the hill in a charge. But the force was not large enough to hold its advantage. Doniphan saw that Reid was already being driven back and out of the second trench. Captain Parsons galloped to Doniphan, shouting to be heard above the sound of firing.

"Sir, can't I support Reid up there? He'll never be able to hold on long enough for the whole column to reach him!"

"Damn it, man," Doniphan shouted, "that's what I ordered you to do in the beginning!"

"DeCourcy must have misapprehended! He told Hudson and me to hold back and wait for your order!"

"Well, you've got it now! Charge!"

As soon as Doniphan saw the two cavalry companies start up the hill, he sent his sergeant major to Lieutenant Colonel Jackson with orders to storm the redoubts on the left with his 1st Infantry Battalion. Then he turned to Captain Thompson, who had been his liaison with the 2nd Infantry Battalion.

"Major Gilpin has the heaviest batteries to contend with in the center," Doniphan said. "Tell him to move his infantry slower than the First Battalion and keep Clark's guns with him all the time. If we can take those redoubts on the right, we'll have their center in a crossfire by the time Gilpin reaches them. It'll cut your losses way down."

Thompson saluted, and rode off. One of the Mexican cannon balls bounded down the slope and Doniphan had to make his horse jump to keep from being hit. He saw both infantry battalions begin their advance. The protection of the wagons had worked out the way Doniphan had planned it but now that phase was over. Now they would find out just how deep the bedrock really ran in Missouri.

Kirby didn't know how long he had been fighting in the trenches. His horse had been shot out from under him at the first redoubt and he had emptied his pistols and had thrown them at some Mexicans. The fighting had passed him by and he stood alone in a trench full of dead and wounded. There was blood all over his arm but he couldn't feel any pain.

A fresh burst of gunfire made him look across the redoubts. He could see that Reid and Hicklin were

328

having a rough time of it. They had gotten into a second trench, but a charge from the Mexican cavalry massed behind the redoubts was pushing them back. Just about the time they seemed ready to break, Captain Parsons came riding over the breastworks. A whole wave of his Missouri Dragoons followed, jumping over the trench in which Kirby stood.

They hit the Mexicans, and then Kirby saw Captain Hudson and his Rangers join them. It broke the Mexican cavalry charge and Kirby saw Mexicans start to run in every direction. He scrambled out of the first trench, and ran to catch up with the volunteer cavalry. Behind him a wave of Missouri infantry came up over the hill. Lieutenant Colonel Jackson was with them carrying his double-barreled shotgun.

"Come on boys!" he shouted. "Every man his turkey!"

Kirby thought that it was probably the closest thing to an order he had ever heard Jackson give his men. The running infantry swarmed around Kirby and carried him over the second redoubt. When he was up on the earthworks, he could see most of the bench land to the east. Gilpin's 2nd Battalion was just moving up the slope toward the Mexican center and the Mexicans had turned their heaviest batteries on him. Doniphan appeared behind Kirby, halting his chestnut horse on a rampart.

"Jackson!" he called. "Forget those trenches on your right! Form a line of riflemen on that rampart! We've got to pour it on their center! Lieutenant Miller, take that battery on Sacramento Hill! We can't let them keep up that cross fire!"

Captain Thompson rode up beside Doniphan and saluted. "Sir, won't you take cover? You make too good a target on this high spot . . . you're too tall."

"Not tall enough to see what's going on if I was in one of those ditches," Doniphan said.

Jackson had run on into the redoubts with some of his battalion, leaving Captain Waldo to form the line of riflemen Doniphan had ordered. Their fire was beginning to chop into the heavy battery on the Mexican center and had already silenced one gun. Lieutenant Miller stumbled past Kirby, trying to gather a platoon for the charge on Sacramento Hill.

"Fall in, soldier," he said. "Get a gun somewhere and . . ." He broke off, staring at Kirby. "What're you doing here?"

Kirby grinned at him. "Same thing as you."

"Well, hop to it, then. We've got to take that battery on the hill."

"You take it. I've got to find Nate."

Nate had lost his rifle during the fighting in the first redoubt and all he had left was his saber. Clouds of greasy black powder smoke hung over everything and he had gotten some smoke in his lungs and couldn't stop coughing. Captain Reid was collecting his Horse Guards for a charge on the Mexican center.

Some of the Mexican cavalry had rallied around the heavy battery. They had tied ropes on one of the guns and were trying to haul it away before Reid's charge

330

captured the piece. Reid jumped his horse clear across the redoubt to the other side, with the Mexican infantry shooting up at him from the trench, and ran alone to the cannon. A Mexican dragoon crossed in front of him, but Reid sabered him, and then rode on to the gun and cut the ropes with his sword.

Nate tried to jump the redoubt the way Reid had but one of the infantrymen below shot up into his mare and the mare stumbled on the rear slope of the trench and threw Nate. He rolled down into the trench and the fall stunned him. He looked up and saw the Mexican trying to reload his rifle. Nate didn't know how he had managed to hang onto his saber but it was in his hand. As the Mexican rammed his ball home and swung the old smooth-bore around to shoot, Nate lunged up with his saber. It went into the Mexican and he dropped the rifle, and fell back.

Nate turned around and saw a Mexican dragoon riding down the trench toward him. The man was galloping his horse across the bodies lying in the bottom of the trench and he had his lance down. Nate was empty-handed and he didn't have time to get out of the trench. If he turned to run down the trench, he would be lanced from behind, and, if he waited, he would be lanced from in front. The dragoon was only a few feet away when Kirby appeared on the parapet.

"Watch sharp, Nate!" he shouted.

He jumped down into the trench between Nate and the dragoon. He didn't have any weapons and he tried to grab the lance with his hands. The dragoon stopped his horse quickly, and then wheeled him into Kirby. The lance went clear through Kirby.

The dragoon pulled it out and turned on Nate, but it had given Nate time to scoop up the loaded rifle the other Mexican had dropped. He shot the dragoon off his horse. The horse scrambled out of the trench and Nate dropped the rifle and ran to Kirby, who was sitting against the side of the trench. Kirby had his hand squeezed over the wound but the blood was coming through his fingers.

"Better git the surgeon," Kirby said. "This is a bad leak in my boiler."

"I don't want to leave you," Nate said.

"Got to git this plugged up pretty quick, Nate. Got to make me fit for Chihuahua. The women there, they say they're ripe on the bough. We'll have a big hooraw in Chihuahua."

He closed his eyes and made a sighing sound. Nate tore off some of his shirt and tried to wad it against the wound, but it wouldn't stop the bleeding. He didn't want to leave but he figured that he'd better find the surgeon as soon as he could. He ran back through the advancing infantry. He could see that the center batteries were captured now and Gilpin's battalion was pouring into the redoubts. Clark had his whole battery in action and was raking the trenches with grape and canister. The Mexicans couldn't stand up to it and they were deserting their fortifications and retreating across the bench land. The plateau was black with running figures and the volunteer cavalry was following them

332

and riding them down and putting them to the saber. Nate figured that it was about over.

Nate saw Charlie Hayes collecting jewelry from the dead bodies and he asked Charlie if he had seen Dr. Moore. Charlie didn't seem to hear and Nate went on until he found the doctor tending a wounded Mexican. When the doctor finished, he went across the redoubts with Nate. Kirby still sat against the side of the trench with his eyes closed and his hand holding his wound. Dr. Moore examined Kirby and said that he was dead.

By nightfall most of the fighting was over. The cavalry hadn't stopped chasing Mexicans down the river and the wounded were still groaning out in the mesquite but the volunteers knew that they had won. Hugh Long helped Nate bury Kirby on the rocky hill. After Hugh went back to camp, Nate stayed for a long time by the grave. A cold wind had come up, whining lonesomely over the plateau, and it made Nate think how far away from home Kirby was. He was beginning to ache all over and feel sick and he didn't know how much of it was exhaustion, or reaction, or grief. He wondered how he could ever have hated Kirby. He remembered hitting Kirby in the fight at Taos and felt a deep sense of guilt. It had been a stupid fight. He had scarcely known Inez, and she had chosen Kirby. He hadn't ever told Kirby that he was sorry. Why hadn't he told him he was sorry? Why had he been so stupid, so hard-headed, so proud?

After the moon rose and the wolves began to howl, Nate got to his feet and stumbled back to camp. Kirby had been listed as a deserter since El Paso, so he wasn't on the books, and, when roll was taken late that night, everybody was surprised to find that only Major Owens and a sergeant had been killed and seven others wounded. They figured that they had killed over 300 Mexicans, wounded as many more, taken forty prisoners. In the redoubts they found a lot of short ropes and a prisoner said that they were to tie the hands of Los Goddamies when they were marched to Mexico City.

The next day Doniphan sent an advance guard to take possession of Chihuahua City and on the following day the whole army marched in with Clark's band playing "Yankee Doodle" and the "Washington's March". It was a bigger city than El Paso or Santa Fé, with a lot of churches and a building that Nate thought must be a palace, and a bull ring. They were given quarters, and that evening Nate heard that Doniphan had liberated James Magoffin and that Magoffin's niece had been with him. The next morning, when he could get off duty, Nate looked up Magoffin where he was staying at one of the houses. He told Magoffin about Kirby, and Magoffin said that maybe he would like to tell Inez privately. He took Nate to a sitting room, and, after a while, Inez came in and Nate told her.

She didn't say anything. She didn't cry. She sat in a tall chair staring past Nate.

"Last night, at the grave," Nate said, "I wanted to say a prayer over Kirby. But Kirby and me, we didn't go to church after my folks died, and I've sort of forgot how it goes. I couldn't seem to think of anything that seemed fitting. I thought maybe . . . maybe you'd know one."

Her voice sounded small and far away. "If you will kneel with me, I will say it in English so you can understand."

"If you want to say it in Spanish, I think I could understand."

There was an image of Mary in one of the wall niches and they knelt together in front of her and Inez crossed herself and said a prayer in Spanish.

When she was finished, Nate said softly: "That's better. That makes me feel better about Kirby." He got up but she remained kneeling, her head bowed. He cleared his throat. "I suppose you'll be going home."

Her skirts whispered as she rose. "I do not know. I realize now that all I ran away from was not wrong. But there is still so much I cannot return to. My uncle, he has offered to take me to his ranch."

She made him think of a nun with the shawl pulled closely around her pale face. He said: "Inez . . . I don't know how to put this . . . we'll be moving again, the rumor is we'll go across and meet General Taylor to the east, near Saltillo. It'll mean another long march, maybe more fighting. But then, what I'm getting at, my year will be up in June and they'll put us on a boat and ship us home. I figure maybe I'll go back to studying law with Colonel Doniphan. He said I'd be real fierce in a courtroom if I'd jist learn to like Byron. What I mean is, I won't be a Missouri volunteer any more, not thinking about anything except how big a hooraw I can pull, I'll be a lawyer, and a lawyer makes a real solid

family man, sort of how a doctor is. I think we should
. . . I'd be willing to marry up with you."

"Nate . . . ," she said hesitantly, "I am carrying
Kirby's child."

He moistened his lips. Didn't she think that he'd
seen that? He cleared his throat again. "Well, the kid'll
have a lot of good in him. He'll be gentle with horses,
certain for sure. Never was a man gentler with horses
than Kirby." He stopped because he saw that she was
crying. He had never seen her cry before.

In spite of the tears, she said: "You are a kind and a
good boy, Nate. I shall pray for you. Do not worry
about me. Our child's father died a brave man. I shall
remember always."

Nate nodded. He took her hand clumsily, and smiled
slightly. But as he turned to leave, a deep sadness
clawed at him. He was sure he, too, would remember.